Hale Yeah, It's You

NICOLE REEVES

Published by Nicole Reeves

Printed in the United States of America

First U.S. Edition: September 2025

Library of Congress Control Number: 2025915913

ISBN ebook: 978-1-7357037-5-6
ISBN print: 978-1-7357037-4-9

Author: Nicole Reeves

Editor: Victoria Freeman

Cover Design: Brenna Jones Design

For every heart whose journey didn't go as planned—
may the twists and turns lead you to a love that feels like home.

CHAPTER 1

THERE'S A FRAGILE SLIVER of time between sleep and waking—when the world is quiet, your mind is still soft with dreams, and the lie you've been trying not to believe almost feels true. It's a fleeting illusion, that warmth, and it's gone the second reality starts to creep in. And when it does, it leaves you cold. Alone. Grasping for pieces of something that never really was.

Still, I chase that moment every morning. Maybe that makes me a fool. Or a masochist.

Whatever it makes me, one thing's for certain: I am not a morning person. And it's far too early to be wrestling with existential dread.

When my eyes adjust to the soft morning light filtering through the windows, I gently stroke the head of brown curls resting against my stomach. My neck is stiff, head too high off the mattress. Last night, our little trio piled into the master bed for our end-of-summer movie night tradition. It's something we've done for years—one last hoorah before the school year starts.

Alayna climbed in the middle, and we made it through two, maybe three, movies before I passed out. I remember laughing until popcorn flew everywhere, covering the sheets and the floor. I'll have to strip the bed later, put on fresh linens. The whole house could use a clean slate, now that summer's over.

It felt so natural, the three of us like that. Comfortable and familiar. We laughed like we hadn't in months. And yet now, with morning creeping in and my muscles protesting, I'm trapped. Caged like a wild animal in a life I used to dream about. One I once prayed for. So why is that happiness suddenly slipping through my fingers?

Despite the pretty picture we paint, something's changed. Or maybe it's me. Maybe I've changed.

Alayna's soft snores continue as I stroke her hair. She hasn't curled up against me like this in ages. The weight of her, the warmth—it tugs at something deep and aching. Tomorrow she starts high school. And it's not only the end of our summer. It's the end of an era.

She's standing on the edge of something big. I can feel it. And while I'm excited for all that's ahead for her, I'm terrified of what that means for me—for us. For this little family we've patched together over the years.

Gone are the days of scraped knees and magic Band-Aids, of dolls and sticky Lego traps in the hallway. Now it's sleepovers and mascara tutorials and late-night calls with boys I pretend not to hear. The tiny tears over spilled juice have morphed into full-blown teenage heartbreaks. She's growing up too fast, and I'm not sure I'm ready.

These next four years will shape her future. College. Dreams. Independence. And I don't know where I'll fit in once she gets there.

"You awake, Keke?" Clay's voice is groggy, thick with sleep.

I shift slightly, realizing his arm is the lift beneath my pillow. A pang stabs behind my eyes, sharp and sudden. Too early for tears.

"Mmhmm," I mumble. "What time is it?"

The bed shifts as Clay moves. His arm slips out from under me, and I drop flat onto the mattress with a soft exhale.

"Few minutes after six," he says after checking his phone. "You heading into the store today?"

I groan. Inventory won't count itself. "Yeah. Already late."

I ease out from under Alayna, careful not to wake her. I press a kiss to her forehead and tuck the comforter around her. In sleep, she looks just like me—a carbon copy, minus the few lines and wrinkles I've earned over the years. Sometimes it's like looking into a time machine.

"Make her some breakfast?" I ask Clay.

He nods. "Go shower. I'll make coffee."

He gives me one of his lopsided grins, rubbing a hand over his scruffy jaw. His sandy blond hair sticks up on one side, boyish and endearing.

"You're the best," I murmur, escaping to the bathroom.

Hot water and strong coffee. That's what I need before I think too hard.

Under the shower spray, I try to convince myself that this morning is like any other. That everything's fine.

But it's not. Something's shifting. Has already shifted. And no amount of rinsing can wash that feeling away.

Twenty minutes later, I'm dressed in my Hale Hardware tee and faded jeans, hair pulled into a damp ponytail. I rush into the kitchen, wet strands soaking the back of my shirt.

Alayna is perched on a barstool, bleary-eyed, curls wild, and arms cradling a pancake-loaded plate.

"Morning," she says as I pluck a popcorn kernel from her hair.

Clay hands me my purple travel mug. "Figured you'd want yours to go."

The kitchen looks exactly as it always has—brown laminate counters, blue tile floors, scarred wooden stools. We upgraded the appliances four years ago, but the soul of the place hasn't changed. My grandmother's kitchen. Now ours.

"What would I do without you?" I ask, sipping cautiously.

"Die a slow, uncaffeinated death," Alayna says, deadpan.

"Such a cheeky child."

Clay laughs. "She's not wrong. You'd live on energy drinks and takeout."

"You're both insufferable," I mutter, smiling despite myself. "But I really do have to go."

"At least take a pancake," Clay says, wrapping a sausage in one and pinning it with a toothpick. He hands it to me in a paper towel. "Can't have you hangry all morning."

"My coworkers thank you," I say. Not that I'll see many today—just my dad and Mike. The fewer people, the better.

"Tell Grandpa he's still my favorite," Alayna mumbles through syrup. "And remind Dad I deserve new shoes."

Clay rolls his eyes. "You'll live until next weekend."

"Take her to get the shoes," I tell him, grabbing my bag. "It's her first day of high school. She only gets one."

He steers me toward the door, mock-scolding. "You're supposed to back me up, not enable her."

"You expect too much from me in the mornings."

"You're lucky I love you."

My heart squeezes. "Love y'all," I call out, stepping outside.

The Idaho sunrise paints the sky in warm pinks and oranges. I take a deep breath of crisp air.

"Purse," Clay calls, slipping the strap over my head. "We all know how forgetful you are."

"Yeah," I sigh. "If only I could choose what to forget."

CHAPTER 2

HALE HARDWARE HAS BEEN on the corner of Main Street and 3rd since 1902, owned and run by a Hale every year since. The big steel-gray building with wide glass windows draws my eye the moment it comes into view. More than any other place in Pinewood, this store is my home.

The Hale sons have all taken their turns at running it—some longer than others. My father, Franklin Hale the Fourth, always dreamed of handing it off to his own son someday. But since he only had daughters, I—his youngest—was named Frankie and raised with the expectation that I'd follow in the footsteps of all the Frank Hales before me.

Growing up between the aisles with my dad and grandpa as my daily companions, I never resented that plan. I saw the shop as mine from the moment I could talk. I'd tell Grandpa all my wild ideas for making the store prettier: pink and purple floors, glitter paint on the walls, maybe even a nail polish display by the register.

Grandpa likely dreaded the thought of my princess-themed renovations, but he'd playfully ruffle my hair, hand me a bag of fresh popcorn from the old cart, and send me off to sort the mixed-up bins of screws and nails. I felt important every time they gave me a task.

It's been nearly ten years since we lost Grandpa, and Grandma not long after. But when I refill the popcorn machine or find myself reorganizing those stubborn bins, I still feel him with me.

Dad handed the reins over on my twenty-eighth birthday—technically retired, though he still shows up most days to hang around. He says retirement is boring, and Mom doesn't mind as long as he stays out from under her feet.

His old truck, a faded red that now leans more rust-orange, greets me in the parking lot when I arrive. He's always the first one here on Sundays, probably sipping coffee and listening to old country on the radio. I hum Dolly Parton's "9 to 5" as I grab my purse and head inside.

The double glass doors are unlocked. The familiar smells of sawdust, grease, and buttery popcorn greet me like a hug. Country music plays softly over the speakers. I toss my keys and purse near the register and call out a hello.

"Ah, my sweet daughter has finally arrived," Dad calls from the breakroom.

I pull my faded blue apron from behind the counter and tie it behind my back, stuffing pens into the front pocket. Inventory days always leave me covered in dust.

Mike rounds the corner first, a stack of mail in his hands. He's closer in age to Dad than to me, but with his endless energy, you'd never guess it. He's been working at the store since he graduated high school and fits in like part of the family.

"Bills and another offer to buy the land," he says, shrugging as he hands me the pile.

Dad follows behind him, cradling his favorite "Best Grandpa Ever" mug. "Don't bother opening it—it's probably insulting."

"Must be a good offer then," I tease, winking. "Still not selling, though."

Mike shrugs again. "Didn't even open it."

I grin. "You know I'm only messing with you. This store's mine now—glitter paint or not."

Dad's smile softens. "Someday, you might not want to run this place. And if that happens, I'd understand. You've spent a lot of your life taking care of the rest of us."

The deep creases in Dad's forehead are on prominent display, and his white hair seems to glow under the fluorescent lighting. Sometimes I forget how old he's getting; in my mind, he's young and strong and larger than life.

I place a hand over my heart and meet his gaze. "This is home, Dad. Dust, spiders, and all."

He pulls me into a side hug, pressing a kiss to the top of my head. "I know, kiddo. I just always pictured more for my girls."

Girls. The word lands like a rock in my stomach. It tumbles around, sharp and unwelcome. I step back and force a tight smile, jaw clenched. I'm not in the mood to think about my sister, Tasha. Not today.

Mike seems to catch the shift in my energy and slides a clipboard into my hands. "Back room's done. I'd start up front and work your way back."

I nod, thankful for the save. "What are you two up to?"

"Couple deliveries tomorrow," Dad says. "Thought we'd get 'em loaded up today."

"If you need help with inventory, say the word," Mike adds.

I look at both of them—matching T-shirts, faded jeans, all part of my day-to-day—and smile. Dad might be taller, and more filled out, especially around the middle, but after all the years of working side-by-side, the two of them have begun to look more like blood-brothers. "Please. Let me finish in peace."

They take the hint and disappear toward the back. As much as I love them, sometimes it's a relief to have the shop to myself.

There are things we'll never agree on, and Tasha will always top that list.

I turn up the radio and get to work. The faster I finish, the sooner I can head out. And suddenly, that sounds pretty good.

CHAPTER 3

"I hope you brought a barf bag."

I try to hold back a laugh as I reach into my purse and hand a small paper bag to Alayna. It's her first day of school, not mine, but somehow I'm as nervous as I imagine she is.

"Ew, I didn't mean literally." She presses the bag back into my hands, her cheeks turning a darker shade of pink.

I bite my lip, my grin breaking through anyway. I love this child with a fierceness I never knew was possible. "Wouldn't want to ruin those new shoes or anything."

Alayna drags her Converse-clad feet across the freshly waxed floor, her eyes darting back and forth along the hall of blue and red lockers. The first day of school is the only day parents are allowed to escort their kids inside—you couldn't have paid me to miss this moment.

"Thanks for convincing Dad to take me. There's nothing better than fresh shoes on the first day of school."

"They do look great." I pat her shoulder, brushing sun-kissed curls back from her face. "It's going to be fine. You got all the classes you wanted, and I know it's going to be a great year. I loved high school. This is a great opportunity for you to explore new interests and figure out what you want for your future."

Alayna rolls her eyes and smirks. "So when you went to school here, you always dreamed you'd grow up to run the hardware store and spend all your free time with me and Dad?"

"Shh, be quiet and keep walking. You don't want to be late on your first day." This day is not about me, and I do not want to talk about my hopes and dreams this morning. I push her along, waving at a few teachers I still recognize. It's been fourteen years since I walked these halls, but so much of it remains completely unchanged.

I could've dropped her off at the door, but her dad forgot to sign a release form for her tech privileges and asked if I could handle it before opening the store. I jumped at the chance—it was the perfect excuse to walk in with her.

"I see Summer—I'm gonna go." Alayna grips my shoulder. "See you after school."

I nod, letting her break away toward her friends. I don't need her to go to the office with me anyway. I know Mrs. Brosnan will recognize me and get me whatever form I need. That old bat has worked the front desk since before I was born, and I don't see her leaving without a fight.

Another parent holds the office door for me as she exits. Her eyes scream for mercy, and I'm sure Mrs. Brosnan is the reason. I nod my thanks and step inside, preparing for battle.

It's like a time warp, right down to the shining vinyl floors and the smell of stale coffee. Mrs. Brosnan, with her mad mop of white curls brushing her eyebrows, sits behind the oversized oak desk. Her head jerks toward me and I swear she grimaces.

"Ah, here to fill out the form for Ms. Phillips?" she asks, already moving from her desk to a small table and chairs normally reserved for kids in trouble. Without waiting for an answer, she presses a pen into my hand and gestures toward a stack of forms. Her steely gaze still has the same terrifying effect it did when I was sixteen.

"Take one and fill it out. And if you don't mind, watch the desk for a moment while I step out. Apparently, my assistant can't be bothered to make it to work on time." She purses her lips and disappears into the staff lounge.

Letting out a long breath, I try not to laugh. That woman could scare a ghost.

I take a seat and begin filling in the form. The part I need to fill out is short, and I think if I hurry, maybe I can get out of here before the drill sergeant returns. I've almost completed the last line when the door swings open beside me. The smell of my favorite blueberry muffins follows a large man inside. I notice his hands first—filled with coffee cups and pastry bags from Bean-Town, the coffee shop down the street. He appears to be struggling to balance the load, and on instinct, I jump up to help him.

"Let me get some of that for you," I say, taking a cup holder from the crook of his arm and setting it down on Mrs. Brosnan's desk.

"Thank you, Mrs..." The man finally looks up, his eyes locking with mine.

I choke on air. My whole body jerks with the need to breathe. I press a hand over my mouth as I gasp and cough and try to breathe through the sensation.

"Frankie?" His hazel eyes sparkle with recognition. The boy I used to know so many years ago stares back at me. The first boy I ever loved. The last boy I ever allowed close enough to break my heart.

The boy I haven't seen since we graduated high school and he hightailed it out of here like a man on the run.

Roman Clarke.

Only he isn't a boy anymore. In a well-tailored suit and tie, his wavy brown hair cut shorter than I've ever seen it, he looks handsome, polished, and put together. He's a fully grown man—and time has been very, very kind to him.

And God help me, my heart recognizes him before my brain can catch up.

There's a moment—a flicker of something unspoken that passes between us—and it lands heavy in my chest. I blink, but he's still standing there, looking at me like I'm a mirage. Maybe I am. Maybe we both are. I'm sixteen again and also not sixteen at all. Time has passed, years have hardened me, I've moved on... but there's a part of me—small, stubborn, buried deep—that never stopped wondering if I'd ever see him again. A part that never stopped hoping he'd come back and explain why he left.

I hate that it's still there. I hate that it still wants anything from him at all.

My mind floods with the memories I've kept locked up tight for years: the warmth of his hand in mine, the way he used to make me laugh until I couldn't breathe, the promises we whispered under the stars. And then—just like that—the sting of his absence. The silence. The way I stared at my phone long after he stopped calling, the way I told myself I was fine.

I wasn't fine.

I steel myself.

"Roman," I finally manage to speak, but it comes out more of a squeak than anything. I clear my throat and try again. "I didn't realize you were in town."

I stare at him, unable to look away. As far as I know, he hasn't been back since that summer—the summer everything changed. I wonder what I look like to him now. My hair's twisted up with a few stubborn curls falling loose, and I'm wearing jeans and a Hale Hardware T-shirt. I didn't dress for nostalgia. I didn't dress for him.

And yet, here he is.

"I thought you would have heard through the local gossip mill by now," he says. "I'm the new principal."

I shake my head, still trying to reconcile this version of him with the one I once knew so intimately. "What happened to Mr. Garrett?"

Mr. Garrett has been a fixture at this school almost as long as grouchy old Mrs. Brosnan. A stickler for rules, he banned pep rallies and spirit days during my sophomore year, after deeming them too disruptive—and would've cut dances too, if the town hadn't raised such a stink about tradition. But beneath his prickly exterior, he's always cared about his students—in his own way.

"He finally retired. Bought a boat and moved to Florida to be close to his grandkids or something. It was time."

"But what about you?" The words come out sharper than I intended, laced with accusation I didn't mean to let slip. My stomach flips, a nauseating swirl of coffee, nerves, and years of unanswered questions. "Why are you back here?"

He laughs, and that laugh... that sound. It stirs something in me I'd sworn was long dead. "I guess I felt like it was time to come home. I saw they were looking to fill the position, and I was more than qualified, so I jumped."

Just like that. Roman Clarke, always jumping. Into ideas, into trouble, into me—then gone before the landing.

I purse my lips, trying to mask the sudden ache blooming in my chest. "An impulsive decision. Sounds about right." I try to make it sound light, sarcastic, but it comes out brittle. Fragile, even.

He looks at me for a beat too long, like he's trying to read between the lines of my words. I don't let him. I pull my fake smile tight and wipe my clammy hands against my jeans.

"Well, congratulations," I say. "And welcome back."

I take a slow step backward, toward the door, like my body knows I need to escape before my heart decides otherwise. One more second in this room and I might say something I'll regret. Or worse—say something I *mean*.

Before I reach the door, it swings open again. My head swivels as Alayna bursts in, her curls bouncing around her shoulders. "Oh good, you're still here! Dad wanted me to remind you that we have dinner plans tonight. And don't be late. You know how grumpy he gets when he's hangry."

Her words are a lifeline—something real, something grounding. But her eyes shift, catching Roman behind me, and curiosity replaces urgency.

"Are you the new principal?" she asks, her earlier nerves replaced by the bright boldness I've always admired in her.

"Guilty, as charged. I'm Dr. Clarke." Roman's gaze drifts from her to me, then back again, like he's trying to solve a puzzle that doesn't quite fit.

"And you are?"

"Alayna Phillips-Hale," she says proudly, chin lifted.

Roman's eyes widen almost imperceptibly, his lips parting for a moment before he regains his composure. "Gotta go though," she adds, oblivious. "Can't be late to my first class!"

She hugs me quickly before exiting the office, as carefree as she came in.

Roman stares at the door she exited through, his Adam's apple bobbing hard as he swallows. His shoulders square and his face tightens into something unreadable. He straightens to his full height, suddenly less man and more... storm.

The room seems to shrink around us, thick with unspoken history. My heart stutters.

He turns to me, eyes sharp now. "Frankie Hale, how old is that child?"

CHAPTER 4

"She's fourteen."

Roman's mouth drops open. And stays that way. He glances at the door Alayna disappeared through, then back at me. "Is this some kind of joke?"

Before I can answer, Mrs. Brosnan bustles through the staff entrance with her usual stormfront energy. "Ahh, Dr. Clarke! Welcome."

He turns his attention toward her, attempting a smile, but it looks like it's been sculpted under pressure—tight and forced. "I brought coffee and muffins for everyone. I'll put them in the lounge. Frankie, do you mind helping me carry them in?"

His eyes pin me with a look that's all challenge and tension and *don't even think about saying no*. I want to tell him where to shove that cup holder, but something in his expression—a mix of anger and something that looks almost like betrayal—stops me.

"Sure thing," I say, casually retrieving the drinks I'd set down earlier. I don't wait for him; I turn and walk through to the staff lounge like none of this is bothering me at all. But inside? My brain is spinning out like a roulette wheel.

Why does *he* get to be mad?

The lounge is empty. No teachers, no witnesses. The door clicks shut behind us and suddenly the space is too small. The air is heavy with tension and the smell of blueberries.

Roman sets his load down with too much force. Coffee sloshes from one of the cups and bleeds into a napkin.

"Alayna Phillips-Hale," he says slowly, his voice low and sharp, like a blade sliding from its sheath. "As in... Clay Phillips?"

I nod once, cautiously.

And then I see it click. Like a lightbulb snapping to life and blinding him.

Oh.

Oh.

My lips twitch. He thinks... oh God. He thinks *Alayna is his daughter.*

It's written all over his face. The timeline. The name. The *age*. He's doing the mental math, rewinding the tape back to the last weekend we spent tangled in sheets and bad decisions before he disappeared from my life without a forwarding address. My cheeks flush with heat—part embarrassment, part memory, part *how dare he*.

He thinks I kept a child from him. Our child.

And for half a second, I *almost* feel sorry for him.

Almost.

But then I remember all the years of silence. Of wondering what I did wrong. Of letting him haunt every corner of my heart, even while I told myself I'd moved on. If anyone deserves to sit in a pool of his own assumptions for a while, it's Roman Clarke.

"Clay is a wonderful man," I say, too smoothly. "And an amazing dad to Alayna. I know you've only just met her, but

I'm sure you'll see soon enough—she's turning into the kind of person everyone's better for knowing."

I turn away to hide the laughter that's bubbling up. It's cruel. I know it is. But I can't help it. The look on his face is *priceless*.

"I'm going to be late for work," I toss over my shoulder. "But again—welcome home."

I head for the back exit, avoiding another showdown with the battle-ax out front. Out of the corner of my eye, I catch Roman still frozen, blinking like the world has tilted sideways under his feet.

I could tell him the truth. Clear it up. Let him off the hook. But I don't.

He left me in the dark for years. He can sit in a little of his own shadow for a change.

Twenty minutes later, I'm no longer laughing as I push through the doors of the hardware store. The familiar scent of cedar and grease hits me like a balm, settling over my raw nerves. This place has always wrapped me in its arms that way. A little chaotic, a little dusty, but solid and consistent.

I might be a little too proud of the way I left Roman spinning in his own assumptions, but the high is already fading. His face keeps flashing in my mind—older, sharper, but still so *him*—and with it comes a rush of memories I didn't ask for. The kind that cling to the inside of your ribs and make you question everything. Where I'm going. Where I *thought* I'd be by now.

What I've actually built for myself in the ruins of what used to be.

Back then, I thought Roman was it for me. The endgame. The happily ever after. But he made it crystal clear that his future didn't include me. That kind of thing leaves a scar, no matter how much time passes. And maybe the years have dulled the pain, maybe I've learned to laugh it off, but sometimes—on days like today—it still stings like it's all happening for the first time.

Not that I've been pining. I've lived a whole life without him. Haven't I?

I shake the thought away and focus on what's in front of me. Mondays are always busy. A stack of boxes waits outside my office, filled with supplies that need sorting and shelving. Dad will show up later to "supervise" from the front counter, sipping his coffee like a king overseeing his kingdom. But the store is mine now. He knows it. I know it. I don't need him to tell me how to run the place.

So maybe my life doesn't look the way I once imagined, but it's *mine*. I've made something here—something steady, something real. The work feels good in my hands, even if it's not glamorous. I never needed a big career, I only wanted to be *happy*. I still do. I still hope that someday that happiness might include love again. Maybe a family of my own.

Someday just... hasn't happened yet.

In a way, I *do* have a family. It's not the one I dreamed of back when Roman and I were scribbling hearts on notebook paper and planning prom outfits, but it's *real*. Messy and unconventional, but real.

Roman and I were high school sweethearts. It was love at first scrimmage—literally: a boys-versus-girls soccer game for charity. We collided mid-field, both going for the ball. I fell. Hard. And not just on the turf. I hadn't even known he existed until that moment. He'd been living in town for a year, but somehow our paths never crossed—not until that one crash sent sparks flying.

That crash changed everything.

The sparks caught, the fire spread, and two years later, I paid the price.

My phone buzzes, pulling me out of the spiral. I sit down on one of the unopened boxes and pull it from my pocket.

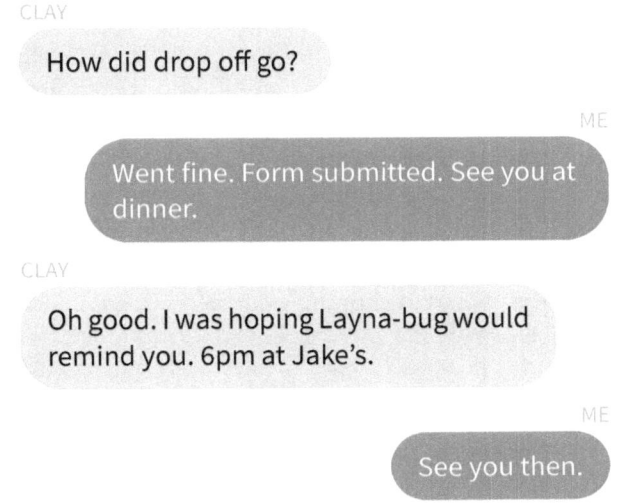

CLAY

How did drop off go?

ME

Went fine. Form submitted. See you at dinner.

CLAY

Oh good. I was hoping Layna-bug would remind you. 6pm at Jake's.

ME

See you then.

I sigh and lean forward, elbows to knees. I don't usually get short with Clay, but I'm off-kilter today. Everything is too close to the surface. My nerves are frayed, emotions rubbed raw. Normally, he's one of the few people who can calm me down.

We've been through a lot together, especially in the past few years. Co-parenting Alayna—unconventional as it is—has only made our friendship stronger.

Clay's another example of young love gone wrong. He fell for my sister Tasha, and for a while, it looked like they had it all figured out. Tasha was two years ahead of me in school, loud and lovely and impossible to ignore. Everyone loved her. Clay was equally as magnetic—smart, funny, the golden boy on every sports team. Together they looked like something out of a teen drama. They left for college as the perfect couple.

Two years later they came back, and Tasha was pregnant. Dad married them in the backyard under the same oak tree that held our tire swing growing up. It should've been a happy time.

But Roman had just left. And I wasn't okay.

I wasn't happy for my sister. Or for Clay. I was heartbroken and confused and angry in ways I couldn't explain. When Alayna was born, I shut everyone out. I went silent. I kept my head down, taking classes I didn't care about at the community college. I didn't know what I wanted. High school graduation had felt like a funeral for the life I thought I was building.

Tasha and Clay moved into Grandma and Grandpa's old place, and I avoided it like the plague. Except for Alayna. I couldn't stay away from her. She was light in the middle of all that darkness. I started slipping over before school and after work, just to be near her.

Eventually, I started coming by more. Tasha loved it. She'd take a nap, run errands, shower in peace. She was so grateful—always thanking me, begging me to stop by more often.

At the time, I didn't think anything of it. I wanted to be there for the baby. I didn't realize I was slowly becoming something else. Something more. A fixture. A third parent, almost.

Clay had taken a job working for the city—steady hours, decent pay. It wasn't glamorous, and it was far from the sports-star dreams he'd left home with, but it was reliable. Tasha, on the other hand, had traded in her big dreams for diapers and dishes. She'd always talked about being the wife of a professional athlete, living in some high-rise apartment with designer strollers and VIP passes. Instead, she was back in our hometown, a stay-at-home mom in our grandparents' old house, surrounded by hand-me-down furniture and chipped paint.

From the outside, they looked happy. At first, anyway.

By the time Alayna was three, I had fully settled into the rhythm of life at the hardware store with Dad and afternoons at my sister's place.

And then, like that first collision on the soccer field, my world changed again.

CHAPTER 5

11 YEARS AGO

"Knock-knock!" I yell through the screen door. "It's me, the world's best auntie, here for her daily snuggles..."

When no one comes to the door, I roll my eyes and let myself in. The screen door slaps shut behind me. Sometimes Tasha and Alayna go back to sleep after Clay leaves for work, so I head through the little house to the kitchen to see if anyone's up. I turn the corner and stop short.

Clay is leaning over the kitchen sink, elbows digging into the old laminate counter, head in his large hands. His shoulders are shaking hard, and there's a strange noise coming from him. Is he... sobbing?

"Clay?" I ask gently, careful not to startle him. "Is everything okay? Where are the girls?"

His sobs grow quiet, and he sniffles a few times, wiping his nose with his sleeve before turning to face me. His voice is gravelly and low when he finally speaks.

"She left us, Frankie. She left us both."

I blink at him, trying to understand. "Who left?"

"Tasha. She's gone."

My head shakes on instinct. "What do you mean, gone? I don't understand—"

"She left me a goddamn note, Frankie. She said she needs to find herself again. That this isn't the life she wanted... That I'm not the life she wanted."

"A note?" My jaw tightens as I grind my teeth. What does he mean she left a note? What does she mean this isn't the life she wanted? Tasha and Clay were like bookends. Destined.

"I found it this morning. I got up to make coffee for work, and it was here..." He gestures to a crumpled slip of paper by the coffee machine. "Waiting for me."

"She didn't even say goodbye?"

My sister wouldn't just leave her family. No. She couldn't do something like that. But even as I fight the thought, I know I'm lying to myself. Tasha's definitely capable of this. She's always done what she wanted, regardless of the damage left behind.

Just like Roman.

"I'm so sorry..." The words sound flat and useless. They don't even begin to cover this. She abandoned her whole family. Her vows...

My heart aches for Clay. And then it hits me. "Wait. Where's Alayna?"

Fear crashes over me like an ice bath, and I cover my mouth with both hands. Tasha leaving is crushing, but the idea of losing my niece—of her being gone too—I might throw up right here on Grandma's old kitchen floor.

Clay rushes over, grabbing my shoulders as panic floods me.

"No, Frankie, it's okay. She's still here. She's asleep in her room. I don't know how I'm going to tell her... tell her that her mother—God, I don't understand how she could do this." Another sob slips out of him.

Relief washes through me, but it's short-lived. He's right. How do you tell a sweet little girl her mama left? Not because she was taken. Not because she got lost. She left—on purpose. She might not get that now, but one day, she will. I pull my sweater tighter, trying to fight off the cold sinking into my bones.

Clay still hasn't let go of my shoulders. I wonder if he needs the contact to stay upright, because I do.

"I took the day off work, but I've got to go in tomorrow. I don't know what I'm supposed to do with the baby." He clenches his jaw, eyes raised to the ceiling like the answer might be up there.

"I'll watch her. At least until you can find someone or get her into preschool or something. It's fine. Dad won't care if I miss some shifts at the hardware store. It's not like he needs me—he's got Mike and, in a pinch, Mom if he really needs help."

Clay shakes his head. "I can't ask you to do that, Frankie. You're about to turn twenty-one. This is your time to figure out who you are and what you want."

"Good thing you're not asking then. I'm offering. And you're going to be quiet and let me take care of my niece while you get things sorted. I know exactly who I am." I lift my chin and meet his eyes, daring him to argue.

As if on cue, Layna-bug cries out down the hall. Her chubby feet slap noisily against the old floor as she runs toward us.

"Mama? Mama?"

Clay's face folds in on itself as she calls for her mother, and I press into him, wrapping my arms around his trembling frame, holding him as tightly as I can. As much as I'm hurting, I know his pain is a thousand times worse.

"What am I going to do, Frankie?" he whispers into my hair.

I don't know how to answer. This solid man I've known most of my life suddenly looks so small. So fragile.

"Keke!" Alayna barrels into my legs, arms lifted. I pull away from Clay and scoop her up, tucking her against my chest. She still can't say Frankie right, and I've gladly taken the nickname.

"Hey, Layna-bug." I squeeze her tight, peppering kisses on her cheeks and the top of her head. Tears sting my eyes. Her warm little body grounds me.

"Where's Mama?" she asks softly, arms tightening around my neck.

"Mama had to go bye-bye for a while, Layna-bug. But your daddy and I are here."

"Mama go bye-bye?" She pushes back to look at me, those bright eyes wide and confused.

Clay touches my shoulder gently and kisses the top of her head before stepping out of the room. He needs a minute to pull himself together, and I hope he can do that. This little girl is going to need him more than ever now.

I hold her even tighter.

"Yes, sweetheart. But Keke will never leave you, okay? Do you understand?"

And right then, I know I'll never break that promise. No matter what it costs me.

CHAPTER 6

PRESENT DAY

Mondays always move fast, but today is a sprint. I bust my butt to get all the boxes broken down and out to the back dumpster before Dad arrives, and when he does, I wave him off mid-stride, skipping lunch without a second thought. He doesn't argue—he never does when I'm in a mood like this. Instead, he takes his thermos to the front counter and keeps busy chatting with the regulars.

I bury myself in the back office, attacking the mountain of paperwork I've been avoiding for weeks. Inventory sheets, vendor invoices, payroll reports... I don't let myself slow down. Not even for a breath. Because I know the second I do, Roman will find a way back in.

And he does.

That suit. That stupid, perfect suit. The way he filled it out, the way his voice sounded deeper than I remembered, more assured. It's like he's a whole new man and yet somehow still the boy who wrecked me. I drop my pen and cover my eyes with my fingertips, pressing hard like I can force the image of him out of my brain.

"Frankie?"

I drop my hands in time to see my mom leaning against the doorway, one hip cocked casually against the frame.

"Everything okay?" she asks, her tone light but lined with motherly concern.

I release a long, controlled breath, avoiding her eyes like they're X-rays. "Yeah. Had a long day. First day of school for the bug and all that."

Her face softens. "Ah, that's right. Was my sweet girl excited?"

"She was. Nervous, too. But you know how she is—give her a day and she'll be running for class president."

Mom chuckles as she walks in and sinks into Dad's old recliner, the one he dragged into the shop after she threatened to toss it. It's cracked and lumpy and matches the couch in the corner that no one sits on unless they're desperate. I've always suspected he bought them as a pair, back when Mom still humored his garage-sale taste.

"She definitely has her mother's spirit," she says with a warm smile.

I bite the inside of my cheek. That bitter taste creeps in, the one I've never fully shaken. She means it as a compliment, but to me, it lands like a slap. Mom's always been the queen of soft excuses, especially when it comes to Tasha. I've long since stopped trying to make her see the truth.

"She's her own force," I say carefully. "That I'll agree with."

My eyes drift to my mom—*Grace Hale*, former pageant queen and present-day perfectionist—with her gray hair pulled back into a low ponytail. We all have the same eyes, the Hale women. Me, Mom, Tasha, and now Alayna. Before hers went silver, we all shared the same head of wild brown curls too. It's eerie sometimes, like we're variations on the same face.

She looks tired tonight. Sad, even. A quiet sort of sadness that settles in the corners of her mouth and eyes. I wonder, for a flicker of a second, if she's more affected by Tasha's absence than she lets on. But if she is, she doesn't say. She never does. I gave up trying to pull it out of her years ago.

"I can close up the shop tonight," she says suddenly, shifting in the recliner. "Or your dad can. Or I'll ask Mike. You've had a long day, honey. You look like you could use the break."

I blink and look at the clock. Quarter to six.

Crap.

"The store's been closed for almost an hour," I mutter, pushing up from my chair. "I completely lost track of time. I'm going to be late for dinner."

"Is that a yes?" Mom asks, eyes twinkling with surprise.

"Actually... yeah. That would be great. I promised Alayna I wouldn't be late tonight, and it's going to take a miracle to keep that promise."

I peel off my dusty work shirt and grab the backup sweater from the hat tree in the corner. It's deep purple and maybe a touch too low-cut for dinner at Jake's, but it hugs in all the right places and makes my eyes look like melted chocolate. I swipe on some lip gloss and run my fingers through my curls, doing my best with what I've got. I've definitely looked worse.

Mom watches me with a curious expression, something unreadable behind her eyes.

"Enjoy your dinner, Frankie," she says finally. "Clay will appreciate the effort. Those two are lucky to have you."

I freeze.

The way she says it—it's not about Alayna. Not exactly. It's the way she emphasizes *Clay*. Like she thinks I'm dressing up for him.

I shake the thought off, grabbing my purse. It's been a long day. Seeing Roman has clearly scrambled my brain.

Before I can escape, Dad appears in the doorway.

"Hey, kid."

He's wearing his favorite blue Hale Hardware shirt, the one with more holes than fabric. Dozens of brand-new ones hang untouched in his closet, but he always goes for the broken-in one. His belly fills it out more these days, but he looks happy. Sturdy, in that dad way. A little slower, a little rounder, but no less himself.

"Have a good night, Dad," I say, pressing a quick kiss to his cheek.

If I let him get talking, I'll never get out of here.

"Take your time," he calls as I rush past. "And tell my grandbaby I said to eat an extra fry for me!"

His laugh echoes behind me as I burst through the front door and jog to my car. The cool evening air hits my face, and I smile to myself despite the chaos of the day. For all our mess, my family is still solid in all the ways that count.

CHAPTER 7

THE PARKING LOT AT Jake's Diner is completely full—of course it is. I circle twice like a hawk hunting for scraps before spotting an elderly woman moving at a glacial pace toward her Lincoln. I throw the car into park and wait as she spends an eternity adjusting her enormous sunglasses, checking her rearview, and then slowly backing out like the fate of the free world depends on her precision.

The clock on my dash glares at me. I'm already ten minutes late. My phone buzzes in my purse for the third time, and I can practically hear Alayna's sass through the vibrations. She's probably wondering if I got distracted by a rogue display of paint swatches again. It's happened before. Many times.

But this is the first day of school. I promised I'd be here. I *need* to be here.

Purse in hand, I half-jog across the lot and hope my deodorant is still working after the stressful day I've had.

Relief washes over me the second I spot Alayna in one of the cracked orange booths near the back, her face lit up by the glow of her phone. She glances up, sees me, and waves. Not a trace of irritation on her face—merely a soft smile that hits me right in the heart. She's too forgiving. Too good.

"Sorry I'm late!" I slide into the booth across from her, trying to catch my breath. The smell of burgers and deep fryer grease hits me like a warm hug. I hope I'm lucky enough to get a slice of the famous apple pie.

Alayna sets her phone down and grins. "I knew you'd be late. I'm glad you're here. Dad ran to the—"

"Restroom," Clay finishes as he slides into the booth beside me. He's swapped out his work suit for his favorite red flannel and jeans, his cologne a mix of leather and citrus that's unfairly comforting.

He gives me a half hug and his hand lingers on my shoulder. "You look awfully nice. How was your day?"

"I'm more interested in hearing about our little Bug's day," I say quickly, my defenses snapping up. There will be no discussion of *this* morning, no uninvited trips down memory lane involving one Roman Clarke. I simply want a greasy dinner with my people. No emotional landmines, thank you very much.

Alayna beams like she's been waiting all day to spill. "It was actually really awesome. The new principal is really cool, and I think it's gonna be a fun year. They're bringing back spirit days and pep rallies!"

"I love a good pep rally," I say, jumping at the chance to steer the conversation toward safe, glitter-covered territory.

"There's a new principal?" Clay asks, his cobalt eyes flicking to me.

Well, crap.

"Yeah, there is. Mr. Garrett retired. Florida, I think?" I say casually, like I'm talking about someone's distant uncle. "Beach life and shuffleboard, you know?"

"Oh, well, that was long overdue. Did you meet her this morning?"

"Who?" I ask, taking the world's longest drink of water. I should have offered the information up, instead of feigning confusion, but I can't seem to get myself together. He knows I'm being weird, I can see it on his face. Alayna jumps in, filling the awkward silence I've created.

"Dad, it's not a woman—it's another man. And he's kinda cute." She giggles and takes a sip of her water like she said *the most scandalous thing ever.*

I nearly choke.

Clay stiffens beside me, the telltale bounce of his leg starting under the table. He leans in, voice low. "Alayna, he's a grown man. That's inappropriate."

She rolls her eyes so hard I swear I hear it. "Okay, *boomer,* calm down. I didn't say I wanted to date him. I'm saying the man is objectively hot. Right, Keke?"

I grab the menu like it can shield me from my own shame. "What's everyone feeling for dinner?" I ask brightly, as if we're not actively spiraling into chaos.

Clay's face is slowly turning pink. He shakes his head. He's still adjusting to Teenager Alayna, and judging by the color rising in his cheeks, it's not going as well as we all hoped.

She's been a heartbreaker since she was seven and declared Nick Jonas her future husband. Clay's been dreading this stage ever since.

"Well," he says, trying to keep it together, "I look forward to seeing what all the fuss is about at family day."

And just when I think we've narrowly dodged the topic, Alayna opens her mouth again.

"I think he knows you already, Dad. He definitely knows Keke."

I choke again. Water goes down the wrong pipe and I break into a full coughing fit. Clay pats me on the back like I'm a toddler trying solid food for the first time.

"Hey—breathe," he murmurs, rubbing soothing circles on my back. "Layna, what's this principal's name?"

She scrunches her nose. "Uhhh... Dr. Clarke, I think?"

Of *course* she got it right.

"Clarke... why does that sound familiar?" Clay's hand stills on my back. "Clarke... Clarke... why can't I place that—"

"It's Dr. Roman Clarke," I interrupt, finally regaining the ability to speak—and regret it immediately.

"*Woah.* Roman? As in your old high school boyfriend, Roman?"

"Boyfriend?" Alayna gasps. "You had a high school boyfriend? You hardly *date.*"

"Excuse you, I *date*," I say, holding back the part where I haven't dated anyone worth introducing to my family. And the one man who was worth it broke my heart and then disappeared like a magician's assistant.

Clay exhales long and hard. "So he's back. Huh. How are we feeling about that?"

We. Interesting choice of pronoun.

I gnaw on the inside of my cheek. How am I feeling? Honestly, I've avoided asking myself that. If I give those feelings names, they might start moving back in.

Then, right on cue, the bell above the door jingles and Mary's voice rings out, cheerful and oblivious: "Welcome to Jake's, take a seat and I'll be right with ya, dear!"

"Speak of the devil," Clay mutters under his breath.

I don't look. I don't need to. I can *sense* Roman in the room like a static charge. My heart slams against my ribs.

And then, bless her, my sweet, loud, traitorous niece says, "Hi, Dr. Clarke!"

Clenching my jaw, I begin to count to ten.

One, inhale. Two, exhale. Three, consider faking my own death...

"Hi, Alayna. How are you this evening? Hello, Frankie. Clay." His voice is like velvet.

I keep my eyes on the menu like I'm studying for a test. "Roman," I manage, my voice almost steady.

Clay's hand tightens on my shoulder before he speaks. "Heard you were back in town."

"Hasn't changed much," Roman's tone is easy. "And yet, some things I don't recognize at all."

I finally look up. Alayna is beaming like he's the newest Jonas brother. Clay looks like someone kicked his puppy. And Roman—Roman is looking at me like I've kept a secret from him for the last decade and he's ready to torture the truth out of me.

"Still the same town," I say, "only... now you're in it again."

He nods, something unreadable flickering across his face. "I won't interrupt your dinner, but Frankie, I'd like to speak with you soon."

His eyes say everything his words don't. He wants answers. Good—I do too.

Clay's hand slides over mine on the table like he's claiming territory. I don't move.

Roman sees it. Of course he does. His jaw flexes, and for a second, there's something sharp between us. Something old.

"I can meet you at the store tomorrow, after work," he says, shifting his weight. "If that's okay."

Clay starts to say something, but I nod quickly. "Yeah. After five. Just knock."

Roman's lips twitch. "It's a date." Then, as if realizing the weight of the words, he adds, "You know what I mean."

The problem is, I *do*.

And worse, so does my heart.

CHAPTER 8

DINNER IS AWKWARD AFTER that. I find myself picking at my food before giving up and pushing the plate away. Clay asks me why I would even *entertain* the idea of talking with Roman, but I brush off his concern. No matter what comes of that conversation, it needs to be had. I need to clear the air about Alayna, and I need him to explain to me what the hell happened fourteen years ago.

Neither of my dinner companions speaks directly to me after that, and I'm content to let Alayna carry the rest of the conversation like a one-woman show. She's good at it—thank God.

She opts to ride home with her dad instead of with me, and I don't blame her. I'm not exactly radiating warm-and-fuzzy vibes tonight. I turn my radio up and drive the long way back to the house, letting the thumping of the bass keep me grounded in the here and now. It would be too easy to drift back into the past. Everywhere I look—every street, every turn—holds a memory of Roman. Of us. Moments I thought I'd buried deep enough to stay buried.

Clay's silver SUV is already in the driveway when I pull in. After it became clear Tasha wasn't coming back and I'd become Alayna's full-time nanny, I'd moved into the guest room at the back of the small house. When Alayna started kindergarten two years later, I brought up the idea of getting my own place. Clay insisted I save my money and the commute, said it didn't make sense to split up what already worked. So I stayed.

Not a traditional family, not a romantic partnership, but something that worked. A parenting plan held together by mutual trust, exhaustion, and the little girl who stole both our hearts.

The darkness pulls at me. I shut off the car but don't move. I sit there, staring at the brick house. My home. My *life*.

What will Roman think when he sees it? Will he think I've settled? That I let this town swallow me whole?

Do I think that?

I shake my head. No. Forget that. Why does it matter what he thinks? I've done the best I could by that girl, and that's more than most people could say. Sure, she isn't my biological daughter, but she became my responsibility the moment my sister vanished without a second thought.

That's something Roman would probably understand—my sister, and her ability to walk away from everything. Like he did.

I don't take risks. I never have. I cling to what's safe, what's predictable. I've stuck to the path that was laid out for me like a set of train tracks, and I've followed it straight through.

Maybe that's why Roman and I would never have worked. He was built like Tasha—all risk and no road map. And me? I like my little life, my job, being near my family. The little things add up to the biggest things when it comes right down to it.

Love. Family. Security. A home.

I have all of those things.

A knock at the window startles me.

"Hey, you coming in?" Clay's voice is muffled through the glass, but his concern is clear. Those deep blue eyes of his look almost black in the moonlight. I release my seatbelt and open the door.

"Yeah," I say, grabbing my bag and stepping out into the night. "I was admiring this little place we call home."

He looks toward the house and smiles. "Yeah, it's not too shabby, is it?"

I laugh softly and lock the car behind me. We walk in silence toward the door, but my steps are slow. My whole body is tight and worn.

Clay stops a few steps short of the porch, turning to face me.

"Look, Frankie, I'm not trying to tell you what to do or how to feel about this whole thing with Roman—"

There's a pause. Not a natural one. It stretches, uncomfortable and expectant.

I narrow my eyes at him. "Then don't." I nod toward the front door. "It's been a long, emotional day, and I'd really like to go inside, take a hot shower, and sleep. Can we talk about this later?"

Clay frowns but nods. "Of course. We'll talk in the morning."

He starts to turn back to the door, but that flicker of hurt on his face keeps me from walking past him.

"But you do have something to say. I can see it all over your face." I cross my arms. "If you need to get it out, let's hear it."

His chin lifts. "We've been lucky to have you in our lives, Alayna and me... and I'd be selfish to ask you to stay, but I do hope you will. We understand each other, I think—both of us have been burned. The ones left behind." He swallows and runs a hand through his hair. "This isn't coming out right. I've tried to ignore it for as long as I can, but I don't think I can sit on my feelings anymore."

My heart skips. My head starts spinning before I can even make sense of what he's saying.

"Clay," I say cautiously, "what are you trying to say exactly?"

He reaches for my hands and I'm startled by how warm his touch is against my cold fingers. He's never done that before—never touched me like this. I study his face, a face I usually know exactly how to read but currently cannot make sense of. He's handsome, boyish and charming, but he's Clay...

"What I'm trying to say, Frankie, is that I think we should try this..." He drops our joined hands to gesture between us. "You and me. Not only for Alayna, but for us, as a couple."

My breath catches. Heat rises in my face. "Like... date?"

He nods, his gaze never leaving mine. "Yeah."

My mother's voice floats in from somewhere in the back of my mind—little comments she's made lately about Clay and me being lucky to have each other, about how it *makes sense.* Are they in on this together? He spends weekends with them all the time. God.

"Would it really be that much of a stretch?" he asks. "We already live like a family. What if we tried it for real?"

My throat closes up. This is Clay. Alayna's dad. My sister's ex. My friend. The man who once, years ago, grabbed my hand during a stormy night when the power went out. We sat on the couch by candlelight and he didn't let go right away. I thought it was simply for comfort. Hadn't I?

"I haven't dated anyone seriously since Mara," he adds quietly, almost like an afterthought—but there's weight behind it. "You remember how that ended." I do. Mara was smart, successful, beautiful—on paper, perfect. But a year into their relationship, she confessed she wanted more. A baby. A fresh start with someone who could give her that. Clay couldn't. Or at least he wouldn't. He's always said Alayna is it for him. His whole world. And the idea of having more kids? He shut it down every time Mara brought it up.

"She wanted to start a family," Clay says, staring somewhere past my shoulder. "And I already have one. I wasn't willing to change that."

I can't breathe.

"Say something, Frankie."

I blink rapidly. "What if we didn't work out, Clay? What if it ruined this thing we have now?"

He sighs, fidgeting with his hands like he's holding himself back from reaching for me again. "I've thought about that too. It's why I've stayed quiet for so long. But my heart knows what it wants. And it's you, Frankie. I want *you.*"

Goosebumps rise along my arms despite the thick sweater. I cross my arms and grip my elbows.

"This is a lot," I whisper. "And given the day I've had, I think I need to sleep on it before I say anything else."

Part of me wants to scream at him for doing this now, for shifting everything under my feet when things were finally starting to settle. And yet... another part of me wonders—*what if it's not that crazy?*

Sure, there've been moments—when we're laughing around the dinner table, or passing the grocery list back and forth in perfect rhythm—when I've realized we live like a married couple. But there's never been anything romantic between us. No kisses. No sparks. No crossing lines.

But have I ever allowed myself to *look* for them?

Could I see him as more than Alayna's dad? More than my sister's ex?

Could he see *me* as more than the woman who stayed behind?

Clay's face tightens, but he nods. He turns and opens the front door, holding it open for me. "Think about it. That's all I'm asking."

I walk past him in silence. The familiar smells of vanilla wax melts and Alayna's potted plants greet me, but they don't bring the comfort they usually do. Everything is different now. Tilted.

My feet don't stop until I'm in my room, the door shut firmly behind me. I wait, listening. His footsteps pause outside my door. My heart stutters. Then—finally—they move on.

I don't want to lose what we have. I don't want things to change.

But they already have, and pretending otherwise won't stop the fallout.

CHAPTER 9

TUESDAY MORNING IS A blur. I wake up later than usual—thank you, melatonin—and barely have time to grab my coffee before flying out the door with Alayna. Clay's unusually quiet, moody even, but I don't have time to dissect his vibe. Honestly, I'm avoiding another heart-to-heart. One was more than enough.

Alayna, on the other hand, seems blissfully unaware of the emotional tension hanging in the air. She's completely at ease, perched in the passenger seat, using the visor mirror to carefully apply her makeup.

We hit the final speed bump in the school parking lot a little harder than I mean to, jostling both of us.

"Hey!" she yelps. "Watch the bumps!"

"Sorry." I wince, easing off the gas. "At least you won't be late. Why didn't you wake me up?"

Students rush past the car in a blur of backpacks and books, fighting the fall wind. A few shout greetings to Alayna, who gives a casual wave like she's been doing this forever.

I pull down my own visor mirror and flinch at my reflection. My hair is frizzy at the temples, a result of falling asleep before it dried. I skipped makeup entirely, and now—sitting next to my flawlessly put-together niece—I briefly consider stealing her cosmetics bag. Not that it matters for a shift at the hardware store... but I'm meeting Roman tonight. And maybe a small, vain part of me wants to look good, if only to remind him I've done fine without him.

"Huh? Oh," Alayna says, finishing with her eyeliner. "I guess I didn't realize you were still asleep. It took me forever to dry my hair, and by the time I noticed you weren't with Dad, you were already making coffee."

"Not your job to wake me up," I mumble, flipping the visor back up. "I just wish I'd had time to get ready."

She clicks her mascara closed and turns toward me. "Dad was in a crap mood this morning. Any idea what that's about?"

I glance at her, surprised. Maybe she's not as oblivious as she looks.

I shrug, aiming for casualness. "How would I know?"

Alayna narrows her eyes, unconvinced. "Come on, you're seriously going to play dumb? He was acting *so* weird last night at dinner. Jealous, if you ask me. I think the new principal—your ex-boyfriend, which I'm still salty you didn't tell me about—really got under his skin. There's totally bad blood between them."

I sigh and focus on the windshield. "Ancient history. High school boyfriends are exactly that—high school. They should stay there."

"I'll keep that in mind," she teases, humming "Bad Blood" under her breath.

"I love you, you annoying little twerp, but if you don't hustle, you're going to be late. And I look like a troll—I refuse to go sign your tardy slip looking like this."

Alayna leans over and blows me an exaggerated kiss. "You always look hot, Keke. Don't even worry about it."

"And that's why you're my favorite niece," I grin, tapping the wheel.

She opens the door with a dramatic eye roll. "Um, I'm your *only* niece."

Then the joke hits. She groans and sticks her tongue out as the door slams shut behind her.

My mind refuses to settle. I spend over an hour wandering the aisles with a broom in hand, pretending to tidy while accomplishing exactly nothing.

When Mom and Dad show up for lunch, I jump at the chance to slip out for a bit. The look of surprise on my mom's face instantly makes me flush with guilt.

"Of course, sweetheart," she says, eyes narrowing. "Is everything okay?"

I nod. "I overslept this morning. I want to knock out a few things at home, if you don't mind."

She studies me like she's trying to see through my forehead but doesn't press. She hugs me tightly and sends me on my way.

I head straight home and dive into the shower, giving my razor a workout I've been neglecting. Afterward, I spend more time on my hair and makeup than I have in years. I hate how much I care—but it doesn't stop me from swiping on an extra coat of mascara or squeezing into my black dress pants, the ones I've been told fit like a second skin.

I try on every top I own before finally settling on a deep crimson sweater. Diamond studs, my favorite black heels, and a healthy dose of doubt later, I catch my reflection in the mirror.

I don't know if I look ready for a date or a job interview. But what I do know is that every inch of this effort feels like armor.

Armor to shield my heart. To hide the fact that Roman still has the power to hurt me, no matter how many years have passed. I won't let him. I'll tell him about Alayna, let him say his piece, and we'll go our separate ways.

Wishful thinking in a town like this—but still. I can try.

As focused as I am on Roman, Clay's words from last night keep pressing at the edges of my mind. That old saying—*when it rains, it pours*—has never felt truer. I'm caught in a downpour with no umbrella, no idea which way is up.

For years, I've kept the wanting locked away. The dream of a real family, of more children, of something that was mine. And in a handful of chaotic days, everything has shifted. The risks I was too scared to take are back, demanding to be acknowledged.

I miss the predictability I used to hate. Nothing is certain now.

By the time I return to the hardware store, it's already three. Mike's car is in the lot. He'll be gone by five—before Roman arrives—and if I have my way, so will my parents.

"You look lovely," my mom says, grinning from behind the register. "Going somewhere after work? Dinner with Clay again?"

I groan. "I have a meeting. It's personal."

She gives me that look. The one that says *I wasn't born yesterday.*

"Whatever you say, sweetheart. But just in case, why don't you work on the books today and let me and your dad handle the grunt work? I'd hate for you to ruin that sweater—red is my favorite on you. Where'd you say this mysterious meeting was, anyway?"

I didn't say where, and we both know it. Her barrage of questions is a fishing expedition. I don't bite.

"You can stay if you want, but Mike and I have it covered. You know Tuesdays are slow."

Right on cue, Dad strolls out of the office and wraps Mom in a hug from behind. "How about we take off and let our daughter run the place for a while, Grace?"

Mom glares at both of us but doesn't protest as she leans back into him.

"Only if you take me out to dinner," she says. "I'm not cooking tonight."

Dad grins. "You *never* want to cook. But I could go for one of Jake's burgers."

"Or a salad?" Mom suggests sweetly.

"Of course not," he says, sticking out his tongue like a five-year-old. "I'll leave the rabbit food to the rabbits."

Mom scolds him, but she's smiling. They're still the gold standard of a good marriage—like both sets of grandparents before them. Leave it to my sister and me to break the streak.

"I love you guys. Thanks for letting me sneak out."

Dad pats my shoulder. "You work too much. It's time to hire someone full-time. Give yourself a break, kiddo. Life doesn't wait."

I wave him off. Between Dad, Mike, and the college students who help out part-time, I have more support than I need. This shop—this life—is mine, the hardware store might not be much, but it's the only thing that feels truly my own. I've always been okay with that.

At least... I used to be.

"Alright, alright," I say, ushering them toward the door. "Get out of here."

I hug them both and watch them leave. Once the door shuts, I retreat to the office, take Mom's advice, and pull up the books. The numbers blur on the screen, my mind refusing to cooperate.

I chew the end of a pencil and rest my forehead against my folded arms.

The next two hours crawl. I can hear Mike humming as he stocks shelves, helping the rare customer that wanders in. I stay hidden in my office, heart racing every time the bell over the front door jingles, knowing it's not Roman. Not yet.

At exactly five, Mike pokes his head into my office.

"I'm heading out. Want me to flip the sign?"

"Please. Thanks, Mike. Tell Mel I said hi."

"Will do. You should come by for dinner soon—she's been asking about you."

I smile. "I miss her. Tell her I'll stop by soon."

Mel, Mike's lovely mother, cooks a mean casserole and hosts a once-a-month ladies' night where she and her friends play cards, drink boxed wine, and gossip like teenagers. I've been her guest more times than I can count. She says I'm an honorary member now.

He nods, ever a man of few words, and heads out. I hear the lock click behind him.

Alone now, I press my forehead to the desk and try to steady my breathing.

Any second now, Roman will walk through that door.

When I finally hear the knock at the door, my whole body lurches from my chair.

There's a crease in my pants from sitting, and I smooth it out with my hands, hastily pulling my sweater back into place. I allow myself two long, deep breaths—and then I head straight for trouble.

Roman has his back turned when I open the door. Another well-tailored suit clings to him in all the right places. From this angle I can see he's not the long, lanky teenage boy I once loved. This man is still lean through the middle, but he's impossibly broad now—muscular, solid, a living piece of art.

Not for the first time since he came back, I wonder how different *I* look to *him*. "Hi, Roman."

He turns, and his dark eyes rake over me, undoubtedly taking the same inventory I did. The way they linger—curious, appreciative—makes me grateful I dressed up. Sexual chemistry has never been our problem. The cool evening wind tosses my curls around my face, but it does little to cool the heat rising in my cheeks. My heart pounds hard against my ribs, as if it's trying to break out.

Roman clears his throat. "Wow, Frankie, you look…" His hands gesture vaguely toward me before falling to his sides.

"You too," I say softly, caught off guard by the sudden shyness crawling up my throat. I don't want him to compliment me. I don't like the way it stirs old hope inside me—hope I have no business entertaining. "Come in. We can sit in the break room."

Roman nods, stepping past me into the shop. I close and lock the door behind him, then lead him through the store. The last time we were in this space together, we were studying for finals. I swallow hard as the memory rushes in—bright and painful.

It's awkward, disarming, having him here. In *my* space. I should've suggested we meet somewhere else, but it's too late now.

The break room is exactly as we left it all those years ago. I never got around to renovating it. Four wooden high-back chairs crammed around an undersized round table. A corner counter with a sink, a microwave, a fridge stocked with drinks and snacks. A time capsule. The air smells faintly of old coffee and dust.

Maybe I *should* finally throw some glitter paint on the walls like I used to dream about when I was little.

"How was your day?" Roman asks, slipping off his jacket and draping it over the back of a chair.

"Huh?" I blink, struggling to focus. I can still see us sitting at this table, drinking root beer, laughing until I snorted soda out my nose. Roman had laughed until his sides hurt. My mom had yelled at us about the mess. I'd spent the next weekend scrubbing the place from top to bottom.

"I asked how your day was." He raises an eyebrow.

"Fine, I guess." I chew the inside of my cheek. "Are we going to talk about the weather, too?" The words come out sharper than I intend, and I regret the tone instantly. But it hangs there, tense and uninvited.

"Okay," Roman says, rolling up his sleeves, his forearms strong and tanned. "If you'd rather cut to the chase..."

"I'm sorry. This is... a lot." I drop into a chair and release a long breath. "Why don't *you* tell me about your day instead?"

Roman gives me a pained look. That same face my heart never forgot. Strong, straight nose. Hazel eyes that see right through me. Dimples absent—he's not smiling. His jaw is so tight it might crack. His hands grip the back of the chair, body still rigid.

"It was fine. The kids are incredible. I'm settling into the job even faster than I expected."

Of course he is. Roman was always good at everything. "That's great. Lots of familiar faces, I'm sure."

He lets out an exasperated breath and finally sits across from me. His hand covers mine—warm, soft—and the electricity is instant. I resist the urge to pull away. "Look, Frankie," he says gently, "you were right. Small talk isn't going to work here."

My phone buzzes loudly in my pocket. I pull it out and glance down—*Clay*.

Roman sees it too. I catch the question in his eyes.

"Do you need to get that?"

"No. It can wait." I power it off. Clay knows where I am. He's probably being protective... or jealous. "Sorry."

Roman smiles, a small, fleeting thing, but enough for his dimples to flash. Then they're gone. "I don't see a ring on your finger."

It's a statement, but I can hear the question it conveys.

"I'm not married, if that's what you're asking. I don't see one on your finger either. No Mrs. Dr. Clarke?" I hold my breath.

"No," he says with a soft laugh. "Haven't found anyone who can put up with me long enough to think about that."

I smirk. More likely *he's* the one who doesn't stick around. "Imagine that."

Roman licks his lips, and my body betrays me—heat blooming under my skin. I remember too well how his mouth once felt against mine. How he branded me with it.

Then, just like that, the spell breaks.

"Are you going to tell me about Alayna, or are you going to make me beg? God, she looks exactly like you."

I blink, reeling at the shift. The image of Roman begging has a certain appeal, but I shake it off. "She's not your daughter."

He doesn't flinch, but his hand tightens around mine. He leans in. He smells like sandalwood and something spicy. I don't know if it's cologne or shampoo, but I like it.

"Frankie, if you're only saying that because—"

"She's not your daughter," I interrupt, firmer this time. "She's Clay's."

I can't bring myself to add *she's not mine either*. Because she feels like mine. And I'll claim her, for as long as she'll let me.

"But she's fourteen," he says quietly, pulling his hand back. "I guess that means you moved on pretty damn fast, huh?"

I laugh, a short, ugly sound. "That's rich."

"What's that supposed to mean?" His voice sharpens.

"I *moved on*? *Me*? You left. You ghosted me like those two years meant nothing. I've been right here, Roman. I wasn't hiding. Any of our old friends could've helped you find me."

The tears burn, but I won't let them fall. Not in front of him. "I think this was a mistake. You should go."

Roman's voice drops, cold and quiet. "You didn't try that hard to reach out either, Frankie."

And he's not wrong.

I lean back in the chair and close my eyes. I had tried. For two weeks, I gave it my all—calls, emails, asking anyone who might know how to contact him. But he never responded. And eventually, I gave up. I wasn't going to make a fool of myself. Not again.

If I hadn't bumped into him the other day, I'd probably still be sticking to that vow to never be the one to make the first move.

"Alayna isn't yours. I didn't cheat, if that's what you're worried about. You left. I stayed. And it's all ancient history now, right? Let's leave it in the past."

I can't believe he thought I'd cheat on him—let alone with *Clay*. Clay was with Tasha. Everyone knew that. Didn't they? But maybe Roman never really paid attention to Tasha; she was two years older, it was possible he didn't remember they'd left for college together. Or maybe he didn't care enough to remember.

Roman drums his fingers on the table. Then he stops. His chair scrapes back sharply.

"You're right. This was a mistake. I wish you and your daughter—and Clay—all the happiness in the world. Thanks for clearing that up."

I want to tell him he's wrong. That it's not like that. That Alayna only looks like me because she's my niece, and while I love Clay, it's never been the romantic kind of love.

I want to tell him that having him here, so close, what a few days ago was only the ghost of old pain, a manageable ache like arthritis before it rains, has now morphed into a soul-crushing weight. I want to tell him that I'm glad to see him. That I still have questions, still care, still *feel*—

But I say nothing.

Even as the walls around my heart collapse, even as every jagged piece tears through me, I don't speak. I don't chase after him.

I let him walk out on me.

All over again.

CHAPTER 10

I SIT IN THE breakroom staring at the scarred table top for a long time after Roman leaves. My memory is a steel trap, and I know that if I climb underneath the table now, I'll find the little heart, with 'R + F 4ever' carved in the center. It was carved with Roman's pocket knife on our one year anniversary.

Those early days with Roman had been easy. It was as if the moment our eyes met, our souls had recognized each other. We'd spent days talking on the phone, filling every second that we couldn't physically be together with each other's voices. Writing notes and passing them between classes, watching each other's soccer practices and games. We were inseparable and yet, we moved slower physically. It had taken two weeks before Roman finally got up the nerve to kiss me, and then I hadn't understood his intentions and he'd met my cheek instead of my lips. I think it knocked his confidence, because he didn't try again over the following few days, and I was not that patient.

I'd waited for him after school, leaning against his black sedan. The grin that lit up his face when he saw me waiting there was more than enough encouragement. I'd reached up on tiptoes, taking his face in my hands and softly brushed my lips against his. Even though I'd been the one to initiate the kiss, he'd instantly taken charge. I saw fireworks, my whole body bursting alive with color. I knew without a doubt, I'd fallen hard for that boy and I was going to keep him forever.

But forever ended up being a lot shorter than I ever imagined.

I rub my eyelids, not letting the burning needles turn to tears. I like the anger better than the wishful thoughts about what could have been.

Despite the absolute failure to communicate we've suffered tonight, I can't help the irrational flicker of hope growing in my heart. Maybe we can never be friends—the scars we've left on each other may never heal enough for us to move past them—but after years of silence, of nothing at all, having Roman back in my life—even like this—is something. I'm not sure if it's a step forward or backward, but it's something.

A glance at the clock tells me it's getting late, almost eight-thirty. Clay and Alayna will be getting ready for bed, dinner finished and dishes done. We have a good routine, the three of us. Guilt gnaws at me for turning off my phone and ignoring Clay's call. As much as I let him into my day-to-day life, I need a moment alone, I need to do this by myself. No one can figure out what my heart wants but me.

And after his proposal last night, I'm not entirely sure where things stand between us.

Clay has never really crossed any privacy lines with me before. We do a lot of family things with Alayna, but it's never felt like more than that. As long as we know who is watching Alayna, the rest is up to our own schedules, our own routines. We have personal lives outside of the house that don't involve the other person.

He's known when I've gone on dates over the years, and he's never asked me questions when I roll in super late, letting me keep my walk of shame details to myself. I do the same for him, never asking about his dates or his relationships. Bringing someone home with a child in the picture means it had better be pretty damn serious, and I never found someone that made me want to risk the peace. Mara being the only exception, Clay has never introduced any of his dates to me or Alayna either, so it's never been an issue we've needed to talk through.

Did his actions this week mean he was worried I'd bring Roman and our history home with me? Was he jealous? Was that what had pushed him into sharing his feelings? His words echo in my head.

My heart knows what it wants, Frankie, and it wants you. I want you.

The problem is, my heart has been broken for so long... I no longer trust it to know what it wants.

Perhaps it wants too much.

With a long sigh, I get up from the table and turn out the lights. My mind bounces around, hitting every nerve like a game of pinball, and I hope like hell that I'll come home to a quiet, sleeping house. I don't have the energy to explain to Clay how tonight went, when I'm still not sure myself.

Somehow I manage to avoid Clay and Alayna for the rest of the week. Clay must have sensed my need for space when I didn't return his call after the meeting with Roman—and then stayed in my room until they left the next morning.

Alayna wouldn't have given me this much space on her own. I'm thankful we know each other well enough that they've granted me this reprieve—even if part of me wonders how long it'll last.

Alayna doesn't need me to drive her to school. Clay's more than capable of getting her there most mornings before work. He'd never admit it if she were listening, but he loves those quiet drives with her. Their father-daughter bond is solid—one of those rare, unshakable things I've always felt lucky to witness.

By Friday, Clay finally breaks the silence. He texts me from the grocery store, asking if there's anything we need that didn't make it onto the fridge list. I lean back in my desk chair, scanning my brain for what we might be out of. I've been so caught up in my feelings, I've barely remembered to eat.

ME

Microwave popcorn & bananas

CLAY

That sounds disgusting

ME

Not together, you heathen

CLAY

Everything good with you?

ME

Yep.

CLAY

Home for dinner tonight?

ME

No. Sunday I'll cook though. Lasagna? I think we need mozzarella.

CLAY

I'll grab some. You got a hot date?

ME

Having drinks with a friend.

CLAY

A certain high school principal?

I stare at the screen. Actually, it's Sarah—my only remaining girlfriend from high school—that I'm meeting. She comes to town once a month to check on her parents, and we've had a standing bar date for years. She's the best friend I have outside of Clay and Alayna.

My head pulses with irritation. Why is Clay asking about my dating life like it's normal conversation for us? It never has been. Then again, I never followed up on the front porch conversation either. I've been hiding. Eventually, I'll have to stop.

I roll my shoulders and shoot off one more text.

ME

No. I'm meeting Sarah. I'll tell her you forgot about our monthly night out. She'll love that.

> Please do not do that. I do not want an angry Sarah coming after me. Have fun. Call me if you need a ride.

Not once in my entire life have I called Clay for a drunk ride home, and I would not start now. Usually if I have too much to drink, I order a ride-share and sleep it off at the hardware store, or if I'm being extra boujee, I'll get a nice hotel room for the night. Clay assumes I spend those nights with Sarah at her parents' house, and I've never corrected him.

There's a lot of speculation that goes on around a small town like Pinewood. Sometimes allowing people to believe whatever they want to is the best form of self-preservation.

People in this town have always assumed things about me and Clay. When I moved in with him, the rumors immediately started to fly. People think we're more than we are even now. When we're out in public they stare and whisper, taking bets on how it will all end. I know it. He knows it. Neither of us talk about it. We know how our dynamics work and that's enough. Alayna has never been confused by our arrangement. I'm Auntie Keke, and that's her dad. The end. Why should I care what anyone else thinks?

Including my mother.

After locking up the store, I fix my hair and makeup in the small employee bathroom. I brought my outfit and supplies with me so I could avoid heading home before my night out. I've decided to wear my normal worn-out skinny jeans and a loose black spaghetti strap blouse. I skip the heels and slide on some plain black flats. One night of heels was enough for this week.

Sarah is already waiting for me at the bar when I get there, even though I'm five minutes early. She looks stunning and put-together as usual: a black pencil skirt and a cream-colored top that might be silk, mile-high chunky heels, and her blonde hair expertly styled. She waves me over, a sly look on her gorgeous face.

"You've been holding out on me," she says, sliding a fresh raspberry mojito into my hand as I take my seat next to her. The barstools here are more comfortable than the booths, but what they make up for in comfort, they lack in privacy. I swivel my head to see who is within earshot, and, not seeing any of the local tongue-waggers, I turn my attention back to my friend.

"Well hello, gorgeous, it's nice to see you too," I smirk back at her. The familiar smell of patchouli wraps its welcoming arms around me.

"Hi," she says, with a dramatic wave of her hand. "Now start talking."

"So your mom was quick with the gossip, then?" I should have known she would hear about Roman's return before I could tell her myself. It seemed like something I should share in person and not over the phone. Besides, I have more news than that to share.

Sarah nods. She takes a long sip from her own drink, a giant pink margarita, and shimmies her shoulders as the alcohol hits her tongue, a move she's been doing for as long as I can remember. "I can't believe you didn't call me the second you found out he was back. Have you seen him yet?"

So she had only heard he was back in town then. I can barely hide my surprise. The gossip mill needs to up its game. "Oh yeah. We met up at work last night."

Her blue eyes widen, and she squeezes my arm, red manicured nails digging into my skin. "Oh. My. Gracious. You better start spilling, and fast, I'm about to combust on this barstool."

"He thought Alayna was his daughter." I let the words hang there, watching them land. "I told him that she's Clay's daughter, but for the life of me, I couldn't tell him that she wasn't mine."

"Holy crap. So he thinks that you and Clay—why would he assume that? How does he look? I absolutely wish I could have been a fly on the wall for that reunion!" She twists a napkin in her fingers, her whole body buzzing with the kind of drama-high only Sarah could enjoy. "How are you doing with all of this?"

I laugh before downing half the mojito. "He looks..." I swallow hard.

Sarah's red lips turn down in a dramatic frown. "He looks what? Frumpy? Old? Did he get one of those pregnant man bellies? Maybe glasses?"

"Worse," I scoff. "He looks even better than he did in high school. He was always too good-looking for his own good, but now... now he's all big and broad and manly. And he wears fancy suits and gels his hair. It's downright rude."

"Figures. Why couldn't he be hideous? Premature balding or something." She laughs, loud and unapologetic.

Even completely bald, that man would be beautiful. "Yeah, it's weird. He looks like Roman, and he sounds like Roman, but we're complete strangers now. And we certainly didn't mend any fences talking to each other the other night. If anything, we're more messed up now than when we were not talking at all."

"Is that what you want then? To mend fences?" Sarah takes another long drink, eyes flicking sideways at me.

Is that what I want?

"I don't know. Maybe?" It's not a lie. I don't know exactly what I want. It's not the whole truth either, because when I think of Roman, I immediately wonder if his lips still taste the same. How they would feel pressed against my neck, or anywhere else on my body. It's strange to look at someone you used to be intimate with and no longer know in that way. It's confusing to all the parts of my body, but mostly my head.

"I wish you would have snapped a picture of him. That's going to drive me crazy. What are the odds I'll run into him while I'm home this weekend?" She wiggles her eyebrows.

"What would you even say to him? I had a hard enough time forming coherent words."

"Hmm. I don't know what I'd say. We don't have a history like you two do." Sarah leans into the bar, resting her chin on one hand. "If I had the chance to talk to Trevor again, I think I'd probably kick him in the balls and that would be that."

I tap my lips with my fingers, remembering Sarah's ex. "You and Trevor didn't shy away from saying everything you wanted to when you finalized the divorce. I'm surprised one of you didn't set the other one on fire to be honest."

Sarah's eyes blaze. "I did consider it, but I'm not going to jail for that knucklehead. We rushed into getting married before we knew each other well enough. I won't ever make that mistake again. Besides, that was more than two years ago now. I'm mostly over it. Actually, I heard last week that he's dating Jarrod."

I cover my mouth to keep from spitting out my drink. "Jarrod, as in his boss, Jarrod? His very male boss?"

"Yep. Explains so much really. I'm kind of happy for him, dang it." She smiles and I know she means it. Even though they weren't right for each other, neither of them were bad people.

"I still hate that he stole you away and now you're not local anymore. If you'd never met him, maybe you would still be here in town with me."

Sarah laughs. "He did steal me, and I would have come back, but you know I love my job too much to leave the city now. I don't think there are enough people in this stuck-up town to keep me in business. At least not enough people with taste. Present company excluded, of course."

"Which reminds me, when are you going to design me a tattoo?"

"You hate needles. I'm not putting you through that. When you get your own place, I'll paint you a mural."

When you get your own place.

She's been telling me to do that for years. As much as she supports the close relationship I have with my niece, she is not a Clay fan. She's convinced that he's holding me back from starting my own life and my own family. After all, playing house with another man doesn't go over well with potential boyfriends.

"Yeah, yeah, I know how you feel about me living at Clay's."

"You get zero benefits from that. You need your own space. I cannot stand that he's okay with you holding Tasha's place."

"I am not holding Tasha's place." I don't even try to hide the grimace on my face as my sister's name leaves my lips.

Sarah glares at me. "Call it whatever you want, but that man has ulterior motives, and you're too blind to see them."

"Wouldn't be the first time I misread a man." I throw my hands up. "I'm apparently an idiot."

"You're not an idiot, Frankie, but you are too nice."

"Well, you're not going to like my other news then."

She motions for the bartender to bring her another drink, even though she still has half a drink left. "You have more news and you're just now telling me? Why do I think I need to be more drunk to hear it?"

I rub my hands over my pants, suddenly nervous about sharing. "A few nights ago Clay told me he has feelings for me. That he wants to see if we could be more to each other than friends."

Sarah's drink sprays from her mouth, garnering us some nasty looks from the bartender and a few people down the bar. "Excuse me, what now?" She attempts to mop up the mess with a drink coaster. The bartender practically growls as he throws a stack of napkins toward us.

"His exact words were 'My heart knows what it wants, Frankie, and it wants you.'"

She stares at me, mess forgotten, pressing her lips together as she takes it all in.

"But now that Roman's back..." I pause, fingers tightening around my glass. "I keep wondering if I'll ever get my own happily-ever-after. And Clay... I trust him. At this point, I probably know him better than anyone. Would it really be so awful to see where that could go?"

I glance at Sarah. She doesn't interrupt, but her brow twitches, her eyes sharp with barely-contained opinion.

"He's been through hell, too. He knows what it's like to be left behind, to hurt. And I know—deep down—I know he respects me more than that." My voice drops into something softer, more uncertain. "You really think he treats me like a placeholder?"

The air between us hangs heavy until Sarah slaps napkins down onto the bar top with more force than necessary. "Listen," she says, each word clipped and vibrating with restraint. "I am trying very hard not to say something I'll regret."

Her jaw tightens. "I am not now, nor have I ever been, a fan of Clay Phillips."

I wince. "I know. You think he's holding me back—"

She holds up one hand, silencing me with a single finger. "But," she sighs, eyes flicking away and then back again, "he's not someone I think would hurt you. Not on purpose."

"Okay..." I shift in my seat, suddenly wishing the barstool had armrests. "So... should I hear him out? Maybe consider a date?"

Sarah shakes her head slowly, like she's trying to dislodge something stubborn from her thoughts. "I don't think it's a good idea. Not because I think he'll break your heart—but because I think you won't let yourself dream past him. So if you have to try this—if you need to get it out of your system—fine. Take him for a spin. But promise me this: if it doesn't work, you'll finally get your own place. Spread those wings. You love your niece, I get it. But you deserve a life that's yours, too."

I nod, but it's hollow. The warmth of Alayna's laugh, the weight of her delicate hand in mine—those things have shaped me more than I ever expected. I can't imagine mornings without her sarcasm over coffee and sing-a-longs on the way to school. But if things ever fell apart between me and Clay, she wouldn't be mine to keep. I have no legal ties, no claim. If he cut me off, that would be it. After eleven years of knowing every freckle on her nose... that kind of heartbreak might just unmake me.

I trail a finger down the side of my glass, watching the condensation slide and gather. Maybe I've lost it—entertaining the idea of romance while everything teeters so precariously. Roman's return, Clay's confession... all of it a dare from the universe. But what if I bet wrong?

"You could always try dating them both." Sarah's voice breaks the spiral of thoughts, her tone light, teasing, as a fresh margarita lands in front of her with a dramatic clink.

I blink. "Date them both?"

Frankie Hale does not date two people at once. That's not how I'm wired.

Roman isn't even speaking to me. And it's not like he's lining up for a second chance. So why do I keep picturing his lips on mine? Why does the thought of him not caring twist like a blade beneath my ribs?

I press the mojito to my lips and drown the ache. "Or maybe I should join a convent," I mutter with a laugh.

Sarah snorts. "We do not have the best taste in men, do we?"

I raise my glass. "To...swearing off men."

She clinks hers against mine. "I'll stick to tortured geniuses with emotional repression issues—preferably painted, dead, and in a museum, and you can binge watch all the best episodes of *Suits*; I know you have a thing for Harvey Specter."

I laugh with her, grateful for the break in the tension. But under it all, I know the truth—I'm still thinking about Roman's mouth and Clay's quiet longing and whether I'm about to blow everything up just to see what sparks.

I'm not worried about Clay. He seems content to let me keep my distance for now. Though, Sarah's confession that I'm only a placeholder for Tasha clings to me like a bad cold.

My biggest fear is still Roman... he lingers in my thoughts like an unanswered question.

And the worst part?

I want him to be the one asking.

Before I can spiral again, I knock back the last of my drink, the sweetness turning bitter at the end. "Yes," I say, but it's more breath than word. Sarah nods like we've made a pact, but my eyes drift to the door—half-hoping, half-dreading. Because no matter what I say, the truth is this: I don't want to keep them far away. I want one of them to fight for me.

CHAPTER 11

A FEW HOURS LATER, I'm pacing back and forth outside of my grandmother's old house. Clay's house. The house where I live but am suddenly too nervous to step inside. It took me over an hour to walk the few miles from the bar to here. I could have used my app to get a ride home, but I'd wanted the fresh air and the time to think and sober up. I was sure a walk was all I needed to clear my head. Once the alcohol wore off, my strange mood seemed to linger. Now that I'm home, I can't seem to get myself to unlock the door and go inside.

Never once have I hesitated like this before.

When I left the bar, what I really wanted to do was track Roman down and retry that conversation we'd started the other night.

Only this time instead of clinging to hurt and pride, I would be honest with him. I'd tell him...

What? What the hell would I say?

"Hi Roman, I'm still as hot for you as I was in high school, maybe more than I was in high school, and I'd like to take you

for a spin and see if we still have the same great chemistry? Won't you tell me where you've been and everything I've missed? Oh, and P.S. Alayna isn't my kid, I just raised her for the last eleven years, because that's totally normal, right?"

Yeah, right.

What would be the point of it all? Eventually, he'd end up leaving me all over again. And that's if he even has the desire to let me in in the first place. He isn't married, but that doesn't mean he doesn't have someone he's dating, or that he would even be interested in me after all this time.

Do I really want to risk falling in love with him again so he can rip my heart out once more? What if the love I felt for him back then no longer applies? We're adults now, surely we're different people.

I let out a frustrated groan and continue to pace.

The truth is, I don't know if he's worth the risk—not only because we don't know each other anymore, but because of everything Clay brought up the other night. Maybe Sarah's right, maybe I've been so busy being a placeholder for Tasha that I haven't allowed myself to plan a real future for me. Maybe I've missed my opportunity to find the man I'm supposed to spend forever with because I've been too scared to really put myself out there. Or maybe Clay's right, and the man I'm meant to be with has been under my nose the whole time. Anything's possible. Life's crazy like that, isn't it?

Pining after my high school boyfriend, or playing house with Clay, working at a job I didn't even choose for myself—those are all safe options. I don't have to put myself out there to do any of those things. I'm blissfully coasting along in mediocrity.

It's time for me to start focusing on what I really want. I need to figure out what I want my future to look like and then pursue it with everything I have. If I don't make the effort, nothing will change. It doesn't have to mean abandoning what I have now; it could simply be about improving the connections and experiences I've built so far, couldn't it?

The front door jerks open and a shirtless, barefoot Clay stares at me with concern.

"Oh, hi," I say lamely.

"Mrs. Lane called to tell me some lunatic is wearing a hole in the ground outside my door."

"Lunatic?" I roll my eyes. "That's rude–"

Clay doesn't wait for me to finish. "I told her it was probably nothing, but that I'd check it out for her. I didn't expect it to be you, I thought you were with Sarah tonight. Are you locked out or something? Why didn't you knock or call me?"

"I–I um–" This was a mistake, I should have gone home with Sarah or got myself a room at the hotel like I usually do. My heart and my mind are such a jumbled mess, and now Clay will see that I'm falling to pieces under all the stress. I shrug, words failing me.

"Frankie, please come inside before Mrs. Lane calls the police." He looks behind me and waves dramatically at what is surely Mrs. Lane peeping through her blinds at us. You'd think she would know what I look like by now, middle of the night or otherwise. Why is the nosey old woman even awake?

"She's probably got her binoculars out now, what with you being all naked and everything." I can't help the giggle that slips through my lips. Maybe I am still a little tipsy. I let my gaze travel the length of him, from his rumpled sunkissed hair to his bare feet. The light from the hallway illuminates him from behind, giving him an almost angelic glow.

When Clay laughs, I jerk my eyes back to his face. "I'm not naked, Frankie. But good gracious, it's cold out here, where's your coat? Come inside." He offers his hand to me.

He's right, he isn't naked, but somehow the navy blue pajama pants he's wearing seem far too revealing. He looks good, too good.

I swallow hard. It's been such a long time since I've thought of Clay as a man. Yes, he was Alayna's father, and my sister's ex-husband, but he was also a smart, dependable, sometimes hilarious, and undoubtedly attractive man.

When you really get down to the bones of it, I'm just Frankie, and he's just Clay. Why does that give me a flicker of hope? "Maybe I should stay out here..."

"Frankie," Clay sighs. His deep blue eyes seem to plead with me. "Please, come inside."

"Fine." I take his offered hand and despite my best efforts to appear put together, stumble over the edge of the welcome mat and fall forward. Clay catches me in his arms, pulling me tight against his naked chest, saving me from face planting into the floor. My fingers flex against his broad chest, my arms pinned between us, his vice grip around me holding firm.

He laughs softly as he kicks the door shut behind us, his breath disturbing the curls around my temple. "How much did you have to drink tonight?"

"Not that much, unfortunately." I laugh, too. Still, he holds me, his skin warming me through my clothes. I realise just how cold my skin is as I feel his heat against me. I shiver in his arms. "Did Mrs. Lane wake you up?"

"Yeah, but it's alright. I hadn't been asleep long. Alyana is sleeping over at Summer's tonight, so I was catching up on some paperwork for work." He presses me closer to his chest. "You are freezing, come with me to the kitchen, I'll get you a blanket and some hot tea or something."

I shake my head. "I don't know, I should probably go take a warm shower and go to bed. It's late. What time is it even?"

Clay holds on, one of his strong hands rubbing the exposed skin on my back. We've hugged a million times before, but this is different. Part of me doesn't want him to let go. I stare up at him, as he leans around me to check his watch.

"It's a little after one." He leans back, his eyes locking on mine. "We have the house to ourselves for the night. And it is late, so if you really want to take a shower and head to bed, I get it. But if you're not set on heading to bed, I'd really love your company. I've missed you this week."

I stare up at him, my heart making a slow flip in my chest. He missed me? He's been so patient with me after I've all but ghosted him since he asked me to think about "us," and right in this moment, I'd be lying if I said I didn't feel anything at all.

But, what *do* I feel?

I can feel his strong arms holding me to him. His familiar scent wraps around us both. I feel warm and safe here in his arms. Somehow, I know he'll do everything he can not to break my heart. My heartbeat accelerates in my chest, and my skin is tingly and alive. Have I always felt this way under the surface? Or am I only now willing to admit there's something more here, or the potential for there to be, because his questions have given me permission to go down that path?

I bite my lip, debating what the right decision is. Conflicting emotions battle inside of me. I still need to talk to Roman, to clear the air and figure out where we both stand. But that doesn't mean I can't give Clay his fair chance too. I'm not tied to anyone, and I promised myself I'd follow my heart.

If only my stupid heart would speak up. I'm floundering here.

"What's going on in that head of yours?" Clay's eyes search mine, his words gentle and low.

He pulls one arm free to cradle my cheek in his hand, his thumb brushing lightly over my mouth. I release my lip, my eyes watching him for guidance. I'm not sure what's happening between us, but I'm not ready to break the spell yet.

"I don't have anything figured out, Clay."

"I'd like to kiss you." His words are barely a whisper. I swallow, a shuddered breath leaving my parted lips.

Alarm bells ring somewhere in the back of my brain. I should tell him that it's too fast. That we should wait and talk about everything, about the risks of changes between us, but my body hums, melting into him as I raise up onto my tip-toes. I let my eyes linger on his mouth as it gets ever closer to my own.

As his soft lips press into mine, I close my eyes and surrender to the moment.

He kisses me gently, barely brushing his lips against my own. He shakes a little as he holds me to him. One hand tilts my head, giving him better access to my mouth, while the other holds me at my lower back. It's almost torture, the way he kisses me so tenderly and slow, tasting me timidly, like I'm the last bite of a decadent dessert.

My pulse echoes in my ears, heat filling my cheeks as I taste his minty tongue. It isn't a fiery passion, but a pleasant lightness envelops me, and I wonder if, when Clay lets go of me, I might float into the air.

Clay pulls back, leaving one last soft kiss on the corner of my lips before pulling me against him in a tight hug. He strokes my hair, and I press into his chest as his heart hammers beneath my ear.

I don't know what this will mean for us. There's so much to say, so much to figure out. I've never imagined what kissing Clay would be like. It's a little like sinking into your own bed after a long day, both familiar and comfortable. There are so many questions swimming in my head, but I don't want to let go of this moment. So, I say nothing. I squeeze my eyes shut and let him hold me.

CHAPTER 12

ON SATURDAY MORNING I wake up in an empty house. I take two ibuprofens for the raging headache I know is coming, and try to ignore the panic beginning to rise at the memory of last night's events.

That kiss.

Clay had stood there in the hallway holding me, and when I didn't speak, he eventually said goodnight and kissed the top of my head before leaving me in the hallway alone. I knew he wanted more, that he'd wanted me to offer to have tea with him in the kitchen, to stay up and talk about things. But I hadn't trusted my own voice or my own feelings. So I didn't stop him when he walked toward his bedroom. I went to my own room, took a shower and fell into my bed.

Now though, in the quiet of the morning, I wish I'd said something. Anything. Because as it stands now, I have no idea where this left us.

After that kiss, I'd hoped clarity would follow. But clarity is clearly on vacation.

I turn on some music and clean the house room by room, giving my nervous energy something else to focus on. I start in the kitchen, scrubbing refrigerator shelves and cabinet doors, tasks we've neglected far too long. Once I start, I can't stop, moving on to the bathrooms, tidying up the living room, and folding the mountain of clean laundry that always lives at one end of the couch. We share the house chores well, but with back to school and our busy schedules, we've let it all pile up.

The music blares loud so I can sing along, letting the words keep my brain busy.

I put my and Alayna's clothes away, glad to see her room is clean and her bed has been made. She's got to be the easiest kid to pick up after, always happier in a tidy space. I know I'm not her mom, but I like to think I've contributed in the same way that a mother would to the awesome young woman she's becoming.

I'm about to bring Clay's pile back to the laundry room when Alayna comes bursting through the front door. She's bright-eyed and full of energy this morning.

"We brought donuts!" Alayna sings as she heads past me to the kitchen with a large box of the sticky goodness in her hands. She turns the music off as she passes the stereo. "I got you a maple bar, I know they're your favorite."

Clay stops a few steps inside the front door, looking around the now sparkling clean house. "We would have helped if you'd waited."

A blush creeps up my neck thinking about us standing in this same spot last night, his lips fused to my own. I lift the stack of clothes in my arms toward him. "Well, how about you put these away and pretend you've helped?"

He nods, but makes no moves toward me.

"How did you sleep?" There are questions in his eyes but I ignore them.

I shrug, bridging the distance between us and handing the stack of clothes over. "Fine, I guess."

"I've been meaning to ask you, how did that meeting with Roman go?" He motions for me to follow him as he puts his clothes away.

"It was fine." I mumble, not sure why he wants to know anything about me and Roman. Unless he's hoping it went terribly so he can feel better about last night.

His room is dark, from the navy blue bed spread to the black furniture, and it smells like his cologne, a mixture of citrus and leather. He'd thrown out everything after Tasha left, starting over fresh with his own style. We spent a lot of time in this room when Layna-bug was small, but the older she got, the less it made sense for me to be in Clay's space like that. Last weekend was a rare throwback to the old days.

He opens dresser drawers, depositing stacks of clothes, before turning back to me. "Think you'll be spending much time with him?"

"What's with the twenty questions, Clay?" I'd expected questions, but I thought he'd want to talk about last night, not my situation with Roman.

Clay shrugs. "Looking out for you is all. I remember how upset you were when he left. It's like we can relate there, you know?"

I do know, but for some reason it doesn't seem right to discuss this with Clay when I don't even know the answers to his questions. I need to speak with Roman. He and I have a lot of unfinished business to hash out.

Alayna pops her head in the door. "Hey, you gonna come have donuts?"

"Yes, I deserve at least two after cleaning up this house." I'm thankful for an excuse to get away. I follow her to the kitchen, ignoring my guilt for once again running from Clay and his questions. Something about the way Clay keeps looking at me has me feeling guilty and confused. My head is a whole mess right now.

Alayna hands me a plate and the two of us sit together at the table, the box of donuts between us.

"Hey Keke," her eyes seem to sparkle as she calls me by my favorite nickname. "I was wondering if you'd be able to pick me up after school on Monday."

"What time?" I mumble through a mouthful of maple donut. I cover my mouth with my hand.

"Well, I have rehearsals all week, and they finish up before five. So if you come right after work I can wait for you out front."

"Rehearsals? Does that mean you got a part in the play?" Excitement makes my voice go up an octave. She's been looking forward to this part of high school for as long as I can remember. We spent many weeks over summer break running lines for the summer drama program, and I watched her love for acting grow. She's a natural, and I cannot wait to watch her on that high school stage.

"It's a full freshman cast, so you're looking at the best modern day Juliet you're ever gonna meet!" She grins before stuffing the last bite of donut in her mouth.

"Woah, baby girl, you got the lead?" I squeal the words, pulling her up out of her chair for a hug. "Look out world, my niece is gonna be a star!"

Clay laughs from the other side of the kitchen. "It's no surprise, none of you Hale girls are fading-into-the-wallpaper types. Much too gorgeous for all that." Alayna and I both roll our eyes. I try to ignore the fact that he's lumped all of the Hale women into one group. Tasha included.

Alayna gives me one last squeeze before turning her beaming smile onto her dad. "Thanks Daddy, remember that when it's time for us to get a costume. Your wallet can be my biggest fan."

This time it's me that laughs out loud. "Don't you get a costume from the theater department?"

Alayna shakes her head, a frown spreading. "No, I guess there was some kind of burst pipe situation over the summer and everything got thrown out. No costumes, no props, even the old set pieces had to be thrown out. I don't think the school has the budget to replace anything. Mrs. Betty is trying to get some donations from local businesses, and running a special where they can buy ad space in the programs, and they've asked some of the parents to spread the word and maybe get a fundraiser going. More people care about football team budgets than theater kids."

Clay pats Alayna on the head. "Don't worry kiddo, I'm sure it'll work out. I'll ask some of the guys at work if they'd like to donate. I'm sure they still need a few tax write-offs for the year."

"I might have some ideas, too." I add, the wheels in my brain spinning wildly.

I can certainly donate my time, the use of tools, wood, paint, and supplies for their set making. I remember my parents donating things of that nature to the school over the years. And Mom and Dad keep begging me to get out of the store; I'm sure they'll be happy to help out for a while so I can build sets with the kids. There's not much they won't do for me, and even less they wouldn't do for our sweet Layna-bug.

"Since you already cleaned up, can we watch some old *Romeo and Juliet* movies? Pile up on the couch like we used to?" Alayna's eyes move back and forth between me and Clay.

"Sure thing kiddo, you in Keke?"

"Yeah, sure. Mike's running the shop today, so I'm not needed at work." I shrug, following my girl into the living room.

My thoughts focus on set design ideas and ways I can make myself useful. Alayna sits next to me on the couch, and I pull her into me, running my hand over the back of her hair like I did when she was little. Clay takes his spot on the other side of her, and just like that, things are mostly normal again.

"Let's watch the one with Leonardo Dicaprio first," Alayna says, passing the remote to Clay. "I think we can get some good costume ideas from that one."

My heart speeds up as I start making plans for the next week in my head. As much as I'd like to claim this is one-hundred-percent only to secure my spot as the best aunt ever, I can't deny the truth. This is the perfect excuse to get closer to Roman. If we are in close proximity at the school, day after day, he'll have to talk to me. I fully intend to get all the answers I long for out of that man. Even if I have to play a little dirty to get them.

"How long do you have before opening night?" I ask, taking a deep breath and holding it in.

"Opening night is in six weeks!"

Six weeks.

There's no way that Mr. Sexy Principal can turn down my offer of help for the school, and Clay can't complain about it when I'm helping our sweet girl get what she needs for the school play.

One way or another, I am going to figure out how to move on from the ghosts of my past, and to do that, I need to work through this thing with Roman. Either we'll find a way to mend what was broken, or at least I'll have the closure I need to put him firmly in the past. Between my feelings for him and this new thing with Clay, I have a lot to iron out, but it doesn't feel impossible.

I've spent enough time sitting around feeling sorry for myself, and as the theater kids would say, the show must go on.

CHAPTER 13

By Monday morning I have everything set up. Since the hardware store is closed Sundays and Mike is willing to take over the Friday and Saturday shifts for a few months, Mom and Dad readily agreed to take over the store the other four days of the week. They all but jumped at the idea of me taking a small vacation from the store. I didn't think anyone cared that much about my overworking tendencies, but I guess they were paying more attention than I gave them credit for.

Sunday, Clay was called into work before the sun came up, saving me from more awkward half conversations with him. Alayna and I spent the day with my parents, and as soon as she was distracted on the phone with Summer, I brought up my proposal to Mom and Dad.

Mom's exact words were, "Yes, please, get a life outside of that dusty place." Dad was beyond thrilled to be needed at the shop again. It felt like a win-win for all of us.

I don't tell Clay my plans, even though part of me wants to. I know he'll be happy for Alayna and the theater kids, and for the fact that I'm taking an active role in the school production. But I also know it will open the door to a barrage of questions about Roman and how I plan to handle seeing him every day.

The thing is, I don't know for sure that Roman will even let me get away with this idea, nor do I believe for a second that he's going to volunteer his own time and be up close and personal with me while I'm working. No matter how much I want that to be the case. Even though we fought the last time we were in the same room, I can't shake off this need to be close to him.

To find closure for the past.

Maybe set the tone for our future.

I wait for the first school bell to ring before heading up to the front door. I don't want Alayna to see me or to hear anything about my plan until I have Roman's approval. Better that she doesn't get caught anymore in the crossfire of my past relationship. It's not her fault I didn't make it clear she's not my child the other night. That one is completely on me.

The double doors at the front of the building are unlocked, but they only lead to a glass box entry where you show your ID before being buzzed into the main building. It's not wide open like it was on the first day of school. Ms. Payton, one of the school secretaries, who was a year ahead of me in school, smiles brightly at me as I walk in. I'm a little relieved, as I was expecting Mrs. Brosnan.

"Frankie! What a surprise! What can we help you with this morning?" Her pretty blonde hair is pulled back into a sleek twist, and I can't help but wonder if she's paying more attention to her appearance due to a certain sexy principal working here. When we saw her in the summer for registration, she looked frumpy and not at all as made up as she is today. Can't say I can blame her for her efforts though; she looks fantastic.

"Hi, Ms. Payton."

"Please, call me Kate. We know each other too well for all that fuss." She taps a pen on her lips.

"Kate." I nod. We don't know each other well at all, but I suppose in this town everyone thinks they know all your business. "I was actually hoping I could speak with Dr. Clarke."

Kate's eyes go wide and she bites the pen in her hand. She obviously knows that Roman and I have a history. "Well, he's a very busy man, let me run over to his office and see if he has time to squeeze you in."

"Thanks, I appreciate your help." I smooth my hands over the black pencil skirt I suddenly regret wearing. Skirts were always Roman's favorite on me, and I was hoping it might help convince him to keep me around. I paired the skirt with a pair of light pink stilettos and a matching pink blouse; the look is feminine but still professional. I look like a sexy, badass business woman, and why shouldn't I? That's entirely who I am now. I swallow, trying to truly believe those words.

"Oh, Frankie?" Kate calls to me, looking back at me over her shoulder. "What should I tell him this meeting is pertaining to?"

I smile, knowing she probably thinks I'm here for personal reasons. I'm sure she's dying to tell the town gossip mill that I've been here asking for Roman. She's not entirely wrong, but I play it cool. "Donations and supplies for the school play."

Her smile falls a little but she nods and walks out of view. I take a seat in one of the two old vinyl chairs and try not to shake my leg as I wait.

The door beside me buzzes before it clicks open. Kate holds it open for me. The warm smile she had for me earlier is gone and she's all business now. "He's ready for you. I imagine you remember which door it is?"

"Thanks Kate, I do." I walk past her, my heels clicking on the freshly waxed floors. My heart pumps hard in my chest as if I've been running instead of sitting quietly in the foyer. I take one last deep breath and then turn the handle for Roman's office.

Roman is sitting behind his desk, his phone pressed to his ear and he's staring out the window. He hasn't seen me yet and I take a minute to look him over. His tie is loose, suit jacket slung over the back of his chair, and his shirt sleeves are pushed up, revealing the tan skin of his arms. He looks tense, stressed. His hair is messed up as if he's run his hands through it a dozen times, and god, the effect is seductive as hell.

"Yes, Mrs. Abrams, I understand what you're saying, but if James doesn't make it to practice, he won't be playing in any of the games. Attendance is important, don't let him make this a habit." His voice vibrates with authority, and my pulse reacts to the sound.

"Wonderful, have a great day." He finishes the call and presses the phone back into the cradle, a little harder than necessary. I've obviously caught him on a stressful morning; hopefully that doesn't mean he won't want to hear me out.

"Rough morning?" I ask softly, letting him know I've entered the office. He looks up, turning his chair forward, his eyes slowly climbing from my heels up to my face. My cheeks burn hot under his gaze.

"Some of these parents have a hard time hearing that their babies aren't always perfect little angels." He sighs. "Come on in, Frankie, take a seat. I hear you have something to tell me about the school play."

Shutting the door behind me, I walk slowly, not trusting my legs to carry me to the chair. He looks so damn good behind that desk, it's disarming. I never would have guessed he'd work in the education field, though I suppose it shouldn't surprise me–he was an excellent student himself.

I sit on one of the old wooden chairs in front of Roman's desk and try not to think about the last time I sat in this chair, when we'd been getting yelled at for our attempt at a senior prank. Apparently the faculty didn't find two dozen chickens running the halls quite as hilarious as we had. Even on his worst day Roman is a lot more pleasant than Mr. Garret, and this time I'm nervous for all different reasons. This time, I'm the only chicken in the office.

I clear my throat and sit taller, "Hale Hardware would like to donate lumber, tools, supplies, paint, and labor. Basically, whatever we have that can be used for the school production. We heard about your unfortunate water damage issue, and we'd love to give back to the community. We can start bringing supplies in as early as tomorrow and work around the clock for as long as you will have us." I say "we," but it's really only me that will be here. I don't offer up that tidbit.

Roman laces his fingers together on top of the desk, his eyes never leaving mine. "That's a mighty big donation, Mrs. Phillips."

I shake my head. "I'm not Mrs. Phillips, Roman. I already told you I'm not married."

He quirks one eyebrow but says nothing. When he stays silent, I continue.

"As you are probably aware, Alayna is playing the lead role, and when she informed us that you needed donations, it was the least we could do. My family has always made it a point to give back to the community, and while the sports teams seem to get most of the fundraising opportunities in this town, we'd like to match that effort for the theater." I swallow, my cheeks turning pink under Roman's steady gaze. He really thinks that Clay and I are a couple, and I've done nothing to clear that up, except to tell him I'm not Clay's wife.

Even at face value, Clay and Roman couldn't be more different. Clay's features are softer, his blond hair and blue eyes both light and welcoming. His voice has become even more gentle after years of fatherhood. Roman, by contrast, is made of chiseled lines, dark hair, and striking hazel eyes. His voice is laced with a dark authority, begging you to challenge him. Yet, somehow I find them both intriguing and loveable in their own ways.

Maybe I've been alone for too long.

Roman's deep voice pulls me from my thoughts. "Well, you'll have to run all this by Mrs. Betty, as the theater is her department, but I can't see any reason why she'd have a problem with it. We'll need to get background checks and badges for anyone who will be working on campus, but we can have those through and back by Wednesday if you and Mrs. Betty would like to get started on Thursday. I'll give you a temporary visitor badge when we finish here, and you can go speak with her. If I remember correctly, she has a free period next."

He sits back in his chair, letting out a heavy sigh.

"It's just me." I blurt out. I don't want to play any more games with Roman, I want a shot at a real conversation with him. This is my chance.

"What's just you, Frankie?" Hazel eyes, today pulling a deep hunter green, stare into my own curiously.

"The background checks, the workers, it's only me. Mom and Dad have to run the store since I'll be here, and Mike only works part time, so we need him to cover the weekend shifts. I'm happy to donate as much as I can to make this a good production for the kids." I smooth my hands over my skirt again, biting my lip to keep from coming out of my skin. It's taking everything I have not to blurt out more, to beg him for answers I so desperately need from him.

"If it's only you, I can print the pass today and you can start tomorrow. But, please clear it with Mrs. Betty so she doesn't think I'm stepping on her toes. And if you need any help, I'm sure the shop teacher, Mr. Daniels, and I can fill in the gaps."

I let out a breath, thankful he's agreeing so easily. "That would be great, I look forward to it. I'll talk with Mrs. Betty and if she agrees, I'll try to stay out of your hair."

Roman stands, his chair bumping lightly against the bookcase behind him. He walks around his desk, stopping right in front of me. I stare at the floor, unsure what he plans to say or do, afraid he's about to take it all back and toss me out of here.

His fingers brush under my chin before he tips my head back to meet his gaze. "Frankie." He says my name like it hurts as it leaves his lips. "I'm sorry about the other night, I was a prick. I want us to be able to talk. It wasn't fair for me to be upset that you've moved on."

My skin is hot under his touch, my lips tremble and I'm not sure I can get the words out, but they need to be said. No matter what comes of the truth, I need to say it out loud. "That's the thing, Roman," I lock my eyes on him. "I haven't moved on. Not in the way that you mean it."

It happens so fast I almost don't register the movement. Roman lifts me up out of the chair, his strong hands are gentle but firm. I am putty in his hands, the warmth in his fingertips scalds my skin even through my blouse. He sits down into the chair he's pulled me from, repositioning me onto his lap, my legs off to the side. My chest is pressed to his, one of his hands holding the back of my neck and the other dangerously close to the slit in my skirt.

I'm trying to catch my breath, but his lips find mine with an urgency that takes the very breath from my lungs. They're soft, two silky pillows pressed against my own. I wrap my arms around his neck, afraid he'll pull back at any moment, but he doesn't. His lips part, and his tongue slides gently against my lips, a quiet moan escaping from me as I taste him.

These are not the lips and hands of a nervous teenage boy. This man knows what he's doing, and what he's doing is wrecking me in all the best ways. It's different than I remember, but somehow in this moment, it's like coming home.

He tastes exactly how I remember. Like smooth chocolate and desire.

I let my fingers knot in his hair as he deepens the kiss. A hunger I haven't felt in years coils tightly in my belly. I press my body into him as much as I can. His fingers singe my bare skin as he rubs circles on my upper thigh, and my body reacts to his touch. I gently bite his lower lip and he groans from the contact, the hand on my neck sliding up to tangle in my hair. It's pure ecstasy and it's only a kiss; I don't dare imagine what anything more could do to me.

We take from each other, kissing and groping and devouring as if no time has passed at all. His lips slide down my jaw, kissing my throat and my collarbones before coming back to my mouth. I can feel the length of him where I'm pressed into his lap. I loosen my hold on his hair, slowing the kiss down, trying to savor the moment. His hand cradles the back of my head as he pulls his mouth from mine. I stare at his swollen lips, before risking a glance into his eyes, afraid I'll see regret in them.

"God, Frankie," he drops his forehead to mine. "What are we doing?"

"I don't know," I answer honestly. My breathing refuses to slow down. The explosive chemistry I'd always felt between us is still there. I want to pull him back to me and never stop kissing him.

"Meet me after school? We can try and have that talk again." He presses a kiss to my forehead and then stands, taking me with him.

"Where are you staying?" I ask, my voice shaking with need and an ever growing fear. I think I might need him, and that scares me, but it also makes me feel alive. I'm unsteady on my feet, but Roman doesn't let go of me, his hands holding my upper arms.

"Do you remember the old Miller house? I bought it. I don't have much furniture yet, but I can make us dinner and we can talk."

Of course I remember the Miller house. We had our first kiss on the back porch of that old house. I wonder if he remembers.

"I remember it."

My chest rises and falls as I try to catch my breath. I want this, I want him to talk to me, to hash out all the things that we've left too long. But part of me is terrified by the intensity of my reaction to this man. The one man I vowed to never give the power of breaking my heart again.

"There's so much I want to say." My voice trembles. I smooth a hand over my skirt, suddenly awkward after we've both lost complete control in his office. I need to tell him the truth about Alayna. I need him to know that I've promised to give Clay a chance. I want to believe that Roman still wants me and that there's a chance for us to find the happiness we left behind as kids... I feel incredibly selfish and crazy, because my wants and needs are conflicting and confusing. I don't even know where to start.

The phone on Roman's desk begins to ring, and he sighs, walking around the desk to pick it up. "Dr. Clarke," he gives me an apologetic look. "Yes, I'll be right down. Give me five minutes."

Roman runs a hand through his sexily disheveled hair. "I hate to run out of here after that, but I have a meeting with a student to get to. I'll let Kate know you need a badge."

I shake my head, my cheeks burning. "Don't apologize, this is your workplace. Go, I'll be fine."

"Please, Frankie, will you have dinner with me?"

The tenderness in his voice breaks through any lingering resolve. I stare at those perfect lips, the lips I want back on mine, hell, all over my whole body. I nod at him, "Yes, Roman, I'll have dinner with you."

CHAPTER 14

ALAYNA CHATTERS A MILE a minute after school. She's perched on the side of the bathtub as I fix my makeup over the sink.

Her ponytail bounces with her animated movements, her hands gesturing wildly. "I can't believe you didn't tell me first! After you talked with Mrs. Betty, she called all of us in at lunch for a special planning meeting. We're having the shop kids and the art kids help us draw up plans for the set. They're going to paint this beautiful mural for part of the balcony scene, it's going to be epic! We already posted some videos to get other kids to volunteer their skills. Ahh, you are the best auntie in the history of the world."

"And don't you forget it." I stick my tongue out at her before turning back to apply mascara.

"Did you know my school has a fashion class? They're going to work on some costume designs for us, we'll have to do a little fundraising for fabric and whatever else you need to make clothes, but it's so freaking cool. And Derek got the part of Romeo... do you remember Derek Gage from middle school?"

"The redheaded guy from the basketball team?" I plug my curling iron in and lean against the counter while I wait for it to heat up, giving Alayna my full attention.

"No, that's Derek Noble. Derek Gage was the class president last year, he's on the soccer team but I can't remember if you've met him."

"Sorry, I didn't realize there were that many Derek's at Pinewood High."

"Well, now you know," she quips.

"Are we happy with this choice for Romeo?" I can already tell she's thrilled with the prospect of kissing this boy, acting or otherwise.

"Oh yeah, he's really nice."

"Nice?"

"And soooo cute." She grins. "I am a little nervous though... I know it's acting, but I've never kissed a boy before. Summer says your first kiss is gross. Was your first kiss gross?"

I let out a long breath as I think back to the memory of my own first kiss. "No, it wasn't gross, but I do remember I was really afraid I wouldn't get it right. I was sure he'd know I'd never kissed anyone before... but then when it happened, that first moment when his lips touched mine, well... it was..." I touch my lips remembering that kiss with Roman. I was two years older than Alayna is now, but I'd never really wanted to kiss anyone before Roman.

"It was what?" She stares at me, biting her lip and hanging on my every word.

"Natural. I didn't have to think about it, I just did what felt right. But you know what the trick is?"

She stands, latching her hands onto my arm and tugging. "No, I know nothing! Tell me!"

"Kiss the right boy."

She groans. "Well that sucks. If Derek isn't the right boy, then isn't that like throwing away my first kiss?"

I laugh and tuck her hair behind her ears. We're the same height now, and it throws me off sometimes that my little girl can meet me eye-to-eye. I pull her into my chest, hugging her tightly. "You don't have to count a kiss for a play as your first kiss, unless it's totally epic and you want to count it. Otherwise, you call it acting and you save the real effort for the right one."

"How did you know your boy was the right one?"

My stomach flips at her question, because it's a valid question even for my current situation. How do I know which man is the right choice, even now?

How did I know I wanted to kiss Roman Clarke back then? Because not kissing him sounded like a fate worse than death. Because when I was around him, the whole world seemed to disappear around me. Everything was brighter, happier, more exciting with him around. "I think when it's the right person, you don't have to think about it. The moment comes and you somehow know."

"Like magic?" Her voice is quiet, innocence radiating from her big brown eyes.

"Yeah, I think it is a little like magic. I know you'll find it, baby girl, you just have to be patient."

She hugs me back, tightening her hold on me. "Thanks Keke, I don't know what'd I do without you."

"I love you too, goofball." I squeeze my misty eyes shut. I don't know what I'd do without her either. She's growing up right before my eyes.

"Wait, why do you look so pretty?" She steps back, taking in my leather leggings and deep violet sweater. It's more casual than the skirt I had on earlier, but I know I look more dressed up than my usual jeans and Hale Hardware shirt. I am skipping the heels tonight though, my black Converse calling my name.

"I'm meeting an old friend for dinner," I say, not wanting to lie to her. I don't really want to explain my evening plans to

Clay, but I'd rather not lie about where I'm going or who I'll be with either. Part of me wishes I had listened to Sarah and moved into my own place this summer. I didn't want to miss a minute of Alayna's life, but now that things with Clay are shifting, it might've been easier to have space to figure things out.

Even thinking about leaving tugs at me. I'd miss the little things—like catching Alayna trying to microwave her socks because "they were cold," or Clay grumbling about glitter somehow ending up in his coffee again. I'd miss dinner at the table, spontaneous dance parties in the kitchen, the constant, comforting presence of family. There are big moments coming—first dates, first kisses, prom, heartbreaks and late-night laughter. And I don't want to miss a second of it.

"Earth to Keke..." Alayna waves a hand in front of my face. "I said, what old friend?"

"Dr. Clarke," I say, watching her face, gauging her reaction.

She wiggles her eyebrows at me. "Oooh, a date with the hot principal? He's like a real life Superman or something, and all those muscles!" She blinks rapidly like some kind of cartoon princess.

I shake my head. "It's dinner and talking, I didn't say it was a date." Though the idea that it might be a date makes my cheeks flush. If that kiss earlier today was any indication, we're even more in tune with each other's bodies than we were as teenagers. His body felt like heaven everywhere it had touched mine. And unlike in high school, we wouldn't have to sneak around.

Alayna laughs, breaking me from thoughts. "Whatever. Adults are so full of it. I bet it's a hot date. He'd be crazy not to want to be your boyfriend again."

Boyfriend. The word bounces around in my head like a pinball machine. Is that even something I want? "Like I said, it's only dinner. And it's been a very long time since he was my boyfriend, Layna-bug."

Her phone buzzes in her hand and she looks down at the incoming message. "Ah, I gotta go, Summer and I are going to watch more *Romeo and Juliet* movies and look for inspiration!"

"Have fun," I say, giving her one last hug.

"You have fun on your not-date." She giggles, making kissing faces at me as she backs out of my room. I can't help but laugh with the little turd.

A soft knock draws my eyes back to my open bedroom door. Clay is standing there awkwardly, a take-out bag in his hand. "What's this about a not-date?"

I bite the inside of my cheek, looking for the right words to tell him. I know that our relationship hasn't been defined, that we haven't even talked about the kiss yet, but we're a team, and I suddenly feel a pang of guilt that I don't quite understand the meaning of.

"I'm having dinner with Roman." The words sound robotic as they leave my lips.

Clay looks surprised, but then he nods. "I brought dinner, but I'm sure Summer won't mind eating what I got for you."

"I'm sorry, I should have told you I made plans tonight. It was short notice and—"

"Frankie, I'm not your keeper. You don't have to check with me before you make plans." Clay shifts on his feet, leaning against the door jamb. He looks handsome in his black slacks and light blue button down. He's still in his work clothes, but his tie is gone. I let myself appreciate the man I know maybe better than any other man in my life, just for a moment.

For years, all I could see when I looked at Clay was my brother-in-law. Even though the divorce was final before Alayna was even five, he was Tasha's ex. The goofy and confident boy who was enamored with my big sister. The guy who always made me feel safe and welcome in his home. The father to the most important human in my life. But there were moments, especially when we were doing family things, the three of us, that I'd sometimes imagine how different it would have been if Clay were my husband and Alayna my daughter.

I never imagined kissing Clay, or anything of the romantic sort, I just pictured myself as more than the fill in for my sister. I couldn't imagine a life without Clay and Alayna in it; I wouldn't want to imagine that. Those nights when we would lay in Clay's bed, Alayna between us, trying to get her to sleep peacefully through the night. The weekends we spent laughing so hard we cried watching her learn to tie her shoes and ride a bike. The many sleepless nights we spent worried about a fever or broken bones or hurt feelings...

We'd done all of that together.

We are bonded in a way that I've never felt with anyone else. It's a type of love, sure, but is it a romantic love? Would he ever love me with the same passion that he'd felt for my sister? The same passion I found with Roman all those years ago? Could we get there if I opened that door and allowed that possibility?

And if we did, what would that mean for our relationship with Alayna? What would happen if we realized that opening that door was a mistake? My head spins with all my questions. So much has changed in a few weeks. My world is all jumbled and confused. I don't know what to think, what to feel.

Clay's still watching me from the doorway, and I can see unasked questions in his eyes. "I know you're not my keeper, Clay. But I also know that we have a system that works here, and I should have had the courtesy to let you know I'd made alternative dinner plans for tonight. I'm sorry."

Clay smiles, but it doesn't meet his eyes. "Be careful, Frankie. We can talk later."

I nod, waiting until he disappears around the corner before turning back to finish curling my hair. I can't help the twinge of fear that snakes its way across my arms, making me shudder. What would it mean if things went well for me and Roman? Would it mean Clay wouldn't want me around anymore? Would Roman be okay with this strange family dynamic that we have here? Am I okay with the thoughts of exploring something more with Clay that are skittering around in my head?

Would Clay take it all back if he knew I still had real feelings for Roman?

Sure, the chemistry is there with Roman—he sets my body on fire—but would he protect my heart the way that Clay would, or would he break it all over again? These two men, one from my past, and one from my present—they're like magnets set so their poles repel one another, and I am stuck somewhere between them. Somehow I can't see any scenario where I'm not forced to choose between two men that I care about, two men that I love, and in the end, how many of us will end up hurt?

CHAPTER 15

THE MILLER HOUSE LOOKS exactly how it always has—the big oak tree that shades the yard, the rose bushes in the front garden, even the beautiful wrap-around porch are the same as when Mrs. Miller tended the house,—but knowing that Roman lives here now makes it seem like a completely different place. If you could see energy with your eyes, I imagine the energy of the house has gone from a calming beach sand to a deep forest green. A forest that threatens to pull you in and never let you go. I stare at the rose bushes as if I might find my strength there, trying to gather the courage to step out of my car and walk the whole ten yards to the front door.

By the time I gather the courage to head to the door, I notice Roman in the front window. He has the decency to turn away and pretend he wasn't watching me, but he's not a very good actor.

I purse my lips, embarrassed that he's seen me out here taking my sweet time. It's been more than ten minutes; how long has he been watching me have an internal meltdown? I shake my head, knowing he's likely still watching me, and finally step outside. I resist the urge to stare down at my shoes as I walk up the path, keeping my head high and my shoulders back with a confidence that I don't feel. My nerves are wound tight, my body still buzzing from the kiss this afternoon. Half of me wants more of that heat, the other half is ready to run for the hills.

Roman opens the door, a soft smile on his lips as I carefully take the two steps up onto the porch. He's wearing a T-shirt and jeans, his hair looks slightly damp and messy, as if he's just come from the shower, white socks on his feet. He looks domestic, and somehow this makes me more nervous than his suit and tie. Here, in his own home, in casual clothes, he reminds me more of the young boy I used to know. My throat works, suddenly tight and in need of water.

"I thought maybe you changed your mind about having dinner with me." He leans heavily on the open door.

"Jury is still out."

He steps out onto the porch, taking my hands in his. "In that case, you should come inside while they deliberate, I hear those verdicts can take a while."

I purse my lips but a laugh slips through. "I see your jokes haven't improved much."

"They still make you laugh though." He grins triumphantly.

"You have me there. I guess I'll come inside."

Roman nods but he doesn't make a move to go back inside. Instead he leans down and presses one feather light kiss on my lips. "I hope you're hungry. You gave me a reason to cook something good in my new kitchen."

I lick my tingling lips, a different hunger building inside my chest. "Oh, I could definitely eat."

Roman turns, leading us into the house. I don't think I'm imagining the awkward nervousness coming off of him. Maybe we're both still shaken from the kiss in his office.

"Make yourself at home, dinner is almost ready," he says, leaving me in the foyer. I slip my shoes off by the door, the aged wooden floor creaking beneath my feet.

Inside the house, it's warm and brightly lit. Roman hasn't changed much inside the old colonial home as far as I can tell. Small white flowers speckle the sky blue wallpaper, and crisp white chair railings and crown mouldings pop against the backdrop. What has changed is the furniture. Where Mrs. Miller had more clutter than she knew what to do with, from what I can see, Roman has barely furnished the large house.

"Looks like you have some furniture shopping to do," I call down the hallway that leads to the kitchen, running my hands over the back of the pale gray couch in the living room. An antique looking coffee table and end tables are the only other furniture in the room. Does the man even own a TV?

"Did you say something?"

Heading down the hallway toward the kitchen I call out to him again. "I said it looks like you have some furniture shopping to do."

I pause in the wide kitchen door frame, taking in the scene before me. Soft music drifts to me from a small speaker near the stove, and Roman has a kitchen towel thrown over one shoulder, his oven-mitt clad hands reaching for something inside the oven. His dark hair has fallen forward over his forehead and his tan arms flex with the movement. This is a man who is confident in the kitchen, and it shows.

My heart squeezes in my chest, and emotion wells in my eyes thinking of how many years we've missed out on being part of each other's lives. The years have passed anyway, and we've both grown into adults with jobs and lives of our own. I wonder who's been lucky enough to share those years with him. While I haven't exactly pined for him or wasted my life waiting for him to return, there has never been another man who has touched my heart in the way that Roman had.

"Did you hear me?" Roman, having placed a delicious looking cheesy pasta dish on the stove, stares at me with concern. "Frankie, you okay?"

I blink back the tears, smiling at him and shaking my head. "Wow, that looks as good as it smells. I think I was distracted by food." My voice sounds watery, even to my own ears.

Roman crosses the few feet separating us and meets my gaze. "I was telling you that I have the hardest time picking out furniture. I can't seem to visualize it in my own space, and I usually end up with a bunch of things that don't match. And since it's only me here, I figure I have time."

I picture his childhood bedroom, an eclectic mixture of styles and patterns, walls haphazardly speckled with movie posters and concert photos, and laugh. "Does it need to match?"

"Well, according to my last realtor, yes." He laughs, his hand reaching up to tuck one of my curls back from my face. "She told me to hide all my furniture in storage and let her stage the place. I think she was right though, it sold during the first open house. Do you know anyone with a good eye for that sort of thing?"

I take a shuddering breath before answering. "You could always go to a furniture store and pick out one piece and then let them match the rest of the items for you."

Roman shakes his head, dismissing the suggestion. "That seems too easy."

"Easy is nice sometimes."

"I think I prefer complicated things." Roman leans down and brushes his lips over mine again. "Sometimes it's worth it to put in a little extra effort."

The microwave dings and Roman pulls back. "I need to grab the bread before it burns. Go ahead and have a seat at the table and then we can eat."

I take a seat in the adjoining dining room, surprised to find that Mrs. Miller's old dining table still occupies the room. Its wooden surface has been resurfaced and returned to its former glory. All six dining chairs as well. Roman has set a table for two, the head chair and one to the left. I choose the seat to the left, toying with the fringe on the woven cream-colored placemat as I wait. Two glasses of red wine have already been poured, and I take a timid sip from my own glass.

"Here we are." Roman places a plate in front of me, loaded with the cheesy pasta, a breadstick, and a delicious looking green salad.

"Wow, this looks fantastic. Thank you. Where did you learn to cook like this?"

Roman takes his seat beside me, motioning for me to dig in. "I took cooking classes in college after I got tired of eating ramen noodles and day-old pizza."

Taking a small bite of the pasta, I savor the flavor explosion in my mouth. Once I've swallowed, I beam at him. "Well, the classes definitely paid off."

"Thank you. I found a love for cooking. The taste testing especially."

We eat in comfortable silence, only the sound of soft music coming from the kitchen and our forks occasionally scraping against our plates. I sneak glances at Roman, catching his eye a few times and earning a shy smile in return. As much as we're strangers to each other now, I'm still comforted by the familiarity of his presence.

"I really am sorry about the other night. I shouldn't have gone off like I did. I didn't come to talk to you with the intention of fighting... it was a lot." Roman fiddles with the stem of his wine glass. "I've missed you, Frankie. I hope Alayna knows how lucky she is, having you for a mom."

Time is up. I need to set the record straight about Alayna, and get closure on how things ended with us the way they did, so that we can start fresh and leave the past where it belongs.

"Speaking of the other night..." I sigh, taking one more sip of wine for courage. "I wasn't as forthcoming with you as I should have been, and I need to set the record straight. While Alayna is my responsibility, and I think of her like a daughter, I'm not her mom. She's my niece, Roman. She's Clay and Tasha's daughter."

Roman goes quiet, staring down at his plate, and I wish I could read his mind. When he doesn't make a move to speak, I continue.

"I should have made that clear the minute I realized you thought she could be your own daughter, but to be honest, I was so hurt by how you left me in the dark... I liked the idea of letting you sweat a little. I know that was wrong, and I'm sorry."

Roman places his hand over mine. "Alayna is your sister's kid?"

I nod, though the admission pains me. "Technically she's Clay's daughter. My sister hasn't bothered to show her face around here since the divorce hearing, and that was more than ten years ago. That's why I stepped in, because she's my niece, and I love her like my own. I've raised her with Clay, and it's totally unconventional and people think it's weird, but it works for us."

"I didn't even remember Tasha and Clay were together." He shakes his head. "But now that you say that, it all makes a lot more sense."

"They came back to town not long after you left for college and Tasha was already pregnant. They were married and moved into Gram's old place. Seemed like they were going to have the perfect start to a good life together."

"So what went wrong?" Roman leans toward me as I speak, giving me his full attention.

"I don't know. I've had years to try and understand how my sister could walk away from her family like that. Alayna was three years old, she needed her mother. She didn't even warn us, she simply took off one day and as far as I know, has never looked back." I rub my chest over my heart, remembering the pain of losing my sister.

"And her marriage, it seemed okay?" I can see the questions in Roman's eyes as he tries to put the pieces of the story together.

I bite the inside of my cheek as I mull over his question. Clay and Tasha had seemed happy. In fact, he'd worshiped the ground she'd walked on. But Tasha was a tumbleweed, and maybe that had been the problem all along. "They seemed good. Maybe they weren't and I refused to see it. I know motherhood was hard on Tasha from the beginning. She was overwhelmed by all of it. I tried to help her as much as I could, but it never seemed to be enough. I think she spent her whole life doing whatever she wanted and as soon as she had a family, she realized she liked her freedom more."

"Are they divorced, Tasha and Clay?"

"Yes." I grimace, remembering the last time I saw my sister. "About a year after she left, Clay tracked her down. She was renting a place a few hours from here and working as a flight attendant. Finally travelling the world like she always wanted to. He served her the papers and she agreed to show up for the custody hearing and to finalize everything. We thought she might try to get visitation or something out of it, but she told the judge she was thankful her daughter had a good life and signed her rights away."

Roman wipes a tear from my cheek. I didn't realize I'd been crying. "I can't imagine how hard all that must have been."

"It broke my heart for Alayna. Knowing her mother doesn't want to have a relationship with her, I can't imagine the hurt that she carries. Tasha didn't even ask to see her while she was in town."

"Did you ask Tasha why she left?"

"I tried. I was so angry with her, I probably went about it all wrong. I asked her how she lives with herself, never seeing her own daughter. I told her she should be ashamed of herself. I called her selfish and thoughtless, and she let me yell at her." My words had been cruel and I'd wanted to hurt her with them.

Even now, my blood still seems to heat when I think of her attitude about the whole thing.

Roman takes a sip of his wine. He's watching me closely. "She didn't say anything?"

"She said something like, 'I wanted a different life for myself. They're doing fine without me, like I knew they would.' And that was the last time I talked to her." And I hoped I never had to speak to her again. My parents could forgive her and talk to her all they wanted, I didn't have to do the same.

"How did Clay take the divorce?" Roman's hand flexes over mine, his body tensing a little every time he says Clay's name.

"Honestly, I think he was relieved in some ways. After a while he dated this woman, Mara, and I thought they might get married at some point, but that didn't end up working out either." I'd been a little relieved when Mara had left. It meant I didn't have to wonder about my own place in Alayna's life. As sad as I'd been for Clay, it felt like I could finally relax again once she was gone.

"But you and Clay, you've never been a thing?"

I expected this was where his questions were leading, but this is where I need to be careful. I don't want anything to be left unsaid. "We've never pursued a relationship before, no. But Clay has expressed an interest in seeing if we could be more than what we are to each other now."

Roman downs the last of the wine in his glass. His face pinches as if it tastes bitter on his tongue. "Do you want there to be more between you?"

"I don't know what I want anymore." I blow out a breath, frustrated, because that's the honest truth. "A few weeks ago, had you asked me that same question I would have laughed at you and told you that having a man in my life was not something I saw in my future."

"And now?"

Roman rubs circles on the back of my hand, the way he'd done countless times when we were teenagers, and suddenly my throat is being strangled with emotion. I've spent years keeping everyone at arms length because I don't trust people to stick around. People can—and will—hurt you. They make you love them and then leave you in the dust. Like Roman left me.

My voice wobbles, but I force myself to ask the question that has always plagued me. "Why did you break up with me that day?"

The circles still, but Roman's hand remains touching mine. "I got scared."

I lift my eyes to his, wanting to see if there is any truth to his words. I am so eager to understand what went wrong. "Scared of what?"

"The future." He shrugs. "Disappointing you. Not living up to the dream in your head."

My body recoils with confusion. "I'm not really following you."

"You had your whole life planned out, Frankie." He shakes his head as if he's back in the moment. "You were going to get married, have babies, take over the hardware store and live happily ever after, right here in Pinewood. And I didn't know the first thing about what I wanted."

"I would have changed my future plans for you, Roman. I would have followed you anywhere." I've never said those words out loud, but as they leave my lips, I know they're true.

"That's what scared me the most, that you'd give up your dreams for some dumb kid who didn't even know what he wanted out of life. I knew I loved you, but I couldn't make myself believe that that would be enough. Maybe loving you was selfish, and I was supposed to let you go. What if it took me years to be ready to get married, or what if I was a shitty father like my own dad had been? It was too much pressure."

"Why didn't you tell me that then?" My heart protests, shattering all over again. Those barely healed cracks splinter down the same lines as I remember the look in his eyes when he told me he didn't think I should wait for him. "Do you remember what you said to me, your last words before I never heard from you again?"

Roman closes his eyes, his free hand massaging the side of his temple. "How could I forget?"

"You said, 'I'm sorry Frankie, but this is it for us. Please don't call me, live your life and be happy.'"

"And did you?"

I want to tell him, no, I've been miserable. But that isn't entirely fair or true.

"Not at first. At first, I tried to find a way to contact you. I called all our friends, I sent emails and text messages, but then—"

"You moved on?"

I let out a humorless laugh. "Then Tasha had Alayna, and I went to school for a little while, and when Tasha left Clay behind, it felt like losing you all over again."

Roman's eyes look glassy, but he remains quiet.

"I didn't even question what I needed to do. I moved into the spare room at Gram's, and I took care of that little girl, and I promised her I'd never leave her. And I haven't. But do you know what else I haven't done, Roman? I haven't let myself get close enough to anyone, because I know how much it hurts when they leave you behind."

I stand, suddenly tired and far too vulnerable. I'm happy that we've cleared the air. I know now why he left, but it doesn't change anything. At least my conscience is clear; he knows the truth about everything, and now we can both move on.

"Frankie—" Roman stands too, but he doesn't reach for me.

"I'm tired, thanks for cooking, you have a real talent for it. I think it's time for me to head home."

Roman opens his mouth, and then closes it. He looks like a fish out of water. If he has something more to say, he chooses not to. I slip back into my shoes and run to my car, pressing my forehead against the steering wheel and holding back my tears.

Maybe the past is meant to stay there.

Maybe I'm not meant to have anyone.

CHAPTER 16

HELPING MRS. BETTY WITH the design plans for the set pieces is a lot more work than I imagined, but I'd be lying if I said I wasn't loving it. The art and woodshop students are full of fun ideas and talent, and the excitement for it all is contagious.

For days, the students have shared their plans with me, drawing out sketches of Juliet's famous balcony and the grand hall, their ideas for a bustling market scene, and the colors and costumes they have in mind. It's refreshing to see teenagers' passion for something other than their phones and social lives. I've been given a backstage pass into a part of Alayna's life that I wouldn't have seen otherwise.

I wonder if this is the part Roman enjoys most about working with students. Seeing them apart from their homes and family, turning into the future adults who will help the world turn. Teaching has never been something I considered as a career, but now I understand why so many find joy in it.

By Friday, we narrow the ideas down to three different cohesive designs, and all that's left is to pick one and get started on the list of supplies to order from the hardware store. Even my parents are eager to hear what the students decide.

Sitting on the edge of the stage, looking out over the empty seats of the theater with Mrs. Betty beside me, brings back a pang of nostalgia for my own high school days. When I'd gone to school here, I'd never taken any of the theater classes that were offered. Being up on the stage in front of people has never been appealing to me. But my sister always loved the spotlight, and Mrs. Betty often confused us for each other in the hallways my freshman year.

She hasn't changed much, still wearing the '60s-style A-line dresses in every color of polka-dot they offer. The older woman has long silver hair that she wears up in a bun or down in a braid, but always with a matching silk scarf tied into it. She must own one of every color, because they always match her dresses perfectly. I wonder if she still sings Broadway songs while walking the hallways.

"With the plans from the last few productions of *Romeo and Juliet* and all of these new ideas, we are going to have a beautiful set in the end." Mrs. Betty beams as she pats my arm. Today's dress is a beautiful shade of sunshine yellow with white polka-dots. She looks like she's ready for a bright summer day, despite the fall weather outside. "You don't know how much the generosity of all of you at Hale Hardware means to us. Your lovely family has been such a gift to this community for so many generations. We would have found a way. As you know, dear, the show must go on! But we are forever grateful that we can continue to put on our show in style."

My cheeks heat under her praise. "You're so sweet, Mrs. Betty. I am happy to help make this even more special for my niece and the other kids in the production. We're happy to give back to the community, and to be honest, I think I'm as excited as the rest of you to be a part of it all."

"Please, dear, call me Betty."

I'd forgotten that Mrs. Betty is actually Betty-Ann Laubenstein, and she'd asked to be called Mrs. Betty after years of botched spelling and pronunciation of her last name. It's strange not to call her Mrs. Betty, but I nod my agreement. "Thank you, Betty."

Betty taps a hand on the stack of design ideas between us. "Well, Frankie, the students have chosen their three favorite ideas, but we're going to leave the final decision up to you. Take the weekend, make your choice, and then let me know how we can help you. If you need extra hands to bring supplies, or whatever you need, say the word, child, and we are at your service. Our lovely new principal has assured me that we can borrow anyone we need to get this job completed." I wonder if she remembers teaching Roman in her own class and if it was strange to have a former student as her new boss, but I don't dare ask.

I haven't talked to Roman since our dinner. He's waved and said hello to me each morning as I entered the school, but otherwise, we've both been preoccupied with our own work and haven't crossed paths throughout the week. My traitorous heart still leaps out of my chest every time I catch a glimpse of him. It's unfair how attractive he looks in those suits. I'm not surprised he told Betty we could have all the help we want; I'm sure he's eager to have this done and me out of his hair.

"That's generous of him."

"He seems to like you. I guess not much has changed there." Betty winks at me. I guess she remembers quite a bit.

"I'm sure we can get this done in no time. I'll make my decision this weekend and spend the beginning of next week at the hardware store making sure we have everything we need. I'll bring the box truck over by Friday, and we can get the truck unloaded and ready for construction the following week. For the next five weeks, or as long as you need me, I'm your girl."

She claps her hands together. "The sooner we get the set pieces finished, the easier rehearsals will be. If you're serious about giving up your entire life, I'll get some volunteers for after-school construction, and we can push through some late evenings to get a head start. Take this next week off to gather what you need and I'll watch for you and your truck of goodies next Friday!"

I am more than ready to devote myself to this project and let everything else in my life stop taking up all of my mindspace. It's a welcome distraction. "Completely serious. You tell me the schedule, and I'll make sure I'm here."

"Wonderful, just wonderful." She hugs me tightly as the last bell of the day rings out. "That's my cue, dear. Tell your lovely parents hello, and enjoy your weekend."

She stands, the petticoat under her dress rustling, and as she walks up the aisle toward the exit doors, she begins to sing, "Singin' in the Rain." I've missed hearing her voice in the halls. I make a mental note to watch the Gene Kelly film with Alayna soon.

I pack up my own things, careful to tuck them deep into my bag so they won't get wet outside. The sound of the students chattering and slamming lockers drifts in from outside the theater. Tonight Alayna has requested chicken and potatoes, and Clay has offered to cook for us. I'm looking forward to a nice, normal Friday night at home with my people.

With everything that's been said between us, I wonder if tonight will really be like the normal Friday night dinners from the last decade, or if everything is forever altered now that Clay has thrown his feelings out there. It isn't that I'm upset with him—of course I always want him to be honest with me—it's just the worst possible timing.

Clay is my rock, the guy waiting for me after work, eager to hear about my day and tell me about his own work drama. We commiserate over parenting woes with Alayna. Cheer each other on for the little wins, and help each other through the disappointments. But it's always felt like family, like a friendship. Can I find a spark there? Do I even want that?

I linger a few extra minutes inside the quiet of the theater, waiting for the commotion in the halls to quiet down as most of the students rush out to begin their weekend plans. I know Alayna will be impatiently waiting for me, but I need these few minutes to compose myself. As exciting as this week has been, it has me even more confused than before about what I want for my own future.

The universe seems to be yelling at me, telling me to wake up and look around. All I have to do is stop stalling and answer the call.

So, why is that so terrifying?

I straighten my back and force myself to leave the theater. I don't have to have all the answers today, but I do need to get out of this school and head home.

Alayna is waiting for me by the front doors. In a pink T-shirt and jeans, she's not prepared for the weather. "It's dumping out there, my hair is going to be ruined," she pouts.

"Where is your coat?"

Her eyes roll so hard I worry they'll get stuck in the back of her head. "Ew. Seriously? No one wears a coat, Keke."

I try to hold back my laughter but fail. I tug at the shoulder of my own thick raincoat. "Actually, smart people dress for the weather."

All around us, students rush out into the rain, not a single one of them wearing a coat. Alayna pulls her backpack from her back and suspends it over her head like a shield.

"You're ridiculous." I pull my hood over my head and push the door open, leaning against it. I unlock my car from the open door, the lights flashing in response, and motion with my hand for Alayna to go ahead of me. She rushes past me and into the downpour, cursing and squealing as she dodges puddles and miserably attempts to stay dry. "Teenagers," I mutter.

"Ah, they're not so bad." Roman's hand holds the door open above my head. I try not to stare at him even as goosebumps break out over my arms.

"Regretting spending so much time here yet?" he asks.

I take a quick breath, steadying my voice. "No, actually it's been really great."

"Glad to hear it. Let me know if anyone gives you any grief."

"Do you have a dungeon for bad students or something?" I laugh.

"Worse. They have to assist Mrs. Brosnan for an entire day."

My head snaps up, and I search his face. He's stone cold serious. "Wow, that's mean."

Roman retrieves an umbrella from somewhere inside his black peacoat. He's practically an ad for some expensive menswear catalog, his hair falling forward over his forehead and his suit peeking out from under his jacket. I bite my lip and shift my gaze away from him as I walk through the doors and into the rain.

Instantly he's behind me, shifting his umbrella to cover us both. The smell of his cologne in the air makes me shiver. "I'll walk you to your car, no sense in getting soaked." He steps closer, not waiting for me to respond.

I stammer a thank you and walk quickly, trying to match his naturally long stride. The air between us is charged and awkward. I can't see through the rain-streaked car window if Alayna's watching or not, but my money is on yes.

Roman side-steps a puddle and I lean into him to keep from stepping into it myself. His arm snakes around my shoulders, likely on instinct, and I close my eyes as the warmth of his body seeps into mine. It's almost a hug, and I hate how much I crave more of his touch. A part of me wishes he'll sweep me off my feet and kiss me like he did in his office.

The more sane part of me knows that's a terrible idea.

"Have a good weekend, Frankie." Roman hugs me to him one last time before dropping his arm from around my shoulder.

"Thanks, you too," I say lamely. It feels like things between us are destined to be awkward forever. I long to go back to the easy, familiar way we used to be. Back when there was no doubt in my mind that he was the boy I would love forever.

"Feel free to call me if you need me. You know, for help with the set or anything."

"I don't have your number." I pause, tugging on the door handle. And I don't want to need him. It will hurt too much when he leaves me again. "I'll stop by your office on Monday and we can exchange numbers then."

"Okay." Roman's voice is low, he almost sounds disappointed. "See you Monday."

I climb into my car, quickly shutting out the rain and my own mixed feelings. Why can't he be cold to me, then it would be easy to write him off forever. Instead, all I can think about is how nice it would be to climb inside his jacket and wrap my arms around him. How much I like his stupid jokes and the way he's always smirking at me with his crooked mouth.

Alayna has the visor mirror down and is trying, unsuccessfully, to control the frizzy mess of wet hair on top of her head. "He walked you to the car to keep you dry? How romantic."

"You're ridiculous," I repeat, but this time I'm only talking to myself.

CHAPTER 17

Dinner is as normal as I can hope for.

Alayna carries the conversation, excitedly talking about rehearsal and not so subtly bringing up Derek's name more than a dozen times. For his part, Clay doesn't question it, but I see his teeth clench a few times, poor guy. I worry how he's going to handle a front row seat to her on-stage kiss.

Watching this little girl become a woman is like watching a flower bloom in fast forward—stunning and impossible to slow down. It's hard to think of her as a young adult when wasn't it only five minutes ago that we were dropping her off at kindergarten and sneaking 'Mr. Blankie' into her backpack in case she got scared?

These memories cling to me lately like static—flickering images I can't shake. She's slipping into her future, and I'm still clinging to the hem of her childhood. Maybe that's part of why I've started craving something more for myself. When she leaves, spreads her wings like I know she will... where does that leave Clay and me?

Clay and I stand shoulder-to-shoulder at the kitchen sink, a well-practiced rhythm between us. He washes, I dry. Alayna bolted the second she polished off her plate, muttering something about homework. We both know it's a lie, but we let her go anyway.

At least Clay looks more at ease tonight. His hair's a mess, sandy strands sticking up in defiance after a long day. The sleeves of his shirt are rolled up, exposing forearms dotted with soap bubbles. There's a softness in his smile, a quiet that settles over him when he's not trying so hard.

"How was your day?" I ask, watching him fill the sink. The faucet hisses, steam rising as he slides the first plate into the suds.

"Can't complain," he says. "It's easier when it's not an election year. No campaign drama, just the usual budget wrangling and pothole complaints."

"Not exactly the athletic career you always dreamed of though, is it?"

Clay pauses, scrubbing at a stubborn bit of sauce. "That dream fizzled out a long time ago. I think it was more about momentum than passion. I liked the adrenaline, the team, the simplicity of it. But a career? Probably not. I like what I have now—being home, stability, routine. My girls."

My breath catches. *His girls.* I know it's not the first time he's made a comment like that, but it hits differently since his confession. I know we've always called Alayna *our girl,* but something about the way he includes me in that now... It unsteadies me.

We've talked about his past—the way everything changed the moment Tasha got pregnant—but I've never asked if he mourned the life he left behind. Maybe I didn't want to know. It's a strange comfort, hearing he doesn't carry that regret like a hidden scar. After Tasha left, everything shifted. For both of us.

A bubble escapes from the sink and floats between us like a tiny balloon. Clay flicks a cluster of suds in my direction, grinning when they land on my cheek.

"Earth to Frankie..."

I blink. "Sorry, what?"

He hands me a dinner plate, and his smile lingers. "I asked how it's been, working at the school all week. You ready to abandon ship and run back to the hardware store yet?"

There's a teasing edge to his voice, but underneath it, I hear something else—like my answer matters more than he's letting on.

I huff, taking the plate. "I actually underestimated how much I was going to enjoy it. Seeing how excited they were to show me their ideas, absorbing that creative energy again, it's like a breath of fresh air I didn't know I needed. I get why people teach now. It's a different kind of reward. It makes me think... maybe I need to rethink what I want out of my own life."

I gently set the plate on the drying rack before taking the next one from Clay. "I thought you liked running the hardware store?" Clay stops washing. He turns his body toward me, pressing his hip against the counter.

"I do love the store. I grew up in those walls, every aisle holds a memory. It's not that I'm unhappy, I just..." I hesitate, running the towel over the dried plate too many times as I gather my thoughts.

Those things Roman said at our dinner left me questioning my own choices. When he said I'd had my whole life figured out, that running the hardware store and starting a family had always been my plan, I'd wanted to push back. But he was right; I'd never questioned the life that was planned for me. Not the way that Tasha had. I'd accepted that I was meant to run the shop. I'd chosen to stay for Alayna's sake, but was that my dream? Was that what I'd wanted for my life? Why had I given up on the rest of my dream so easily?

"I can't help but wonder if I'm living my own dream, or if I settled for the one that was handed to me."

The thought hits like a stone skipping across my chest. *I want more.*

"Are you thinking about leaving the store?"

I snort. "No. I'd never do that to Dad. He says he'd understand, but I know it would break his heart. Honestly, it might break mine too."

"What's the issue then?"

"It's like I've just been skating by in every aspect of my life because it's comfortable, but I haven't stopped to ask myself what I really want in such a long time that I don't even know anymore. I just know I want more."

He exhales, tension leaving his body. "Okay. Then what's the 'more' part?"

"I don't know yet." I lean back against the counter. "I've just been... drifting. Going through the motions. I want to want something again. I want to feel like I'm moving toward something that's mine."

Clay studies the plate like it holds answers. "Is Roman the 'something more' you're talking about?"

I wince. "No. That's not what I meant... Maybe I'm being stupid."

"Sorry." He curses softly, rinses the last plate, then hands it to me. "That was unfair. You haven't said much about your date with him. And now you're working together, talking about changing your life... I guess I'm a little jealous."

I can't blame him. I've avoided this conversation with everyone, even Sarah. Because saying it out loud makes it real, and I'm still trying to untangle it all. But the change I'm craving—it's not about a man. It's about me.

"I should've told you sooner," I say, placing the last plate on the rack. "I've been hiding. The dinner with Roman? It was... hard. We talked about the past. That might be where we leave things. I haven't really spoken to him since."

I don't want to cut Roman out of my life, but what chance do we have when we can barely spend an hour together without saying or doing something that hurts the other person? Once the project at the school is finished, I may never hear from him again. We're virtually strangers at this point. My heart aches even admitting that to myself.

And if I'm not careful, I might hurt Clay and end up a stranger in his life too.

Clay rinses the sink in silence. The water rushes down the drain, leaving only the brittle quiet between us.

"After all this time, I'm not sure what else I expected," I whisper. My voice vibrates with a sadness I can't quite shake.

He dries his hands and pulls me into a hug. "Aw, Frankie."

His hand settles on the back of my head, fingers sifting through my hair. I let myself fall into him. It's familiar and warm, like a favorite blanket you forgot you still had.

His heartbeat thumps beneath my ear. A little fast.

Maybe we don't have fireworks, but we have something solid. Something I don't want to break. It seems like he's waiting for me to bridge the gap between us, both literally and figuratively, but I'm still not ready to make that leap. I might never be ready.

"What do you think about doing something this weekend? The two of us. Alayna's staying with your parents overnight tomorrow."

I gently disengage from his hold. "What do you have in mind?"

He shrugs, rubbing his arms. "That bar in Spokane—the Quiz and Quench? They're doing the '90s Sitcom Trivia Challenge again. We could head down early, grab lunch, do some shopping, then go win that golden Q."

The last time we went, we almost won. Back when Sarah and Trevor were still together, and we went as a group. This would be different. Just the two of us. A real date. An out-of-town date even.

The hairs on the back of my neck rise as little tendrils of fear prickle my skin. If it goes badly, will we ruin the balance at home?

But he's already opened the box, the words have already spilled out. I can't stuff them back in and pretend none of this ever happened. So my only choice now is to put my big girl panties on and see where this leads us.

"Okay," I say, ignoring the pit of fear in my stomach. Clay finally lifts his eyes to mine. "But we're not coming home without that trophy."

He laughs, and the tension between us cracks enough to let something hopeful in. "That trophy is as good as ours."

We've earned our sitcom credentials. Alayna was a terrible sleeper, and we spent years glued to old reruns during the midnight shift. We probably know more about the Tanner family than our own extended relatives.

But I wonder, not for the first time—

Who are we without Alayna in the middle?

CHAPTER 18

THE TWO-HOUR DRIVE TO Spokane flies by in a blur of music and half-dreams. Clay streams an upbeat playlist through the car speakers, singing along as his fingers tap out rhythms on the steering wheel. I drift in and out of sleep in the passenger seat, lulled by the warmth of the seat heater and the steady hum of the tires on the road. I've always been a terrible road trip companion. Not that I've had many chances to improve.

Outside of the occasional drive to visit Sarah, I haven't ventured far from home. When Roman got into Berkeley, my first thought wasn't excitement for him—it was how far away California sounded. I've never seen the ocean. The closest I've been is Eastern Washington, and that hardly counts. The furthest south I've traveled was Salt Lake City for a shopping trip, and after the nightmare that was Utah traffic, I never went back. Someday, maybe, I'll take a real road trip. See something beyond the borders of familiarity. But I'd have to stay awake long enough to enjoy it.

Clay doesn't seem to mind that I sleep. He hums along to the music, perfectly content behind the wheel. He never complains about being our chauffeur—mine and Alayna's. We've mastered the art of being passenger princesses, and he's leaned into the role like he enjoys it. I think, deep down, he does.

There's a strange comfort in the silence between us. We don't fill it with small talk or forced laughter. Simply existing in the same space feels natural. Still, I keep wondering—has he thought about kissing me again? Is that on the table tonight? Has he imagined something more than burgers and trivia and the low hum of flirtation we never quite address?

I try not to think about it too much. But the truth is, I already have.

That kiss—it was sweet. Both familiar and easy. But now that Roman has kissed me too, I can't help but compare. Not the kisses themselves. Not even the men. But the way each one made me feel. Clay's kiss warmed me from the inside out, like slipping into a favorite sweater. Roman's felt like a lit match pressed against my skin—unexpected, dangerous, and impossible to ignore. Neither felt entirely safe. Kissing is risky business. And my heart? It doesn't do well with uncertain things.

There's a warning simmering in my gut, but I can't quite translate it.

Clay gently shakes my shoulder when we cross into the city limits. "Hey, we're here. You hungry?"

"Sure. I could eat." I slide my sunglasses down, shielding my still-blurry eyes from the sharp glare of the late afternoon sun. It's bright enough to fool you—like it could be a summer day. But the chill in the air and the bare trees don't lie. It's fall, through and through.

Still, a cold shiver runs through me that has nothing to do with the weather.

It's already after four, and we haven't eaten since breakfast; Clay is probably starving. Alayna had slept in this morning, and no one in our house dares to wake her early. She's a storm cloud when she's tired, and Clay and I had no desire to get caught in the downpour. Instead, I'd taken advantage of the time while she slept, choosing my favorite plan for the play and filling out an online order form for the supplies we would need to achieve it. It was nice to check off an item on my to-do list, and it helped distract me from my nerves.

Clay and I had debated if we should tell Alayna about the trip as we shared eggs and toast, but in the end we decided not to tell her we were heading to Spokane without her—it felt too loaded, too strange to explain. So when she took her time with her shower and curled every strand of hair and blended her makeup to perfection, I didn't rush her. I didn't tell her we had plans. How do you explain something like this? *"Hey kid, hurry up—your dad and I are going on a maybe-date, but don't worry, we don't know what we are either"*?

Of course, Clay told my mom. Thought it was smart to let someone know we'd be in Spokane. In case of emergencies. And maybe he's right, but I can practically hear the wheels turning in her head from here. She's been watching us closely for weeks, all but bursting to say something. I hope she keeps it to herself, at least around Alayna. If this becomes a thing—if it's ever real—we'll tell her. Together.

Clay takes the exit, pulling into a strip mall. "Burgers? Pizza? What do you want, Keke?"

The nickname makes me flinch—not because it's new, but because it isn't. Alayna's been calling me Keke her whole life. Eventually, everyone else did too. Clay saying it now, in the context of whatever this is, feels... off. Like he's trying to mix the past and present into something that doesn't quite fit.

"Whatever you want is fine. I'm not picky."

"Aw, come on," he says, grinning. "Without the opinionated kiddo here, we can go wherever you want. You don't have a single craving?" He reaches over and gives my shoulder a squeeze.

I don't. Not really. I could eat anywhere. Alayna usually makes the call, and I find something on the menu. But Clay's looking at me like this is part of his plan—to make today special. And I want that. I want to want that. But everything in me is still off-kilter. Maybe it's nerves. Maybe it's hunger. Or maybe it's something I'm not ready to name.

I force a smile. "A burger does sound pretty good."

"That's my girl. Burgers it is." He turns back to the road with a little smirk, clearly pleased.

I rub my hands over my jeans, trying to ground myself. I don't want to disappoint anyone, but there's a hollowness in my chest I can't quite shake. Like I'm playing a part again, trying to please everyone around me. That scares me more than I want to admit. Maybe I need food. Maybe I need to relax. Or maybe... my gut is waving a red flag, and I'm pretending not to see it.

"This place look good?" he asks, pulling up to a faded plum-colored building with "Billy Bob's Burgers" painted across the front. There's a small line outside. Usually a good sign.

My stomach growls. "Guess my stomach thinks so." I'm quiet. And weird. But I can't snap out of it.

"Well, what are you waiting for?" Clay hops out of the car and jogs around to open my door. "Let's get you fed. Can't win trivia night on an empty stomach! Need that brain food."

I try to remind myself—this is Clay. One of my best friends. Not a stranger. Not someone I have to impress. We can just hang out, like we always have. There's no pressure. No expectations.

But the truth lands hard as he opens the door for me. No matter how this night goes, things are going to change.

After our meal, Clay and I wander into a shopping mall to kill time. Our stomachs full, we browse a few stores, chatting about the holidays and making notes of things Alayna might like for Christmas. Despite our best efforts, the conversation always circles back to her.

As the afternoon fades, Clay grabs our bags from the car and suggests we find a restroom to change into something more bar-appropriate. It's a little like sneaking into a party you weren't supposed to be at, the kind where you change in the locker room at school. I linger in front of the mirror, applying mascara. My hand shakes more than usual as I run the brush over my lashes.

"Wow, you look great." Clay's voice makes me jump, his grin wide as I step out of the restroom. I'm wearing a tight pair of jeans and a long-sleeve black shirt with lace trim and bare shoulders. It's simple, but I feel sexy as hell. The black peep-toe heels are the perfect finishing touch, lifting me enough that I almost meet his gaze.

He looks good too, his dark eyes warm and velvety against the deep blue of his button-down shirt. His caramel-colored oxfords give him a polished yet casual vibe. It's almost annoying how effortlessly he pulls it off. "You look good yourself."

"Shall we?" he asks, offering me his arm. I slip mine through his, the scent of his cologne surrounding me as we head back to the car. The silence is different now, a little less comfortable. My palms are clammy, my nerves unexpectedly on edge. I count my steps to distract myself from the ridiculous jitters twisting in my stomach.

The Quiz and Quench is buzzing when we walk in. The crowd's always interesting, a mix of ages and styles, from hipsters to cowboys, all equally at home here. The bar is huge, lively, and brightly lit, with gold and blue décor that reaches from floor to ceiling. This isn't a place for drowning your sorrows in solitude. It's a place for meeting people, for having fun, and maybe leaving with a trophy.

Clay signs us up for the trivia contest as I grab a seat by the stage. A live band is covering "Sugar" by Maroon 5, and I sway to the rhythm. The line at the bar is long, so by the time Clay returns with our drinks, they're announcing the start of Trivia Night.

"Raspberry Mojito?" I raise an eyebrow, eyeing the mint sprig and raspberry-colored liquid.

"Yeah, hope that's okay," Clay says, nodding to his own drink. "Got myself a vodka soda if you'd prefer that."

I shake my head and take a long sip. I'm surprised he remembers my favorite drink. We've hardly been out together where alcohol was involved. "No, you did good."

"Alright, ladies and gentlemen, please take your seats. My name's Larry, and I'll be your host tonight for '90s Sitcom Trivia!" A man in a *Gilmore Girls* T-shirt and khakis adjusts his glasses as he announces the rules. Our waitress, whose name tag identifies her as Candy, hands each table a whiteboard and dry-erase markers.

Clay pulls our bar stools closer, sitting next to me, close enough to whisper answers without the other teams hearing. His body radiates warmth, but it does nothing to shake the chill running down my spine.

Larry clears his throat. "Remember to write your answers clearly, and don't let your neighbors peek! I'll tell you when to raise your boards and then announce the correct answer. We've got six teams tonight and three rounds. At the end of each round, we'll eliminate the two lowest-scoring teams. In the final round, the last two teams will compete for the bragging rights and the coveted golden Q trophy. So, let's get those big brains warmed up, and let's get started!"

Clay and I scan the competition. Table one is a group of college girls giggling and taking selfies, dressed in matching pink shirts. Table two, a pair of older women with white hair, is sizing up the room. Table three features a biker couple surrounded by empty beer bottles—definitely not to be messed with. Our table is number four, and at table five, two younger men are too busy flirting across the bar to care much about trivia. Finally, at table six, a couple close to our age is making out, looking very much in love.

Looks can be deceiving. I'm not ready to count anyone out yet.

"You ready to bring this baby home?" Clay raises his glass with a grin.

"Bring it on." I clink my glass against his, my first real smile breaking through. This night can be fun, if I stop being such a worrywart. I take another long sip, preparing for the challenge.

Larry kicks off the game, and the first round of ten questions is laughably easy. I'm impressed when the college girls hold their own, and not surprised when the guys at table five and the biker couple at table three are out after the first round. The remaining teams are all tied with a perfect score of ten.

Candy brings us a fresh round of drinks, and I take a cautious sip. The second mojito's stronger than the first, and I wince. Clay shakes his head at me. "Lightweight."

Round two's questions get harder, but Clay and I keep getting them right. When Larry asks, "On *The Nanny*, what's Fran's catchphrase, often directed at Mr. Sheffield?" Clay leans in, whispering, "Oh, Mr. Sheffield!" exactly the way Fran Drescher always said it. I can't help but laugh, drawing glances from our rivals. Teasingly, I poke him in the stomach, and in return, he kisses my cheek. My skin burns where his lips touched me.

"Alright teams, that's the end of round two. It looks like tables one and four are tied with perfect scores of 20! To the rest of you, thanks for playing, and grab one more drink on the house!"

Clay pats me on the back. "Hell yeah, it's down to us and the college girls. We've got this."

I rub my hands together. "Woo!"

Candy brings us another round. Normally, I only drink when Sarah and I meet up, and even then, we're more about fries and gossip than getting tipsy. But tonight, I can't deny the alcohol is kicking in. My cheeks are warm, my nerves easing.

Larry resumes the trivia, throwing questions from *Friends*, *Seinfeld*, and *The Nanny*. The college girls are holding their own. I wonder if any of them were even born when these shows aired. We're still tied, one question left to go.

"Alright, ladies and gentleman," Larry says, stressing "man" as he gestures toward Clay, the only guy left in the competition. The crowd erupts in laughter. "What was the name of the Conner family's dog in *Roseanne*?"

My hand freezes over the whiteboard. *Roseanne* was never my favorite show, and I often switched to music when it aired. I glance at Clay, who pulls the marker from my hand.

"Don't worry," he says, smiling. "I know this one." He writes 'Freddy' on the board, making sure no one else can see.

"Are you sure?" I ask, although I'm zero percent confident. I glance nervously at the girls, who look as lost as I'm certain I do. I never watched *Roseanne* much, and dogs and I don't mix. After being chased and bitten by Mr. Miller's dog back in second grade, I've never trusted one again.

Clay's eyes crinkle with that grin of his. "Yes, Frankie. I'm sure."

"Okay folks, hold up your answers!" Larry announces, squinting as he reads our boards.

The girls have written 'Comet' in a messy scrawl. I'm pretty sure Comet was the dog from *Full House*, but what are the odds it's the same name on two shows? I'm hoping they're wrong.

"We have a winner!" Larry claps his hands together. "Table four, please come up and claim your trophy!"

My eyes dart between Clay's mischievous grin and the bold black number on the laminate tabletop. "We won?"

Clay grins and swings me up, lifting me off my chair and into his arms. "Told you we had it!"

Applause rings out, and a few people shout congratulations. The college girls congratulate each other for making it so far. My head spins with excitement as Clay's lips brush mine. He holds me by the shoulders as his kiss deepens, and I'm light-headed, unsteady on my feet. He tastes like vodka, and his body is warm and solid against mine.

"Congrats, lovebirds," Larry calls out, his voice booming from behind us. Clay pulls back, his lips curling into a smile. When I turn around, Larry is holding the golden Q trophy, grinning as he offers it to us.

"Thank you," Clay says, accepting the trophy with a triumphant whoop.

Candy comes over, snapping a photo of us before reminding us to follow them on social media.

I'm watching everything from the outside, detached. Two people, on a date, a few drinks, a fun game, a kiss... We had fun today. There's nothing wrong with the way it's gone. This should be exciting, like the start of something new. But the more I try to convince myself of that, the more my gut tells me it's not.

We shake hands with the other teams, finishing our drinks, riding the high of victory. Sarah will probably try to steal the trophy when I see her. She still talks about how we were robbed the first time we played

"Well, gorgeous," Clay wraps his arm around me as we stand near the doors of the bar. "I think we drank a little too much to drive home tonight. What do you say? Should we check the hotel down the street and see if they have any rooms?"

He isn't wrong. The drive home would be reckless, and there's a part of me that wants to be done with tonight. But I suddenly wish we'd thought this part through. Last time we were here, Sarah let all of us crash at her and Trevor's place. This time, it's just the two of us. My stomach tightens, not with hunger, but with something else—something I can't quite name. The thought of a hotel room with Clay, alone, without Alayna... it shifts something inside me.

Maybe getting tipsy wasn't the solution after all. The buzz that once softened the sharp edge of my nerves now feels like a haze, blurring everything I should be thinking clearly about. My gut twists as I realize I've ignored the nagging feeling all night—the one that said something wasn't right. It's there now, like a whisper I can't shake. I should have listened to it sooner, but now I have to figure out how to pull back without making a mess of this.

I take my phone out of my purse and send a quick "9-1-1" message to Sarah. I tell her I'm in town and need a place to stay before I have the chance to overthink it. She doesn't know I'm in town, but her place isn't far. If the hotel has a room, I'll get Clay checked in and then crash with Sarah. I need to find a way to soften the blow for him, to avoid turning this into something it isn't. My pulse quickens, and it doesn't have anything to do with the alcohol.

CHAPTER 19

WITH HER FEET PROPPED up on the desk, and her lips loudly smacking gum as she scrolls through her phone, the girl behind the desk at the hotel clearly isn't thrilled to see us. She glances at us for a second before going back to her screen. "Do you have a reservation?"

Our walk across the street felt like it took forever, the air thick with silence. Clay's stumble beside me as we enter the lobby makes it clear he's more drunk than I thought. I'm surprised he doesn't drop the trophy he insists he should carry. He's never been much of a drinker, and he's definitely overestimated his tolerance. And he called *me* a lightweight. I lower him into one of the plush chairs across from the desk, before I turn back to the girl.

The hotel looks like it's been recently renovated. Clean, bright, with muted grays and blues decorating the floors and furniture. If things were different, this place wouldn't be terrible to spend the night. But things aren't different, and it feels more like a trap with each passing second.

"We don't have a reservation, no. But we'd love a room if you have one available." I reach for my wallet, gently placing it on the counter. I catch the eye-roll she gives before she drops her feet to the floor with a thud and starts clicking away at her computer.

I should be used to dealing with rude service, but something about tonight has me on edge. I glance at Clay again. His face is flushed, his breathing deep and slow, like he's in some kind of stupor. He's slouched, but there's something soft about the way he looks right now, his features unguarded, and that hits me harder than I expect.

I can't trust myself to drive. The buzz in my head is starting to fade, leaving behind something sharper, something anxious and regretful. The weight of the situation is pressing down on me—this mess I've created. At least one of us is sober enough to deal with this.

"We only have one room left. Double bed, no patio, first floor. It's two-fifty for the night, plus a hundred-dollar deposit for damages. No pets, no smoking," the girl says, and glances at Clay with a look that suggests she's already imagining him causing trouble. If she knew the half of it.

I bite back a laugh and pull my credit card from my wallet. "Sounds great."

She doesn't immediately reach for it. Instead, she stares at me, blue eyes cold and judgmental. "I need your ID first."

"Right." I force a smile, handing her my driver's license along with the card. She huffs, her fingers tapping the keyboard in frustration before she swipes my card through the reader.

"How many keys?" she asks, not looking at me as she slides the cards back over.

I try to be polite, but I'm not in the mood for her attitude. "One is fine, thanks."

I glance back at Clay again. He's still slouched in the chair, eyes closed, head resting awkwardly on one arm, his other hand has a death-grip on the golden Q trophy. For a moment, it's like I'm looking at a younger version of him—vulnerable and tired.

His hair's messy, a little wild, and the overhead light hits it in a way that almost makes him look angelic.

Guilt churns in my stomach. I chew on my lip, watching him. Clay's always been handsome—there's no denying that. And he's an amazing dad, so patient with Alayna, so steady, so good at everything. But I don't know how to get past this friendship of ours. Why can't I let myself see anything more with him? Why can't I give my heart to the one person I'm sure would never try to break it?

Because it still belongs to someone else.

Will he hate me tomorrow when he's sober enough to realize I left him here? Will we be able to recover from whatever mess this is that we're making of everything? Could I fix this? Would I even want to? The questions hit me one after another like bullets. Each one leaves a hole in me.

My pulse quickens as the weight of everything starts to settle in. This, whatever it is between us, can't stay the same. We're all changing. Growing. And no matter how hard I try to hold onto what we've built, time continues moving forward. Sarah's right, it's time for me to leave the house, to build something for myself. I've been coasting for too long, never letting myself hit the gas on my own dreams.

I blink back tears. Focus, Frankie, focus. One problem at a time. And right now, that problem is getting this drunk man to his room.

I hope he can walk there. If he can't, there's no way I can carry him. He's solid muscle, dead weight, and I'm not nearly strong enough. Thank God it's a ground-floor room. At least we won't have to deal with stairs or an elevator ride.

Roman's face flashes in my mind. His strong arms, lean body. The way I want him here, now, instead of Clay. My heart skips, but I shut it down. I don't have time for that tonight.

I hear that voice again in the back of my head: *Roman's the one who broke your heart. What makes you think he won't do it again?* But I push it aside. People change, right? Years have passed, he might be different now.

I'm different now.

If I don't at least try to figure out what could be between us, will I ever stop thinking about him?

I shake my head. One problem at a time. Focus.

The girl hands me the key. "Room 103, to your left, right past the elevators. Breakfast at six."

I don't say anything in response. I take the key from her, nod, and head for the door.

My phone buzzes in my pocket.

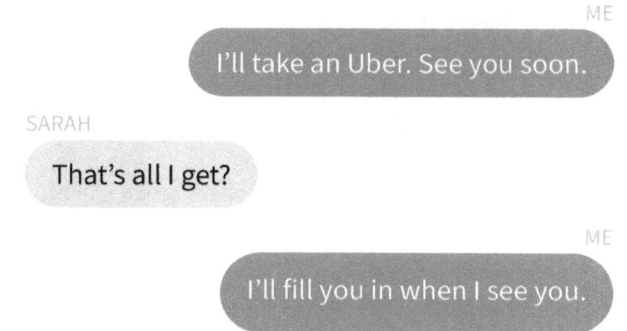

SARAH

Inking for another hour. Where are you?
Can you Uber to me?

I glance at the screen, guilt tightening my chest. I should have told her where I was. But I didn't. Not yet.

ME

I'll take an Uber. See you soon.

SARAH

That's all I get?

ME

I'll fill you in when I see you.

She follows it up with an eye-roll emoji. But then a text comes through reminding me that she loves me. I smile, the weight of it all lightening a little. She's going to lose it when I tell her I'm here alone with Clay. It's easier to wait until I see her face-to-face than risk a hundred questions through text.

The lobby's quiet now. Soft piano music filters through the ceiling speakers, and the faint bubbling of a fish tank is the only other sound. I shake Clay, nudging him awake with my shoulder. "Let's get you to bed."

He mumbles something that sounds suspiciously like, "That's what she said." He leans heavily on me, his weight almost too much to bear, and we slowly make our way to the room. Room 103's the second door down the hall.

Thank heavens.

I use the wall to prop him up while I swipe the key. The door swings open with a soft click, and I pull him inside, dropping our bags to the floor as I steer him toward the bed. We're pressed so close, it's hard to breathe. His head falls against mine, the heat of him seeping through our joined skin.

"You smell so good," he sighs, his voice soft, like he's telling me a secret. "Like a fruit smoothie."

I can't help but laugh, the sound almost too loud in the silence. "It's the shampoo Alayna bought me."

Clay laughs with me, and then suddenly, he flops backward onto the bed, dragging me down with him. His arms wrap around me like he's trying to pull me into him, his breath warm on my neck. I hear the trophy hit the ground beside us and hope it has survived the fall.

"Hey," I laugh, trying to push him off. "You're going to wake up with a killer headache in the morning. You need some sleep."

"I can sleep when I'm dead," he jokes, his voice a little more awake now.

"You might actually wish you were dead tomorrow," I tease, getting up from the bed. I snag the trophy off the floor—it's still in one piece—and cross the room, tucking it into one of our bags.

Clay sings something so terribly off key that I can't even recognize which song it is, but I can't focus on that. I dig through my purse until I find the ibuprofen, then glance around the hotel room. Two complimentary bottles of water sit next to the sink—thank my lucky stars. I grab a couple of pills for both of us, snatch the bottles, and head back to him, one in each hand.

He's almost completely undressed now—stripped down to his boxer briefs and socks, his body sprawled across the bed in a mess of limbs. My heart skips, and I immediately look away. It shouldn't be any different. I've seen him in swim trunks a thousand times, so why is this so... wrong? My body is tight, like there's a line I can't cross, even if my gaze keeps drifting back to the way his muscles move under his skin.

"Does it feel hot in here? Or is it you?" He grins, his eyes still half-lidded.

I press a bottle of water into his hand, hoping it distracts me. My eyes flick to his body again before quickly looking away. "Take these," I say, showing him the pills.

He grumbles, but eventually takes them, swallowing the pills with a loud gulp of water. When he's done, he tosses the bottle across the room and pats the space next to him on the bed. "Now come sit with me."

My heart stutters, and for a moment, I'm frozen. What am I doing here? What am I doing to him? I sit down carefully, not touching him, even though I can still feel the heat of his body radiating off him.

"Trivia Champions!" Clay whoops, grinning wide. "We did that!"

I can't help but smile, relieved at the momentary shift. "We did, we rocked it."

"We make a great team," he winks. "Imagine what else we might be good at."

The innuendo hangs in the air between us, thick and uncomfortable. I wince, trying to hold my ground, but it's hard. If I were into him that way, maybe it'd be cute, but it makes me uncomfortable.

"What are you thinking about?" he asks, studying my face.

I shrug, trying to smile, but my lips are stretched too thin. "I had a really great time tonight," I say, the words heavy as they leave my tongue.

"Okay..." His forehead creases, confused. "Then why does your face look like that?"

I want to say more, but the words are tangled in my throat. "I think I've just realized no matter what I do, things are going to change," I say, my voice quiet. "And I don't know how I feel about it."

He stops moving, his face going serious. "Change? What do you mean?"

I hesitate, unsure if I'm ready for this conversation. But I can't keep running from it. "I know you wanted to see if we could be more than friends, but I—I just don't think I can get there. I like our relationship the way it is. I think we make great friends, Clay..."

"Is that all we are, Frankie?" His voice sharpens, his eyes narrowing. "When we kissed, you didn't want more of that?"

I shake my head slowly, heart shattering inside me. "No. I don't think I do."

"What if we give it more time?" His voice shakes, desperate. "What if you come here and lay with me? We can talk, we—"

"I'm meeting Sarah. She can drive me home in the morning. We'll talk more at home." My voice cracks, but I get the words out. "I care about you, Clay. You and Alayna mean the world to me. But you and I? I don't think that's what I want."

His eyes go wide. His fingers reach for me, and I slide away, needing space. I can't bear to stay here any longer. The hurt in his eyes is like a weight on my chest, and it makes it hard to breathe.

"Please," he chokes, grabbing my wrist gently as I move. "Stay. We have time. You might change your mind."

"I'm sorry." My words are barely a whisper. "I'll see you at home."

Clay drops back onto the bed, covering his face with his hands as his body shakes with silent sobs. My hands tremble as I gather my things quickly, wanting to get out of this room, away from him, but I can't stop my heart from breaking.

As much as this hurts, with each step I take toward the door, the churning in my gut subsides, and I know I'm making the right choice.

I glance back one last time. His eyes meet mine, and my own tears burn at the back of my throat. But I have to leave.

As I step into the hallway, the door begins to close, and I hear him call out, one final plea.

"Please, Tasha—"

And my heart shatters.

CHAPTER 20

MY UBER DRIVER SHOWS up in less than ten minutes—something that would never happen in Pinewood—and I'm grateful for the swift response. I climb into the back of the silver Prius, clutching my bag to my chest like a lifeline. The driver is a middle-aged woman with short neon pink hair and a lip ring. She grins at me through the rearview mirror. I hope she can't see the remnants of my tears. My lip still wobbles slightly. I need to get out of here.

"You're headed to the tattoo shop on Garfield?" Her eyebrows rise in question. "It's pretty late. You need me to talk you into it or out of it?"

A smile touches my lips. "Neither. I'm heading there to meet a friend. She's one of the artists."

The woman turns in her seat to fully face me, flicking the ring in her lip with her tongue. "Please tell me it's Sarah!" She pushes up the sleeve of her lime green sweater, revealing a gorgeous tree with animals intertwined in the roots, twisting up her arm before disappearing beneath fabric. "She did this one.

I'm waiting for her to come back with some ideas for my other arm. She's brilliant!"

"She's a great friend, too," I laugh. "Known her most of my life."

The woman nods, clearly pleased. "Well then, let's get you to your friend. You can tell her Mags says hi."

After I promise to let Sarah know that Mags is impatiently waiting on those new sketches, we're off. The drive is short, and as we pull up to the old brick building, I can't help the swell of pride for my best friend. She's made a big name for herself here, and even though I wish she'd move back to Pinewood for selfish reasons, I know she's where she's meant to be.

I thank the driver, adding a sizable tip in the app before stepping out. The tattoo shop is buzzing—people milling around outside despite the cool air. It's clearly a hot spot on a Saturday night. I tuck my bag under my arm and head inside.

Sarah's easy to find. She's in her chair in the corner, cleaning up, wiping everything down and talking with her fellow artists. She hasn't noticed me yet, and I take a second to watch her in her element.

She's wearing black skinny jeans with over-exaggerated holes in the knees, a band T-shirt, and her long hair is pulled back into a high ponytail. She looks every bit the fun, outgoing girl that she is. Her straight teeth flash as she laughs freely. Her charisma is contagious. It's what drew me to her in the first place.

Someone yells from the front door and Sarah's eyes finally scan the room. When she sees me, she waves me over. "Hey girl, almost done here and then we can go."

I nod, but the motion stirs something in my chest, and the emotions I've been holding back start to rise again. I hear Clay's voice in my head, calling me Tasha. On one hand, it confirms that I'm doing the right thing—stepping away from the idea of something romantic with him. I've always known he was still in love with my sister. Probably always will be. And while I know it's possible to love someone new after a heartbreak like that,

I'm not sure he could ever really see me without seeing her. We're too intertwined. There's too much history. Not enough distance for it to ever be a real, clean start.

But still, it hurt. Had he let me stay all these years because it felt like keeping a part of Tasha close? Maybe that's my hurt talking. But thinking about it makes my stomach ache.

Please, Tasha—

Sarah grabs her purse and says goodbye to her coworkers before taking my bag from my shaking hands. "Hey, babe. You okay?"

I choke back the tears in my throat and nod—then shake my head no. Sarah pulls me into a hug, and the familiar smell of the herbs she loves, the warmth of her arms, it's more comforting than I expected. I squeeze her back tightly.

"Aw, you should've told me it was this bad. I would've moved a little quicker."

"It's fine. You're fine." I shrug against her. "Mags says hi. And hurry up with her tattoo sketches."

Sarah laughs. "She's a character. I'm glad she was available tonight to drive you. Some of those drivers out there, man... they're creepy."

Tears leak from my eyes as I try to smile. I wipe them away on her shoulder. "She was nice."

"Let's get you home," she says into my hair, then pulls back to look me over. "We can talk once you're settled."

My shoulders sag in relief. I wipe my nose on my sleeve and follow her out the back to her car. Once inside, she tosses my bag into the back seat.

"I'm stopping for greasy tacos and caffeine," she announces. "Then, you're getting into comfy PJs, taking a hot shower, and spilling your guts."

"Thanks, Sarah." I manage a real smile. "I knew I could count on you."

An hour later, I'm curled up on Sarah's couch in sweats, an oversized T-shirt, and a pair of neon pink slipper socks—the same kind she gave me years ago in a care package labeled *Emergency Cozy Kit*. I'm freshly showered, still faintly smelling like her citrusy shampoo, and stuffed full of greasy tacos and too much guacamole. The tension from earlier begins to loosen its grip as I sink into the soft, familiar suede cushions beneath me.

Across from me, Sarah's trying her best to be patient, but the questions are practically buzzing off her skin. She's gotten better about her anxiety over the years—therapy, breathing techniques, a yoga class she actually stuck with—but when it comes to the two of us and our long, messy history? Her calm has limits. Honestly, I'm impressed she let me finish my shower, let alone eat two tacos without commentary.

But I can see it happening. The exact moment her restraint starts to unravel. Her leg starts bouncing, her fingers twitch like she's debating whether to grab a notepad or shake me, and she lets out this quiet little hum—like she's trying to keep her brain from exploding.

Then she smiles, tight-lipped but trying.

"Alright," she says, soft but not subtle, "now that the queso's gone, it's time to spill. What the heck happened tonight? I'm happy to see you, obviously, but what brought you to town in the first place?"

I take a slow sip of water, stalling. Sarah's more than a friend—she's my person. Always has been. The one who reminded me that some relationships stick, even when everything else falls apart. Even when my sister left. Even when her marriage ended. She's been my lighthouse in every storm. More of a sister than Tasha ever was. What we have isn't as simple as friendship—it's something we've chosen, again and again.

"I was on a date with Clay."

Her eyes flare. She flinches like she's been burned.

"Excuse me, what? It sounded like you said you were on a date with Clay. But I know my best friend would've told me that before she went on a date. So... please elaborate. Quickly." She grabs my leg and leans in.

"He wanted to see if we could be more than friends. I agreed to go with him to the bar, try to win that trivia night we lost before. And the thing is... that part was fun. But afterward..." I trail off, trying to collect my thoughts.

"Nuh-uh, back up," she says, standing and pacing the small space in front of me. "You and Clay? When have you *ever* thought of him that way? That jerk's been holding you back since Tasha left. He takes advantage of your relationship with Alayna and now he wants you to what—be his girlfriend? I know we talked about this at the bar, but I didn't think you'd actually try this thing with Clay."

I groan, guilt washing over me. "I know. I wish I'd called you last week and spilled everything. It would've been nice not to be so alone in all of it. I just... I think I was afraid that saying it out loud would spook me. And I was curious."

"Curious?" she scoffs.

"I'd never really considered it before..."

Sarah barely hears me. "It's the timing that annoys me. What has him suddenly declaring his feelings, Frankie?"

I could pretend nothing had changed, but that'd be a lie. A voice in my head is screaming the truth: Roman. Roman came back to town and suddenly Clay felt threatened. I knew it then, and I know it now. But that wasn't the part that truly bothered me.

"Calm down," I say. I know Sarah is only acting this way because she's jealous she hasn't had a play by play of my drama. The dramatics are her own love language. "I need to get this next part out, and I don't have the strength to say it twice."

Sarah stops pacing. Her face softens and she kneels in front of me. "I'm sorry, girl. Tell me. I promise—I'll be quiet."

"When he kissed me the first time..." Her eyebrows jump, but she zips her lips like a mime. "It was nice. Not like... set-your-blood-on-fire hot, but it felt good. But the trivia game, celebrating, even the stuff we do with Alayna—it all felt like friendship. Like he's meant to be my brother, whether by law or because he's her dad. It didn't feel like it could be more than that."

I swallow the lump in my throat, holding up a hand to stop her from jumping in.

"I hated hurting him. But no matter what happens with Roman—or doesn't—it had to be said. So I took him back to the hotel, sat next to him, and told him I thought we should stay friends. He was upset. So was I..."

Sarah strokes my hair, nodding encouragement.

"But as I was leaving, he begged me not to go. Only... he said 'Please, Tasha...' Not Frankie. Tasha."

Sarah pulls me into her arms, wrapping around me tight. "Oh, sweet girl. I'm sorry."

It wasn't that I hated Tasha. Or even that, in his drunken state, he thought of her. It was the reality of it crashing in on me. He still loved her. She was always going to be his Juliet—the woman he loved and lost, the mother of his child. Even if we had tried, even if the chemistry had been there, I'd always be in her shadow. I'd always wonder if he looked at me and wished he was seeing her.

And if I was being honest... Roman was probably that person for me.

Only now, I had the chance to see if what we had was real. To get it back—or finally let it go.

"We knew that though, didn't we?" Sarah says softly. She wipes my tears with the sleeve of her pajamas. "He never stopped loving Tasha. Even as the rest of us learned to live without her, he didn't have to. He had you. That wasn't fair to either of you. I bet he's terrified now, Frankie."

"You think losing me will finally make him grieve her?"

"I think it's a start."

Sarah shifts beside me, taking my hand. "Are we gonna talk about the other elephant in the room?"

"I assume you mean the elephant who looks way too good in a suit and tie?" I laugh, even though I'm still shaky.

"How's it been, seeing him again?"

A lightning strike is dull compared to the electricity I feel around Roman. The chemistry is still there—but was the rest of it just a fantasy I held onto for years? Would it still be real if we tried again?

"It's confusing, Sarah. I'm definitely attracted to him. That's never been in question. But what if that's all it is?"

Sarah smiles, eyes glassy. "You know I don't regret my marriage, right?"

"Of course," I say. "I was there for all of it. Trevor doesn't regret it either. There was real love between you."

She nods. "Yeah, I joke about Trevor, but I really did love him. We didn't work out, and that's been a blessing too. Sometimes people come into your life to teach you something. Even if it doesn't last, loving someone like that—it's always worth it."

Fresh tears slide down my cheeks. Her words hit me like a finger poking right into my chest.

"So I should stop fighting the fear and just... go for it?"

The couch shakes as Sarah nods. "What's the worst that can happen? You're already miserable. But you could find real happiness—or finally close that chapter for good. Either way, you win."

I nod, a new resolve building inside me.

"Somewhere out there is a man dying to love you the way you deserve, babe. But you have to be ready to accept that love."

She doesn't know how much I hope she's right. "Okay, boss lady. Where do I start?"

"First things first—you move out of that house."

Normally this is where I'd argue with her. I'd talk about Alayna, how our arrangement works fine. But the words taste sour now. Sarah's right. She lost herself too after her marriage ended, but look at her now. What if I was brave enough to take her advice this time?

Decision made, I square my shoulders. "You have any vacation days?"

I watch shock move across her face, her eyes widening before she breaks into a megawatt grin.

"Oh girl, do I ever."

Warmth floods my veins as I make the decision. "Then I guess you're coming home with me tomorrow."

CHAPTER 21

THE HEADACHE I WAKE up with Sunday morning makes me question every life decision that's brought me to this moment. I barely slept. My brain wouldn't stop replaying the kiss with Clay—the way I felt nothing—and then the moment he called me *Tasha*.

All night, Sarah's words had looped in my head. Her fierce brand of honesty forcing me to face what I've been avoiding for years: it's time to move on. Time to stop doing only what's expected of me and finally start choosing things because *I* want them. I've been coasting through my own life, letting the current pull me along. That has to change. I need to be the one steering.

Having Sarah in my corner helps more than I can say. We've always been each other's constants during the worst storms. There's something sacred about being able to speak your truth—however ugly—and knowing you'll be met with love, not judgment. We're each other's safe harbor, and I pray that never changes.

I still remember holding her the morning she walked away from Trevor for good. It had taken months of breakdowns, late-night calls, false starts, and quiet sobbing in parked cars before she finally made the decision. She fought like hell for that marriage—counseling, temporary separations, even a desperate second honeymoon—but in the end, it was Trevor who asked her to consider letting go. They were exhausted. Unhappy. Done.

She showed up at the hardware store that Thursday, her hair clinging to a tired ponytail, her eyes red and puffy, and without a single word I knew it was over. I wrapped her in my arms and held her in the back office for hours while she cried. She didn't have to explain. I rubbed her back and reminded her she wasn't alone.

Now it's my turn to lean on her.

Sarah hums cheerfully as she pours us coffee and packs an overnight bag. The caffeine takes the edge off my headache, but anxiety still curls in my chest like a cold fist. She's not that shattered woman anymore. She's rebuilt herself—stronger, lighter, freer. It shows in everything she does, from her art, which now bursts with color and life, to the confident way she carries herself. She's thriving. And watching her makes me believe I can thrive, too.

She plants her laptop on the coffee table with a bright smile and claps her hands. "Okay! I pulled up a few short-term rentals I think you'll like. We can tour a couple this afternoon and, if we find the right one, maybe get you moved in this week. Some are even furnished," she adds, a little too casually, "since I know you don't exactly have furniture of your own."

The reminder hits harder than I expect. I don't own much—a meager collection of clothes, books, personal things. I've always been content with the leftovers at Clay's house. The idea of starting from scratch makes my stomach twist.

"Are you sure the gallery won't miss you this week?" I ask, chewing at the inside of my cheek. "I feel bad pulling you away from work like this."

Sarah snorts. "I already talked to Randall this morning. He basically begged me to take vacation time. Said if he had to watch me re-label another storage drawer out of boredom, he was going to lose it. He promised to send you a housewarming gift for getting me out of his hair."

She pulls her blonde hair into a messy bun, her eyes scanning me. "You're having second thoughts."

"Not exactly," I murmur. "Just... feeling the weight of it." I stare down at the ridiculous pink slipper socks on my feet. If only every life decision felt as easy as putting those on.

Hesitation presses against my ribs. It's not that I don't want this—I do. But I hate how it all unfolded. I should've had this conversation with Alayna years ago, back when Mara first moved in and I started questioning my place in the house. Maybe then it wouldn't feel so sudden. Would Alayna be hurt? Would Clay forgive me for shaking up their lives with no warning? I'm not abandoning them. I just need space of my own. That doesn't have to mean I stop being part of their family... does it?

Will Clay still let me be a parental figure to Alayna if I'm not living under his roof?

I shake out my arms, trying to chase off the dread. This is the right move. I have to believe that. I turn back to the laptop, rubbing my sweaty palms on my pants.

The first two listings are depressing—drab, outdated, barely kept up. I'm not buying, but I still want a place that feels like home, not like a last resort. Even if I could fix them up, I don't want to.

"See anything you like yet?" Sarah asks casually, picking lint off her pajama pants. She's trying not to hover, but I see the anticipation in her eyes.

I try to sound casual. "Any of them near Clay's place? I'd like to be close enough to take Alayna to school."

She perks up. "Actually... There's one two blocks away on Elm Street. Right next to the park, with a porch that faces the community garden."

She clicks on the listing and I lean in. A small brick house fills the screen. Two bedrooms. Two bathrooms. Warm hardwood floors. Built-in bookshelves around a fireplace. Tasteful furniture that makes it cozy but not cramped. Sunlight pours in through wide windows, bathing everything in soft gold. My heart gives a quiet kick.

I click through the pictures again, slower this time. I can already see Alayna curled up on that couch, doing homework or sketching. She could have her own room. Her own space with me.

The excitement buzzes up through my chest, loosening something inside me.

Sarah watches me with a quiet smile. "Is this the one?"

"It feels right," I whisper, swallowing hard. "There's a number listed—I'll call while you shower."

She pulls me into a tight hug, the woody scent of her skin triggering a thousand memories. "Promise me something?"

"Anything."

"Let yourself enjoy this. No guilt today, Frankie. Let yourself be excited. Dream big. You deserve to have something that's yours."

I almost tell her about my plans for the hardware store—about the little spark of ownership I'm finally ready to fight for. But it feels good keeping something just for me.

"Thank you, Sarah," I say instead. "I promise. I will."

We meet the listing agent at the house on Elm Street at five o'clock. She's smartly dressed, with gray hair and kind eyes, and introduces herself as Kay. Walking through the rooms and imagining myself living here is like finding the final long-missing piece of a puzzle.

The front door has a large stained-glass window, and the last rays of sun cast dancing rainbows across the living room walls. As if the house isn't charming enough on its own, the deep soaker tub in the master bathroom seals the deal for me.

"I'd like to rent this house if it's available right away," I say to Kay as we step back out onto the front porch.

"I'm happy to hear that. When I told Mrs. Melanie your name, she was thrilled. She's more than happy to give you the keys and fill out paperwork later this week. Apparently she considers you family and isn't worried about a deposit." Kay smiles and hands me a keyring with a little Vegas dice keychain attached.

Mel. I blink in surprise. I had no idea this was the rental she always talked about—her first home in Pinewood, the one she brought her son Mike home from the hospital to. No wonder the house is so beautifully kept.

"Wow. Small world," I murmur, turning the keys over in my hand. "I'll have to make sure I don't miss any more of her ladies' nights after this."

Kay laughs. "She *does* throw a great game party, doesn't she?"

Sarah squeezes my arm, her voice soft. "It's kismet."

I nod, unable to deny it. The house glows in the warm orange light of the setting sun, and tears sting my eyes before I can stop them. If I needed a sign that I'm making the right decision, this is it. I love Mel—she started building her own life here, and now it's my turn. I can feel the love that's soaked into the walls over the years. All her cooking and singing must've left something behind—some invisible thread of joy still humming through the air.

Kay hands me a business card. "Come by my office on Tuesday and we'll sign paperwork and get your first month's rent paid. The address is on the card. Congratulations, Frankie—I think you're going to feel right at home here."

"Thanks, Kay," I say, smiling through the blur of emotion. "I think so too."

After she drives off, Sarah and I sit side by side on the front porch steps, taking it all in. The fall air smells like falling leaves and promises of change. My phone pings in my pocket, and Sarah lifts an eyebrow.

"Who's texting you?"

I pull my phone out and stare at the message.

CLAY

Can we talk?

I turn the screen so she can see. She winces.

"I know I'm not Clay's biggest fan, but... I do sorta feel bad for the guy. A little bit, anyway."

"You want to go see your parents tonight?" I ask.

She rolls her eyes. "You're going to go talk to him, aren't you?"

I laugh—nervous and a little guilty. "I think I owe him an explanation at least. I don't want to leave like my sister did. I want us to still be a family after all of this. I just... don't know exactly what that looks like."

Another ping. Sarah snatches my phone before I can reach for it.

CLAY

Are you coming home tonight?

"Geez. He's persistent." She holds the screen up for me. "Fine. I'll drop you off so you can put him out of his misery. But don't let him guilt you, okay? This house is meant to be, and you deserve it, Frankie. You deserve to have a life outside of them. *Okay?*"

"Okay," I say.

And this time—I'm really starting to believe it.

CHAPTER 22

When I reach the front door, I hesitate. Technically, I still live here. I haven't even told Clay about the rental or my plans yet. But my hand hovers above the doorknob, as if the metal might burn me if I touch it.

A car door slams behind me, and I'm temporarily saved from my own hesitation.

"Hey, Keke!" Alayna bounces up the driveway, my parents waving from their truck as it pulls away. She looks adorable in her flared jeans and oversized pink hoodie. "GG and Pops said to tell you they love you."

"GG and Pops?" I laugh. "Since when do you call them that?"

"Since I said it once as a joke and Grandma laughed so hard milk came out of her nose. It's not exactly lively over there—I've got to bring the comedy show, you know?"

She takes a bow, and I swat at her arm, grinning. "You're too much sometimes. I love it. They do too."

She scrunches her nose at me and gives me a suspicious look. "What are you doing out here?"

"I just got here. I was with Sarah."

"Ooh, I love Sarah. Is she inside?" Alayna doesn't wait for me to answer. She steps around me and bursts through the front door, her backpack thumping against her back. I follow quietly. Her enthusiasm is a sharp contrast to the weight in my chest.

"I'm home!"

Clay is standing in the kitchen doorway. The rich smell of beef stew wraps around us—Alayna's favorite. Our eyes meet. He greets his daughter warmly, but there's tension in his posture when he looks at me. I haven't replied to his texts. I didn't know how. Some things are too big for screens. They need tone, eye contact, the space between words.

And Sunday nights are family dinner nights. I'm not heartless. This is my family—even if things are shifting. They deserve to hear it from my mouth.

"Is dinner ready?" Alayna's practically drooling.

"You just came from GG and Pops' house. There's no way you're starving."

Alayna doubles over in laughter, clutching her stomach. Clay throws his hands up.

"Do I even want to know?"

"It's not that deep, Dad," she says between giggles, her cheeks pink.

"Lucky for you, little lady, dinner is ready. Go set the table."

She groans dramatically but drops her backpack and heads toward the kitchen. Clay approaches me, eyes shadowed, hair a mess. He looks like I feel—wrecked.

"Are you having dinner with us?"

"Of course," I say. "I need to change, but I'll be quick."

He nods, but as I start to walk past, his hand gently catches my arm.

"Are we okay? You didn't answer my texts, and I wasn't sure..."

A knot tightens in my throat. *Are we okay?* No. Not yet. Maybe not ever in the way that he means.

"We'll talk after dinner, alright?"

He sighs, lets go. I think I see something flicker in his eyes—something like hope—but it's bruised and tentative.

"Yeah, sure. I'll help Alayna with the table."

I rush upstairs, change into green joggers and a white T-shirt. If I'm going to tear my life apart, I might as well be comfortable. I stare into the mirror for a long moment, whispering all the reasons this is right. This is necessary. Then I take a breath and head back downstairs.

Dinner is quiet. Alayna's halfway through her second helping. Clay pushes food around his plate like it personally wronged him. I try to memorize the warmth of this house, the soft clinking of silverware, the familiar hum of family—because it might be a while before I get invited back.

Alayna chatters about her weekend with my parents, about Grandpa teaching her how to fix up the old Toyota. I smile, even as I ache. It's good that she's bonding with them. Good for all of us. Especially if Clay doesn't want me around after tonight.

"That rusty truck?" Clay shakes his head. "We'll find you something newer and safer. And maybe your grandpa can show you how to change oil or something less... advanced."

Alayna rolls her eyes. "Yeah, okay, Dad."

"Maybe get a job before worrying about your license," he adds.

"What did you two do this weekend?" Alayna is quick to pivot.

Clay shrugs. "Boring adult stuff."

"Keke said Sarah's in town. What'd you *really* do?"

Clay shoots me a panicked look. I shake my head slightly.

"Actually... I wanted to talk to you both about why Sarah is in town." I set down my fork, heart pounding.

Two pairs of eyes lock on me.

"Is she moving back?" Alayna asks, dropping her bread. "She can share my room if she wants!"

I smile sadly. "No, she's visiting. We found a place to rent, but not for Sarah. I'm the one who's moving."

Clay's glass tips over with a clatter. I grab my napkin, blot the water, but my hands are shaking.

"It's time," I say. "I love being here, love being part of this family, but I need my own space. I'm not going far. Nothing has to change, really."

Alayna grabs my hands. Her eyes are wet. "You don't have to move out to have your own life. What about driving me to school? What if I need you? What about Dad?"

Clay is still as a statue, face drained of color.

"I'll still be around. You'll have your own room at my place. I'll pick you up, we'll do dinners—"

"But why leave?" she whispers. "It won't be the same."

"Can we have a minute, kiddo?" Clay's voice cracks.

Alayna's hands slip from mine. Her lip trembles. The heartbreak on her face is cutting me to shreds. "How can you just leave us?"

"It's not like that—"

"Frankie, let her go," Clay says, voice harder now.

The sound of her running, the slam of her door—it echoes through me. I'm gutted.

Silence presses in like a weighted blanket. I can't breathe.

"So one bad night and you're running?" Clay finally says, rubbing his jaw. "Is this because I pushed too fast?"

"Clay," I whisper. "Can I ask you something?"

He nods.

"When I first moved in, we were both grieving. For me, it's softened over time. But for you... it's still raw, isn't it?"

His jaw clenches. "Is this about me calling you Tasha?"

"If she walked through that door, if you had a chance to have her back... would you take it?"

His arms cross, defensive. His breathing speeds.

"Of course I would. I hate how she left us, but she's Alayna's mother. She gave me the greatest gift I've ever known. But that's not reality, Frankie. She's not coming back."

"I know. And I don't want to be her. But I also don't want to be her *replacement*. I know you wanted more with me. For a while, I thought maybe I wanted that too. But I can't do it."

He stares at me, stunned.

"I don't think you see *me*, Clay. Not really. Not when she's still living in every corner of your heart."

"I don't need you to be her. I just want *you*."

"But I don't think that's true," I say, arms folded tightly around myself. "We've been playing house for so long, maybe we forgot it wasn't real. I don't want to be what's convenient. I want to be chosen."

He pushes back his chair with a screech. "Playing house? Is that what you think we're doing here? So this—this whole life—meant nothing to you?"

"That's not fair. I love you. And I love Alayna. But I need more than this. I need to be loved like you loved *her*. This thing between us, it's not—"

"Not what? Not enough? You keep saying you need more, Frankie. But now I'm offering you more and you're rejecting it." Clay's face is heated, even his neck has gone blotchy and red. I hate that I'm hurting him, but I have to be honest.

"I need you to understand what I'm telling you. We both deserve to be loved for who we are, fully, completely. No ghosts in between. I'm not trying to hurt you, but it's not me that you want."

"Oh, I understand, I just don't agree with you." Clay's voice is louder now, desperate.

A fat tear slides down my face before falling off the end of my nose. I'm angry; I don't want things to end this way, but I can't seem to get us back on the rails. I wanted this to be a gentle goodbye, and now it's like I just threw a bowling ball into a glass cabinet that holds every fragile piece of our life together.

"I'm not abandoning you, Clay. I still want to be a part of this family, always. But it's time for me to have my own life too."

He stands. "Then go. Just go."

My hands tremble. I take a step back from the table. The table where we've shared thousands of meals. Where we've celebrated birthdays, cried over homework, laughed together until our stomachs hurt. The scars in its wooden surface all have memories attached to them, and even this memory will be etched into its history now. If I could see the surface of my own heart, I imagine it would look like this table. All the scars of my life, the highs and the lows, tattooed into the tissue.

And now I've left this mark on all of us.

"Are you going to be okay?" I ask.

He turns his back, heading for his own room. "Not your problem anymore."

The door slams after him and I flinch. They're upset now. But maybe, one day, they'll understand.

In a final act of love, I clean up our dinner mess. I save the leftovers for Alayna to have later. I move through the motions like a ghost.

Four boxes. Two suitcases. Eleven years, packed tight. It's a stark reminder that I haven't taken up any of my own space in a very long time. How is this all I have to show for a lifetime of living? Somewhere along the way, I'd stopped living my own life and existed only to care for my family. I don't regret the years behind me, but it's a helpful reminder that I'm doing the right thing now.

Once I've loaded my car, I do one final sweep of the house, letting my hands trail over every surface, drowning myself in the memories. Even though I know what I'm doing is right, that it's time for me to leave this chapter and start a fresh one, I can't help but wish it had gone down easier. Gentler.

My heart is in my throat as I turn off the lights in my room one last time. I'm leaving this house, but I wish Alayna would talk to me, so that I could assure her that I'm not leaving her.

Walking out without hugging her, telling her I love her face to face is wrong. I need her to know this isn't goodbye. I'm not my sister.

I knock on her door. "Alayna? I'm heading out, but I'd like to talk to you first if you'll let me."

The door vibrates with a heavy thud, as if she's thrown something at it. "Go away. I don't want to talk to you."

I rub the sore spot on my chest as I lean my forehead against the cool wood. "I love you. Call me when you're ready to talk, I'm only a few minutes away."

Music blares through the door and I know I'm not going to get through to her tonight.

If they need time, I can give them that.

CHAPTER 23

IT'S ALREADY DARK BY the time I pull up to the rental house. I think about calling Sarah—ask her to come over, sit with me—but even the thought of talking everything through tonight is impossible. Instead, I grab the bare essentials: comforter, pillow, phone charger, one suitcase. I shut the door behind me and let the silence swallow me whole.

The master bedroom has a mattress with a single fitted sheet stretched tight across it. No blanket, no personality, but it'll do. I toss my pillow and comforter down and collapse on the bed fully dressed. The moment Alayna ran from that room, whatever energy I had left drained right out of me.

Why did I think it would end gently?

Maybe because they're my family. And we always talked things through—hard conversations around kitchen tables, tears in living rooms. But this wasn't that. Not this time.

The weird thing? I don't feel awful. Not like I thought I would. Sure, the disappointment stings, and I hate how hurt they looked. But underneath that, there's something steadier.

Like I finally stepped onto the right path. I've always been scared of change, but this kind feels different—like hope. And even if my family isn't cheering me on right now, I can still keep walking. Maybe they'll catch up.

Sarah was right. It's time to put myself first. To dream a little. Maybe even to believe I deserve more.

I pull the comforter up to my chin and sink into the unfamiliar bed. Tomorrow starts something new—and this time, I'm the one in charge of where I go. One step at a time.

My phone vibrates loud and sudden on the nightstand, dragging me out of a deep, dream-heavy sleep. I grope for it, blindly, eyes still closed.

"Hello?" My voice is rough with sleep.

"So, how did it go? Do I need to come help you pack and escape? Or did you head to work like a lunatic? You didn't update me last night. I've spent the last three hours listening to my dad explain the joys of term life insurance, and if you don't rescue me soon, I'm running back to my apartment and into the arms of daytime television."

Sarah's voice pours through the phone in a breathless rush, her words hitting me like cool water. I blink slowly, my brain still catching up.

"I just woke up," I mumble, yawning into the phone.

Her groan is pure drama. "Should I come over? Do you need coffee? Is everyone gone for the day? Are you okay?"

I sit up, brushing sleep from my face as her questions fire off like popcorn. "No. Yes. Probably. And... maybe?"

There's nothing from Clay or Alayna on my phone—no texts, no missed calls. Monday morning has come and gone without me. Clay's taken Alayna to school plenty of times. But this is different. Like I've handed off something important. Like they've let me.

"Wait—did you say *no*? I shouldn't come over?" Her voice pitches up in alarm.

"Yes," I say gently. "Don't come to Clay's house."

"What? Did that jerk talk you out of it already?"

Even without seeing her, I know she's pacing, eyebrows knitted, mouth twisting with frustration. She's trying to connect dots with half the picture. I smile, heart warming.

"I'm at the new place. Bring coffee and I'll explain."

Silence. Then a dramatic sigh of relief. "Fine. I'm grabbing coffee and coming your way. You better be ready to spill everything."

I grin. "Bring food, too. I'm starving. Love you."

"Love you too, brat," she huffs, and hangs up.

I fall back onto the bed laughing. Having Sarah here, even if only for a few days, was the best decision I've made in a long time. She makes everything a bit lighter, even the hard stuff. And if I'm being honest, I don't know if I would've taken this step without her.

While I wait, I wander through the little house. The furniture is solid, clean, nothing fancy—but it all matches. It's a blank slate, waiting for my touch. I run my fingers along the empty bookshelves, already picturing them filled. I've never had a space that was truly mine before. Not even my room at Clay's—it always felt temporary, like I was passing through.

But this? This is mine.

Maybe I'll add some plants. A splash of color here, a rug there. Maybe even a cat—if Mel doesn't mind. The idea makes me smile. I've always loved cats. And it'd be nice, not being completely alone here.

My thoughts tumble faster than I can keep up. Curtains, throw pillows, maybe some framed prints. It's not just decorating—it's claiming the space. Breathing life into it. Turning a rental into a home.

I still need to talk to my parents eventually. There's a good chance Clay or Alayna will beat me to it. But that can wait. Today isn't about damage control or guilt or any of the heavy stuff. Today is about beginnings.

I head toward the bathroom, ready to shower, get dressed, pull myself together. My best friend is bringing coffee and carbs, and we've got a full day ahead of us. Shopping, planning, dreaming a little.

And I'm going to enjoy every single minute of it.

No guilt. No second-guessing.

Just the first real step forward.

By Wednesday afternoon, the house already seems warmer. Not in the temperature sense, but in the way light feels when it filters through a canopy of trees—gentle, familiar, golden. Sarah and I dip into my savings and go a little wild, and I don't regret a single cent. With her creative eye and my cautious heart, we find a balance that feels like me—maybe the truest version of me I've let exist in a while.

It's not the lease that makes this place mine. It's laughing with Sarah in the middle of a rug aisle, arguing over lamp shades, carrying oversized plants like trophies back to the car. It's choosing things just because I like them, because they make me feel something, because they're mine.

Now, rainbow-colored pots dot the white bookshelves, plants spilling over like they belong there. Clear bookends frame leather-bound copies of the stories that have carried me through different versions of myself. I've added a few framed photos from my old room—Alayna at various ages, my parents smiling in grainy prints, my grandparents, and the chaotic, hilarious photo of Sarah and me mid-laugh on a mechanical bull during my twenty-first birthday.

The cream-colored couch we started with doesn't stand a chance against Sarah's decorating spree. Now it's draped with pillows in goldenrod, sage, and burnt orange. A macrame wall hanging with little wooden beads stretches beside the door, reminding me of mountain peaks. The rug beneath the coffee table blazes with reds and oranges—like a sunset we've dragged inside and dared to walk on. This house has more than furniture now. It has personality. It has joy.

It has Sarah's fingerprints all over it, which makes it even more like home.

I drop onto the couch with a sigh, letting my body sink into the soft cushions. "This place looks like it belongs in a magazine."

Sarah flops beside me and leans her head against mine. "There's something magical about starting over. It's like your soul exhales and remembers what it's like to be free. I'm glad I got to be here for this part."

I slide my arm behind her, pulling her into a half hug. "Thank you. For everything. I don't think I could've done this without you."

She grins. "I think I said the same thing when I finally left Trevor. And I meant it. We were always supposed to find each other."

"I wish we'd met before high school. We would've been absolute terrors as kids."

"Nah," she says, eyes twinkling. "It was perfect timing. You were the first genuinely kind person I ever met. That's why I fell for you so fast."

"And you were the first person brave enough to stand up to Gracelyn. You had me at 'evil spirits.'"

She laughs. "We really do have the best origin story."

I let myself slip into the memory...

Freshman year. Third week of school. Mr. Hewitt's Algebra class. Sarah had recently transferred from the Catholic school across town, and Gracelyn, resident queen bee with a venomous tongue, took one look at her and decided she was a target. The thing was, no one ever stood up to Gracelyn, because doing that typically meant immediate social suicide.

"Ew, something smells really gross," she'd said, sniffing dramatically. "The new girl smells like she's been rolling around in wet dirt."

Mr. Hewitt tried to shut it down, telling her to focus on her math sheet, but Gracelyn wasn't done. "I heard you were poor. What are you, homeless or something?"

Sarah didn't look dirty at all. Gracelyn was clearly threatened by Sarah's effortless beauty. She was tall and naturally lean, her hair looked like spun gold, thick and shining in the sunlight. She had her own funky style that few could pull off, and I personally thought she looked like the coolest girl in the room.

"Seriously, Mr. Hewiit, I can't be expected to do math when she smells so disgusting. Can't you send her to the nurse for a shower and some decent clothes? I think that would be the charitable thing to do." Mr. Hewitt's mouth had dropped open, but Sarah didn't even flinch.

She lifted one shoulder in a shrug and said calmly, "It's patchouli. Used for centuries to ward off evil spirits. Maybe that's why it bothers you."

I laughed—out loud, in class, in front of everyone. Sarah turned to look at me, and in that instant, I knew she was going to be important.

After class, she walked right up to my desk, grinning widely and wiggling her fingers. She asked, "Think she's going to cast spells on me now?"

"Honestly," I replied, "she does kind of seem like she needs an exorcism."

Gracelyn shoved past us, glaring daggers with her eyes. I'd never seen her back down from a fight so fast, and I figured I'd pay for it later, but at that moment, I didn't care. I wanted to know Sarah.

"That was pretty impressive," I beamed at her, offering her my hand. "I'm Frankie."

"Sarah, Wearer of Patchouli." She laughed, returning my handshake.

"I like it, my mom wears something similar. She's a big fan of oils and herbs."

Sarah followed me into the hallway. "You're the first person who has been kind to me. Thanks for embracing my weirdness."

People rushed around us to get to their next classes, and I searched my brain for something clever to say that would impress her, but all that had come out was, "Hey, weird is cool." I cringed, but Sarah's smile remained.

"I'll find you at lunch. We should probably stick together, who knows how many demon friends Miss Fancy-pants has at her disposal." Sarah squeezed my arm before heading the other way. We met for lunch that day, and every day after that, too.

Our journey to "best friends" had been instant and effortless, and she was right: it was like the universe had sent us to each other when we needed it the most.

Back in the present, Sarah pulls away and stands up. "Alright, I'm heading home. You need a little space to settle into this new life, and I'd like to sleep in my own bed tonight."

I pout dramatically. "Fine. Go back to your fancy city life. Leave me to my peasant existence."

She snorts. "Peasant? Please. Your life is about to get a whole lot more interesting now that Clay won't be holding you back."

"I don't think it's fair to blame Clay for that," I say gently.

"Okay, then should I blame you?" She dodges my immediate attempt to swat at her. "Joking aside... maybe part of you *was* holding back. But, now you're not."

She pauses. "Now, what's the plan with Roman? I always liked him, even if he was an idiot for breaking your heart."

Sarah means well, but I frown.

My first instinct is to defend Roman, and it surprises me a little. I always defend the people I care about—well, besides Tasha. That part isn't new. What throws me is that I don't blame Roman anymore. Not really. For a long time, I held on to resentment, clung to the sharp edge of how he left me behind. But standing here now, in this new chapter of my life, I can finally see it for what it was.

A gift.

It broke my heart. That summer, I felt like the biggest idiot—naïve, discarded. But I also learned more about myself in the years that followed than I ever could have as part of a pair. I had to grow up, and somehow, I did—not all at once, but in small, quiet ways that added up over time: every school event I showed up to for Alayna, every time I stayed when it would've been easier to run, I was slowly learning how love comes through in the everyday moments. I started to understand what love actually costs, what it means to stay, what it takes to hold your own heart together when someone else walks away. Things you don't fully grasp when you're young and desperate to believe in forever.

If Roman hadn't ended it, I would've followed him. I know that now. I would've left this town, left behind the version of me who showed up for my family, who helped raise my niece, who built a life that mattered. I would've missed every moment of watching Alayna grow into the fierce, hilarious, beautiful girl she's becoming. I would've missed the chaotic, joyful partnership Clay and I forged in the wreckage of our respective heartbreaks. We wouldn't have raised her the way we did—not if I'd been living across the country or tangled up in someone else's future.

Somehow, in the last few weeks, the way I see all of it has shifted. The past is softer now. Wiser.

And hope—thin and bright like morning light—flickers under my skin.

Maybe Roman was never the villain in my story. Maybe he was just... early.

Maybe it wasn't our time back then. But maybe, just maybe, it could be now.

I don't know what's going to happen. But I can't deny how fast my heart beats just thinking about his name. There's something electric in the possibility, something I haven't felt in a long time. Not like this.

"Hey. Earth to Bestie." Sarah shakes my shoulders, pulling me back. "Where'd you go just now?"

I blink, smiling. "Sorry. I think you're right, Sarah."

She raises a brow, grinning. "I'm always right. But what am I right about this time?"

I breathe in deeply, the air suddenly full of potential. "For better or worse... I think my life is about to get a whole lot more interesting."

CHAPTER 24

ON FRIDAY AFTERNOON, MY box truck loaded with wood, nails, paint, and more power tools than we could ever possibly need, I pull up to the back of Alayna's school. I still haven't heard from her—or Clay—and it's getting harder and harder not to take it personally. Alayna's read every message I've sent but refuses to reply. I wonder if I'll run into her today, or if she'll avoid me like the plague.

Mrs. Betty waves at me from the double-door entrance at the back of the theater. Her rust-colored skirt catches the wind and blows around her ankles, showing off a pair of white vintage kitten heels. Say what you will about her style, but the woman is consistent. I wave back, wondering if she plans to help unload lumber and tools in those heels.

My own outfit is far too casual in comparison, but it's after school hours, and I know I'll probably be sweaty and dirty by the end of this unload. My faded sky blue Hale Hardware hoodie covers a matching T-shirt and a pair of worn-out jeans.

I won't win any fashion contests, but at least it's practical—and my sneakers won't cause me any injuries.

It doesn't take long to get the door open and pull the built-in ramp out. I've brought a flatbed cart and a couple of hand trucks to make things easier. Filling one with a stack of boxes, I push it down the ramp and toward the double doors.

Betty is no longer standing in the doorway. Instead, I'm staring at the back of a man I'd recognize anywhere. Blue suit, brown oxfords, and perfectly styled hair—Roman turns to greet me as I approach. Like Betty, his outfit seems all wrong for today's activities, but he looks so good I'm not complaining.

"Good afternoon, Ms. Hale. Mrs. Betty went to grab the volunteers, but you're welcome to roll that right on through to the storage room."

His formal tone throws me off, so I make sure to match it. "Thanks, Dr. Clarke."

A handful of teenage boys pass me, heading toward the truck. With this many hands, we'll be unloaded in no time—and I won't have to worry about Betty hurting herself in her heels. Plenty of capable help. No need for her to lift a thing.

"This is so exciting," Betty says as I move the boxes to the corner of the storage room. "I peeked into your truck—you're sure we're not putting you out, keeping so many tools here at the school?"

"Not at all. We don't have many equipment rentals these days. Most folks either buy their own tools or hire out the work. Honestly, I could probably sell a lot of these at a discount when we're finished. Maybe I'll even donate a few to your woodshop if there's a need."

That would make my dad proud. He still talks about how much woodshop meant to him, how it sparked his love of the family business.

"You're such a sweet girl," she hums. "Like your mama and your daddy."

"And hopefully my niece?" I ask, fishing for anything she'll give me. I can't remember the last time I went this long without talking to Alayna—maybe never.

"I see you in Alayna," she says thoughtfully. "More fire in her, though. That may serve her well in the future."

"Is she still around?"

Betty's face scrunches. "No, she wasn't feeling well. I thought you knew she left early today—Mr. Phillips picked her up before the last bell."

So she *is* avoiding me—and Clay's helping her do it. I'm not sure how that makes me feel.

"All right, dear. I'll let you get back to it. The students are beyond excited to get started on Monday. Unless you need me, I think I'll head off for the weekend."

"No, you go ahead. This shouldn't take long, and Dr. Clarke and I can handle the students. Thanks, Betty."

Forty-five minutes. That's how long it takes to get everything unloaded and organized for Monday.

Roman dismisses the boys, and I thank each one as they head past me and out to the parking lot.

"I'll lock this door," Roman says, nodding to the storage room and pulling a keyring from his pocket. "I don't think the kids would steal anything, but I'll sleep better knowing it's secure."

"Sounds great." It's awkward again, and I don't know how to fix it. Only that I *want* to fix it—desperately. He's taken off his suit jacket, and his shirt sleeves are rolled up past his elbows. I watch, transfixed by the flexing of his forearms, as he turns the key in the lock and tests the handle.

When he turns back to me, I swallow the drool pooling in my mouth. It should be criminal for one man to have this much sex appeal.

"I guess I'll see you Monday?" I ask.

Isn't that what he said to me last Friday? Heat blooms on my cheeks as I remember our conversation. I'd agreed to meet him Monday morning to exchange numbers—and then my weekend exploded into chaos, and I completely forgot.

My hands fly up to cover my mouth. "Oh my gosh, Roman—I completely forgot to come by on Monday."

Roman fiddles with the keys in his hand. "If you don't want to exchange numbers, I get it. We can communicate through email or something less personal if that's what—"

"Hand me your phone." I cut him off, not willing to let him think I've been avoiding him. He opens his mouth, then closes it and pulls his phone from his back pocket. He unlocks it before handing it over, and our fingers brush during the pass-off. His hands are warm, mine are shaking.

As I type my information into his phone, I apologize. "I had a crazy weekend, and then Sarah spent the week with me. I feel really bad. I'm sorry." I press the call button, letting my phone buzz in my pocket a few times before I end the call. Now I have his number, too.

Roman eyes me curiously. "Sarah, as in Patchouli Sarah?"

Sarah's going to love knowing her old nickname stands the test of time. "One and the same."

"Are you two still thick as thieves?" He leans against the wall, clearly in no rush to leave.

"She moved to Spokane about ten years ago. We have a standing date at Cliff's Bar once a month when she comes down to check on her parents. I don't see her nearly as often as I'd like, but she loves the city and she's doing really well there."

"I'm glad. I always liked her."

"Funny, she says the same thing about you." The words are barely out before I realize I've admitted Sarah and I have been talking about him. His dimple flashes, and my cheeks flare with heat.

"Ah, so you told her I'm back in town, then?"

"She's my best friend, Roman. I tell her everything—nothing is too small to leave out, not even the mailman's mismatched socks."

His laugh is deep and warm and washes over me like a blanket. Goosebumps rise along my arms. I want more of that laugh. I want more excuses to keep talking to him. And as I watch him bite his lip, trying to suppress the next wave of laughter, I find myself wanting him to kiss me again.

"I need to lock up my office and grab a few things—walk with me?" Roman gestures down the hallway, and I nod, not ready for this time to end. We fall into step, the quiet of the school becoming more and more welcoming.

"Have you reconnected with any of your old friends since you've been back?" I ask. I honestly have no idea if he's kept in touch with anyone—or if they even know he's here.

Roman nods. "A few of the guys from the old soccer team invited me to play weekends in their adult league. We meet every other Sunday and sometimes grab a few drinks after. Not too many familiar faces left around here, though."

He's right. Most of our old friends left town for bigger lives. Just like he did.

Only now he's back—and I can't help wondering how long he'll stay this time.

"I've seen them playing at Chase Field a few times. I'm glad you connected with them. You were always a natural." I'm surprised the gossip mill hasn't picked up that detail yet. Roman, shirtless and sweaty, running across a field? That's like small-town catnip. I'd bet money Kate's seen him play—maybe she's just smart enough to keep it to herself.

Roman slows as we approach the main office. One glance at the front desk, and I sigh with relief. Kate and Mrs. Brosnan are already gone for the day. No gossip brigade to dodge. Roman follows my gaze and smirks like he knows exactly what I'm thinking.

"You should join us for practice sometime," Roman offers.

I shake my head, trying not to laugh. "I think my soccer days are behind me. But I'd love to come cheer you on."

Roman ducks into his office, and I wait outside, cheeks warming thinking about the last time we were alone in there. I don't regret the kiss—but dinner at his house had been a disaster. Today is different, though. I can't quite put my finger on why. Maybe it's because I finally realize I don't hold our breakup against him anymore.

"Alright, I'm all set." Roman shuts the office door behind him, hands full—papers in one, a large lunchbox in the other. He's slipped back into his suit jacket. "The janitors are already hard at work, but it looks like everyone else has gone home. I'm officially off the clock. Hello, weekend."

"Big plans tonight?" I ask.

Roman exhales. "Actually, I have a date at Jake's Diner in about an hour."

I bite the inside of my cheek and nod. A surprising wave of jealousy rises in my chest, and I tuck some loose hair behind my ears to distract myself. "With Kate?" I guess.

Confusion flickers across Roman's face. He blinks a few times. "No... with a cheeseburger. Why would you think I was meeting Kate?"

"I don't know why I assumed that. She seemed very... interested."

He runs a hand over his jaw, his smile deepening. "That's flattering, but no. Just a cheeseburger."

"Jake's sure does make a good one," I say as I head for the front doors, eager to escape the embarrassment.

"Would you like to join me?" His voice is husky.

My eyes snap to his mouth. "At Jake's?"

"Yeah. Unless you know somewhere with a better cheeseburger."

He's asking me to dinner. Again. Even after the disaster of our last attempt. My heart does a cartwheel inside my chest and I leap on his offer.

"Technically, the best cheeseburgers in town are found in the food truck outside the post office," I say. "I can pick you up in an hour and take you there. Let you be the judge."

Roman's lips curve up. "Okay. But if Jake's turns out to be better, you owe me a second date to make up for it."

"And if the food truck wins?" I ask, enjoying this flirty side of him.

"Then I'll owe you a celebratory dessert."

It doesn't escape me that Roman is making future plans for us. The blood in my veins moves like liquid mercury; I'm on fire from the inside out. And even though it's scary, the excitement is stronger.

Sarah's voice echoes in my head. *It's time to start living your life—and stop running from your future.*

"You've got a deal."

CHAPTER 25

By the time I return the box truck to the hardware store, race home, and throw on something more presentable, I'm already running late. A quick spritz of perfume, a swipe of mascara, and I twist my messy hair into a hasty claw clip before squeezing my feet into a pair of Converse. Casual, but still... kind of cute, right? We're only heading to a food truck, after all. Maybe a little "I'm not trying too hard" is the move.

As I slide into my car and crank up the volume, Luke Bryan's sultry croon wraps around me, enough to distract from the nervous flutter building in my stomach. I'm excited to see Roman again. This seems like a fresh start, a chance to bury the past and see if there's still something real between us. The conversation earlier today felt like *us*. Playful. Easy. No sharp edges.

Roman's already waiting on his front porch when I pull up. Gone is the sleek suit I last saw him in, replaced with a pair of perfectly fitted jeans and a deep green henley that makes my pulse skip. He waves, flashing that signature grin as he strolls down the steps like he knows exactly how good he looks—and I can't even be mad about it.

"Ready?" I call out through the open window, barely managing to keep my voice from shaking.

"Ready for the best cheeseburger in town? You bet," he says, pulling open the door. He shifts the seat back before folding himself into my tiny sedan, looking oversized and effortless at the same time. His smile alone dissolves my hesitation about not taking his truck. He doesn't seem phased by the tight fit. If anything, the way he settles in makes the car feel... cozy. Intimate.

"The curly fries aren't half-bad either," I say, pulling away from the curb. "But I'm not gonna crown them as the best yet."

"We'll see if your cheeseburger judgment holds up. A bet's a bet, my friend," he teases, hazel eyes flickering with mischief.

The words hit like a warm gust of nostalgia. I grin. "As I recall, I won the last bet we made."

Roman swallows, eyes drifting to the window. "Priest Lake," he murmurs. "You did win that one. Never thought you'd actually take the plunge into that freezing water."

"Freezing doesn't even begin to describe it. I swear my teeth were seconds from shattering." My fingers tighten on the steering wheel as if they can still feel the icy bite of the water.

He laughs, head shaking. "And the look on your face when you came up for air? I thought you were gonna pass out. But somehow, you were laughing. I was seriously worried I'd have to tell your parents I killed you."

I chuckle at the memory. "We took Alayna there last summer. It's a lot nicer when the weather doesn't try to murder you."

"You and Clay?" The question slips out so casually it takes me a second to register the way his hands still slightly on his thighs. I wonder if he's picturing that cabin weekend we shared, the quiet hours wrapped up in each other. That week with Clay had been completely different—full of sunscreen and snack bags and two middle-school girls who never stopped singing. There'd been no romance, no quiet conversations by the firelight.

"Yeah," I say softly. "Alayna brought Summer. They're basically Sarah and me, the younger and louder version. It was sunshine, Taylor Swift on repeat, and two giggling girls splashing in the lake."

My heart tugs at the thought of her. If Alayna keeps avoiding me much longer, I might have to do something drastic.

When we arrive, the food truck is buzzing. A line winds out onto the sidewalk, every table packed with people laughing and digging into foil-wrapped masterpieces. I snag a parking spot and try to ground myself, but old memories swirl around me like steam from the grill.

"Being a mom really suits you," Roman says quietly, his voice unexpectedly gentle. I glance over, caught off guard by the tenderness in his expression. "You light up when you talk about Alayna. It's obvious how much you love her."

"I'm not really her mom, though," I say, almost instinctively.

Roman shrugs, completely unbothered. "Doesn't matter what you call it. You're what she knows. You're the one showing up, day after day. That's what counts. And it's beautiful, Frankie."

His words wrap around my heart and squeeze tight. "Thank you," I whisper. I didn't know how much I needed to hear that until I did.

"Do you think you'll have more kids someday?" he asks.

The question knocks the air out of me. *More.* Not *your own.* More. Like Alayna counts already. The distinction touches something buried deep.

I don't answer right away. I haven't let myself dream about that in a long time. Not since life demanded everything from me just to keep things afloat. The dream of having a child with someone I love, watching a life grow inside of my own body, has been buried so deep, I'm not sure if it is wise to let it surface now.

Roman notices my hesitation. "Sorry," he says quickly. "Too personal. Let's go stand in line before I say something else awkward." I see him reach for the door handle as if it's a parachute ripcord and he'll hit the ground if he doesn't pull it immediately.

But I don't want him to retreat—not when we're finally peeling back the layers again.

"Let's settle this bet first," I say, giving him a smile that I hope tells him I'm not scared. "Then we'll tackle the tough stuff."

He exhales a small laugh, his shoulders relaxing, ripcord abandoned. "Well, in that case, hurry up."

We head toward the line, and I'm relieved not to recognize anyone. I don't want to make small talk with strangers—I just want to be here with *him*. His arm slips around my shoulders and I lean into him without thinking, our bodies fitting together like a familiar melody.

"Is this okay?" he murmurs.

I tuck my head against his chest. "More than okay."

By the time our order's ready, two seats have opened at the end of a crowded picnic table. Roman grabs them, setting down our plates while I unwrap straws.

He snaps a photo of the food. "What's that for?" I ask, laughing. "Starting a food blog?"

"Well, if these are the best burgers in town, I'm going to need photo proof for my rave review."

The woman next to him gives him an appreciative once-over, and I can't blame her. He looks even better than the burger in front of me.

"Enough talk," I say, picking up my burger. I know this one well—it's a masterpiece of crispy lettuce, juicy tomato, the perfect amount of pickle, and a sauce that sings.

He dramatically rolls up his sleeves and takes a massive bite, eyes fluttering closed. "Mmm."

"It's not polite to talk with your mouth full."

He winks. "I wasn't talking. I was moaning. I thought you'd remember that sound."

The girl next to him chokes on her soda. My cheeks burn, but I can't help grinning. "So does that mean I won?"

He nods excitedly. "I have to finish all of it, you know, for science. But unless I find a cockroach in here, you've definitely won."

The food is phenomenal, but it's Roman who makes it unforgettable. I can't stop staring. The laugh lines near his eyes invite you in, like a secret only you get to keep. His shirt brings out the golden flecks in his hazel eyes, and I want to reach across the table and brush his hair from his forehead, kiss him there, maybe never stop.

The more he talks, the more I see the boy I loved. But now he's layered in experience and strength, like time distilled the best parts and made them richer.

He tells me about his students, his hopes for the school, and the possibility of helping coach soccer. He wants to show the kids who are hard to reach—but who need it the most—that he's approachable. His hands move as he talks, expressive and sure. It's clear his whole heart is in it—and it's downright sexy. Especially the part where he's making plans that sound long-term.

"What about you, Frankie?" he asks, finishing off his fries. "What's next for you?"

I hesitate, remembering how he admitted my dreams had been part of the reason he'd left me behind. But this Roman is older, wiser. He seems interested in knowing who I am, and where I'm going, so I let myself share the truth with him.

"I'm thinking of teaching classes at the shop. Maybe on weekends, maybe week-long specialized projects. You know, hands-on stuff—fixing things, DIY projects. I want to help people feel capable, especially in a small town like this where funds are tight for most people. What if they had access to the tools and training to do some projects for themselves? Unclog a toilet, install a ceiling fan, resurface a table, fix a sagging fence... imagine the money they could save and the pride they'd get from learning a new skill. I have the space and the tools, experience in almost every trade, I know I could make it fun and informative. Maybe even get my dad to teach a few things. I don't have all the details figured out yet, but I'm really excited about it."

Roman's grin is wide and real when I finish. "You'd be amazing at that. Would you ever want to teach some of those skills classes at the school?"

I light up. "I'd love to work with your kids."

"That's pretty damn cool, Frankie. This town's lucky to have you."

"You really think I can pull it off?"

"I have zero doubts." He hums in approval, popping the last fry into his mouth.

As I take my last sip, a fat raindrop hits my nose. Then another, splattering on the table. Around us, people scramble, covering food, dashing to cars. I hadn't noticed the storm rolling in—I've been too focused on the man across from me.

Roman grabs our trash and tosses it. Then he turns back, holding out his hand. I take it without hesitation, our fingers threading together like two puzzle pieces.

"Thanks," I say softly.

He opens my car door for me like it's nothing, like we do this all the time. I sink into the seat, watching him jog around to his side through a curtain of soft rain.

I'm soaked. I'm smiling. And my heart is thundering like it suddenly remembered what it means to be alive.

CHAPTER 26

THE SMILE NEVER LEAVES my lips on the short drive back to Roman's place. The rain hasn't dampened the mood—if anything, it's heightened it, wrapping the world in a hush that's intimate, secret. The rhythmic sweep of the wiper blades and the soft percussion of rain on the hood create a comforting soundtrack, a private melody for just the two of us. Our date is winding down, but I find myself wishing I could slow time, stretch these moments until they spill over and become something more.

The rain intensifies, the windshield blurring more with each drop. I should focus on the road, but all I hear is Roman's voice. That low, husky rumble as he recounts the chaos of the last soccer game he coached—one of the seniors pranking the assistant coach, a ball that sailed through a car window, the kind of nonsense teenage boys will always find hilarious. I laugh, already imagining the scene, but what really stays with me is the way Roman lights up when he talks about his students. There's something magnetic about it—about *him*. It pulls at me, makes me want to see him on that field, commanding attention, completely in his element.

As I ease into his driveway, the rain thrums harder against the roof, a steady roar. Roman turns in his seat, his hand resting gently on my thigh, the warmth of it spreading like wildfire through me.

"Are you in a rush to get home?" he asks.

Home. The word feels different now. It's not Gram's house, not the place I left or the one I found. It's become a feeling I haven't quite named. A place I haven't quite claimed.

I turn off the car, shifting to face him. "No," I say, voice softer than before. "No big rush."

"Good." His grin is slow, deliberate. Dangerous in the best way. My heart hiccups in my chest.

He opens his door, then jogs around to mine like he can't get to me fast enough. I don't even get a chance to protest before he's pulling me out of the car, our fingers tangling. He tugs me into the downpour, and I let out a breathless squeal as cold water soaks my shoes, the grass squishing underfoot.

"What are we doing?" I laugh, the wind stealing the words from my lips.

"Recreating history," he shouts, eyes gleaming as he leads me around the side of the house.

He unlatches the wooden gate in one swift motion, and we press forward. The rain is relentless now, pounding against my sweater until it clings to my skin. Every step pulls us deeper into a memory I hadn't let myself revisit in years.

And then—we're there. The wraparound porch appears through the curtain of rain. Even stripped of its summer blooms, the place is still enchanted. The ivy crawls along the lattice, clinging to the bones of the house, and the rosebushes stand tall despite the season. And the weeping willow—God, that tree—it still guards the space like a keeper of the past.

Roman pulls me up the steps, through the familiar curtain of ivy, into the shadowed alcove where he once kissed me for the first time. My breath catches.

Back then, he was nervous, fumbling, a boy on the edge of something he didn't yet understand. But tonight? He's a man—steady, sure—and everything about him says, *I remember, too.*

The memory flickers between us like lightning in the storm. But this time, I stay rooted in the now.

He presses me gently against the brick wall, cold and solid at my back. Rain trickles down his face, catching in his lashes. His hands frame my jaw, reverent, like I'm something precious. I reach up and pull the clip from my hair, letting the wet strands fall free.

His eyes lock on mine, and suddenly there's no air left to breathe. Everything is in his gaze—questions, memories, hunger, hope. I wrap my arms around his waist and pull him to me.

It's the only invitation he needs.

He crashes into me like a storm surge, lips on mine, hands in my hair, breath tangled with mine. His kiss is demanding, aching, slow and searing all at once. Our mouths find their rhythm, and I forget the chill of my clothes, the rain still falling around us. The only thing that exists is *him*.

His tongue teases mine, deliberate and slow, coaxing and claiming. My fingers grip the fabric at his back, and then, desperate to feel more, pull him closer, memorizing every inch. He groans into my mouth, the sound vibrating straight through me. His hands trail down to my waist, then slide up underneath my shirt, warm fingers against my chilled skin.

When he breaks the kiss to drag his mouth along my jaw, down the column of my neck, I shiver—but not from the cold.

"You taste even better than I remember," he murmurs, his lips brushing the sensitive spot beneath my ear. "I don't know how I've survived so long without you."

The words splinter something in me, then knit it back together. I kiss him again, trying to tell him without saying it—*I missed you, too. I've never stopped.* My hands slide under his shirt, across his bare back, and he lets out a breathy curse against my mouth, one hand gripping my hip, the other fisting into my hair.

Our kisses slow, deepen. I pull back just enough to speak, my breath shaky. "I've missed you."

Roman looks at me like he's waited a decade to hear those words. "I've missed you, too," he says, his voice rough with emotion. He leans in, brushing his lips against mine again, soft and slow this time, almost like a question waiting for an answer.

"Tonight was wonderful," I whisper, kissing him one more time.

"For me, too." He closes his eyes and rests his forehead against mine, his breath warm against my lips. We're soaked, clothes heavy and plastered to our skin, mascara undoubtedly smudged all over my cheeks.

I laugh, wiping at my face. "We're a mess."

Roman grins and uses his sleeve to gently clean the black streaks from beneath my eyes. "I got so caught up in recreating our first kiss, I didn't think about how wet we'd get."

"It was worth it," I say. "Even if I look like a drowned raccoon."

"Prettiest drowned raccoon I've ever seen," he murmurs. "I don't think it was raining this hard the first time. And we definitely had to be quiet so no one would hear us sneaking around."

I run my fingers through his soaked hair, sweeping it away from his forehead. I've wanted to touch him like this all night. "No one has ever kissed me like you."

Roman stills. Then slowly, he takes my hand from his hair and places it over his heart.

"I've never kissed anyone the way I kiss you."

The weight of his words, the truth in them, steals my breath. I see it in his eyes—this isn't just nostalgia. It's real. It *always* has been.

Maybe he's kissed others. Maybe I have, too. But none of it matters. Because right now, right here, the only thing that matters is *us*. And this time, it's not about chance—it's about choice.

I shove aside the fear, the ache of the past, and kiss him like my life depends on it. I grip the hand that's still pressed to his chest and pull him impossibly closer, until our hearts are beating in tandem. Until the past and the future blur, and all I can feel is *this*—this moment, this man, this love that's endured.

Roman matches me, breath for breath, heartbeat for heartbeat. His hands roam my back, my hips, like he's relearning me. And I let him. I want him to.

For the first time in a long, long time, I believe I could have it all.

When it gets too cold to stay outside, Roman invites me in to dry off and clean up. I'm grateful for any excuse to linger—part of me is terrified that when I leave, the spell might lift, the magic will fade. I want to hold onto this night for as long as I possibly can.

"There are fresh towels in the bathroom," he says, nodding toward the door down the hall. "I'll find you something to wear while your clothes dry." His voice is calm, but the pink flush in his cheeks tells me he's not as unaffected as he's pretending to be.

By the time I peel myself out of my soaked clothes, I'm shivering. I step into the hot shower, letting the water hit my skin in soothing, steaming waves. Slowly, the chill works its way out of my bones. I wash myself with the soap Roman uses, breathing him in with every lathered handful. My hair smells like him. My skin is already memorizing his touch. When I finally step out, the bathroom is wrapped in a fog of warmth. I towel my body dry, then pause when I catch my reflection in the mirror.

No longer a drowned raccoon—I almost laugh at the thought. My eyes are bright now, still soft at the corners from smiling. My lips are swollen and pink from kissing, and there's a new flush across my cheeks. There's something alive in my expression, something wild and awake. I recognize myself, but I also don't. I look like a woman in love.

A soft knock taps on the door. "Want me to set these clothes outside for you?" Roman's voice carries through the wood, lower now, quieter—like the intimacy of the night has seeped into his every word.

I crack the door open, gripping the towel tight with one hand as I reach for the clothes with the other. He's standing there barefoot, in a fitted T-shirt and gray joggers, his damp hair curling slightly at the edges. God, he looks good. Soft and safe and sexy all at once.

"Thanks," I say with a smile, my heart thudding as our fingers brush.

"I'll throw your wet ones in the dryer and start a fire," he offers, that nervous smile tugging at the edge of his mouth like he's waiting for me to laugh or pull away.

Instead, I nod, closing the door to gather my soaked clothes. I wedge my bra and underwear between my jeans and shirt—somehow the act seems more intimate than being naked in front of him. It's been so long since we've been like this, but everything is new again, charged.

When I hand him the bundle, he smiles knowingly, his fingers brushing mine again before I close the door and lean against it with a quiet breath. The clothes he gave me—an oversized T-shirt and a pair of boxer briefs—make me laugh. The briefs settle low on my hips, borderline scandalous, but the shirt is long enough to cover what needs covering. My legs are bare, and my hair's still a mess of damp curls, but I feel beautiful. Wanted.

I twist my hair back into my clip and leave the steamy bathroom to find Roman.

He's kneeling in front of the fireplace, adding logs to the flames, the light dancing across his face. My breath catches. "Do they fit okay?" he asks, glancing over his shoulder.

"They'll do," I say, tugging at the waistband playfully before sinking into the loveseat.

He joins me, the heat from the fire and the nearness of his body making the room seem warmer than it is. My foot accidentally brushes his and he jolts.

"Geeze, Frankie, your feet are popsicles." He laughs, reaching for the quilt draped over the back of the couch. He pulls it over us both, gently shifting me until my legs drape across his lap. "Let me fix that."

His hands wrap around my feet—strong and warm. He rubs slow, deliberate circles into my arches, and I nearly melt. My eyes flutter closed as the stress leaves my body in waves.

"I thought you hated feet," I murmur, sighing as he presses a thumb deeper into the ball of my foot.

"You remember that?" he asks.

"I remember a lot of things." *I remember everything, when it comes to you.*

"I do find most feet repulsive." He chuckles. "But I haven't found a single inch of you I don't want to touch."

My eyes fly open. He grins, cocky and sincere, and I squirm against the back of the couch, but his hands keep working their magic.

"Are you warm enough?" he asks.

"Mmhmm." I pat the blanket. "I could get used to this."

"Me too," he says softly, and his hands never stop moving.

The fire crackles in front of us, the scent of smoke and soap and rain weaving into something comforting. Somewhere behind us, the gentle thump of tumbling clothes hums in the dryer. The rain taps softly at the windows, as if trying to remind us that the world still exists beyond these walls. But in here, it's only him and me.

"You asked me a personal question earlier," I say, shifting enough to thread my fingers through his under the blanket. "About kids. I told you I'd come back to it."

Roman turns toward me, his eyes searching mine.

"I do want to have more children someday," I say. "I love Alayna, I really do, but I'd be lying if I said I didn't want to experience creating and carrying a child with someone I love. It's always been a dream of mine... to share that."

His gaze drops to the fire again, unreadable for a moment. "I wasn't sure," he admits quietly. "If I wanted that. If I could be that."

"You weren't sure... or you're still not?"

His fingers tense around mine. Then he looks at me, eyes raw and vulnerable. "The day you walked into the school with Alayna... when I thought, even for a second, that she might be mine... it hit me harder than I expected."

"I'm sorry I let you think that," I whisper.

"Don't be. I made the assumption, not you."

"But I should've said something."

He shakes his head. "No. I'm glad you didn't. Because I found myself wishing it were true... I wanted it to be true. I wanted her to be mine. Ours."

Emotion tightens my chest as his voice goes soft. "Working with kids, I always felt protective, like a mentor. But now... now I want it all. I want to love someone so much that your love creates a whole new person. The late nights, the lullabies, the messy, beautiful chaos of parenthood. And I have you to thank for that."

I sit up, climbing into his lap and wrapping myself around him like he's the center of my universe. "You'd be amazing at it," I say, pressing kisses along his jaw.

"That means everything coming from you," he murmurs, his arms wrapping tight around me. "I know we're not there yet. I'm not saying I've mapped out our future, but I want to be clear—I'm open to it. I want that life... with you."

Words stumble over themselves in my brain, tangling into a heap on my tongue, refusing to unscramble into anything coherent. There are at least a dozen ways I could respond to such a romantic declaration, but my tongue stays paralyzed. So I do the only thing I can think to do—I press my lips against his and kiss him. I kiss him with every piece of love I've ever stored up for him, praying the words will bleed through our kisses and settle into his soul.

The dryer buzzes, abrupt and uninvited. We both laugh, breathless against each other, the blanket around us suddenly too warm.

I know I need to go soon, give us both space to breathe, to make sense of all that's happened tonight. As much as I want to stay here in his arms, I don't want to rush things. Maybe call Sarah, work through all my feelings. Maybe sit in the quiet of my own room and replay this all again in my mind.

But as I rest my head against Roman's shoulder, there's one thing I don't need to overthink—my heart is his, as it always has been. Maybe he never really let it go.

CHAPTER 27

ROMAN AND I HAVE been texting all weekend—little jokes, lighthearted conversations, nothing too heavy. Like we're both afraid to break the spell that Friday night wrapped around us. We're living in a bubble, and one wrong move could pop it. Maybe that's what happens when you have a history—everything is a little more delicate, it's been cracked before and you don't want to press too hard in the same spot.

As much as I want to race back to his place and pick up where we left off, I don't want to ruin whatever magic we've stirred back up.

Still, that night with Roman relit a fire in me—a fire that clearly never burned out. I want him. No matter the risk, I want him.

The rest of my weekend is quiet and oddly blissful. I add a few potted plants around the apartment, lounge around in my underwear, read half a novel, and blast music without worrying if anyone else likes my playlist. There's no one to hide from, no one to cater to or tiptoe around. The freedom is intoxicating.

But also a little lonely. A double-edged sword. After so many years of sharing my space—my life—it's strange having so much of it to myself. I'm still figuring out how to take up space again.

By Sunday afternoon, I can't keep the date to myself any longer. I sprawl out on the couch in my pajamas, prop my phone up on the coffee table, and hit Sarah's contact.

"Hey hey, gorgeous! How's the new place treating you?" Sarah's voice booms through the speaker.

"I'm currently taking up the entire couch, staring at the ceiling fan, and wishing my bestie was here to bask in the sunshine with me."

"Wow, you sound suspiciously chipper for someone who was drowning in an existential crisis last week. What did I miss? Please don't tell me you let Clay talk you into another round of bad dates."

I sit up, grabbing a bottle of neon pink nail polish and propping my toes on the table. "Nope. Still haven't heard from him—or Alayna."

"Ugh. They'll come around," she says, her voice softening.

Will they, though? Alayna's avoidance tactics are becoming an Olympic-level event. Clay's never frozen me out like this before, and it stings more than I want to admit. I hate that I still check my phone, hoping to see his name pop up.

"It hurts," I say quietly. "I really thought Clay would come around by now."

"Don't get me started on Clay. I'm trying to be a good person here, but he makes me want to fight someone. Preferably him."

I laugh in spite of myself. "Well, I *did* have a date on Friday... but not with Clay."

"Oh my god. Wait—did Dr. Hottie *finally* get his act together?"

"You and your nicknames. You know he asked if I was still hanging out with 'Patchouli Sarah'?"

Sarah snorts. Loudly. "I *love* that nickname. I should put that on my nametag at the shop. No, I'll make it permanent. I'm getting it tattooed."

"You should. It'll be a great icebreaker for your next hookup."

"Okay, enough stalling. Give me details. All of them."

I hug myself, grinning before I can stop it. "We went to the burger truck. It was... easy. The conversation flowed. Then it started raining, and when we got back to his place, he whisked me out to the back porch and recreated our first kiss."

"Shut UP. The doctor's got moves."

And foot rub skills, but I keep that detail for myself.

"We were drenched, so he gave me clothes to change into and dried mine while we warmed up by the fire."

"Naked?" she screeches.

"*No*, perv. I just said I wore his clothes."

She's wheezing now. "What a gentleman."

"It was kind of magical, honestly." I pause, fingers brushing over my collarbone like the memory is still sitting there. "I think I'm in real trouble, Sarah."

"It's about time. I'm so happy for you, babe."

And I *am* happy. It's a physical thing—like I'm lit up from the inside, electricity humming under my skin. I hope Roman feels it, too.

"I hope my family can be happy for me someday."

"They will be. They *love* you. And they'll come around."

"Remind me again why you live two hours away?"

"Because the universe knew we were too powerful to share a zip code. We're a threat to the local ecosystem. Gotta spread the beauty around."

"Right. Can't hoard the charm and sarcasm." My sides hurt as I laugh.

"You have selective memory. You ignore anything you don't like."

It's meant as a joke, but I hear the truth in it. Maybe that *was* me for a long time—trying not to see what hurt. But I'm not doing that anymore. I'm not hiding from myself. I'm breaking out of my shell; I can feel myself emerging.

"Alright, enough about me. What are you working on for the next gallery show? I want to brag to all the art kids at school."

"Oh, you know. Life, death. Big existential themes."

"Sarah... I'm trying to be serious here."

"Frankie, you're the most serious person I know. I'd be more shocked if you said you were trying *not* to be serious." Sarah snorts again.

Sarah missed her calling as a comedian; my cheeks already hurt from smiling. This is why she's the best friend I could ask for, because we balance each other out where it counts. "Ha. Ha. Just tell me about your work."

"Okay, okay. It's a series called *New Beginnings*. A pregnant woman cradling her belly. A teenage girl mid-first kiss. A man waiting for his bride. A clown wiping off his makeup..."

"A clown?" I blink.

"Making sure you're still listening."

I laugh. "You really feel like a clown?"

"Sometimes. But I'm ready to take the stage makeup off and just be myself again."

"You thinking about dating again?" I ask, nudging her the same way she always does me.

"I... maybe agreed to a date next weekend. Met him at the shop. Which is normally a no for me." She sighs.

"I'm glad you're putting yourself out there, maybe he'll be nice." I smile, knowing she's already considering backing out. That's just how she is.

"It *would* be nice to have someone warm me up by the fire. Naked or otherwise." She laughs.

"We were *not* naked."

"Like you'd tell me if you were."

Touché. I shake my head, smiling. "Let me know when your next show is. I'll be first in line when the doors open."

"You'll be the first person I call. Love you, babe."

"Love you, too, lady."

CHAPTER 28

Mrs. Betty beams at me Monday morning as the bell rings for class change, only adding to my already bubbly mood. We've been flying through the first set build, and the iconic balcony scene is finally starting to take shape. The kids are surprisingly handy with the power tools.

"I'd say we're moving faster than a cheetah on roller skates!" Betty claps her hands, grinning. A few students snicker as they head out of the theater.

My chest swells with pride as I watch them go. They're seeing their work come alive, piece by piece, and there's nothing quite like it. Maybe I should've been a teacher after all. But at least the hardware store classes will give me a little taste of that—if things go the way I hope.

"I'd say that's pretty accurate." I laugh. "I don't see any reason we won't finish with time to spare."

"Stunning sets for a stunning performance. I'm tickled pink." Betty pats my arm and turns to wrangle a group of students near the paint trays.

The theater is buzzing with energy—bright lights overhead, tarps protecting the wood floor, paint cans and brushes scattered in various stages of use. Everything's in motion.

I keep glancing toward the double doors, hoping to see Roman through the glass. I missed him first thing this morning—his office was empty before school started—and I can't shake the feeling of anticipation curling in my gut. It's ridiculous how much it reminds me of being seventeen again.

Betty's definitely on to me.

Just have to get through the school day and then I can track him down. But for now, I'm trying not to spiral about Alayna. I scan the students filing in, but she's not among them. My heart races a little faster. Where is she?

Did Clay let her stay home again? Is she sick? I step into the aisle, trying to peer out into the hallway. A couple of students rush past as the second bell rings, and then... nothing. The hallway goes still. My shoulders sag.

I start to pull the door closed, but as I do, Roman turns the corner.

I step into the hallway, a small smile tugging at the corners of my lips despite the knot of nerves tightening in my stomach. He smiles back, but there's a weight to it. The usual spark behind his eyes is missing, and my pulse only stutters harder.

He stops in front of me, running a hand along his jaw. His suit jacket is missing today, his sleeves pushed up, the top of his button-down undone. His navy slacks are slightly wrinkled, and he looks like he could use a stiff drink. There's something important behind his eyes.

"Hey, you," I say softly, reaching out to touch his forearm. His skin is warm under my fingertips, comforting in a way I didn't know I needed.

"Hey, Frankie." He exhales. "As much as I want to be just Roman right now, I'm here in a principal capacity. I need to speak to you as Ms. Hale—the guardian of Ms. Alayna."

My stomach drops. "Oh God, is she okay?" I tighten my grip on his arm.

"She's fine—physically. But I need you to come with me. I'll explain once we're there, if that's alright."

I let go of his arm, suddenly hyper aware of how inappropriate it is to touch him right now. My mind reels. Alayna's never been in trouble. What could she possibly have done?

I nod, forcing myself to stay calm. "Yes, sir. Lead the way."

Roman flinches slightly at the 'sir,' and his eyes soften with something like regret. Still, he nods and turns toward the front office. I count tiles on the floor as we walk, anything to distract from the panic tightening my chest. I'm a mess—splattered paint on my shirt, jeans, and even my tennis shoes. I can only pray there's no dried primer on my face.

Kate looks up from her desk as we enter. Her golden hair is twisted into the same elegant updo from the other day, and her pink business suit fits her like it was tailored for her curves. I stand a little taller, trying not to shrink. It feels like I'm the one in trouble and not my niece.

"Ms. Payton, please hold my calls," Roman says without looking at her.

"Yes, Dr. Clarke." Her tone is neutral, but I swear there's a flicker of something in her eyes as she glances at me.

Alayna is already seated in one of the worn chairs in front of Roman's desk, her back to me. My heart thuds.

"Please, come inside and have a seat, Ms. Hale." Roman's voice is gentle, but there's tension in it.

Alayna turns at the sound of my name. Her eyes are glassy, rimmed red. I rush to her, crouching in front of her chair.

"Are you hurt?" I scan her, head to toe. Nothing broken. No bruises. I brush a tear off her cheek.

"I'm sorry," she whispers, voice barely audible.

Roman gestures to the chairs. "If you'll sit, we can begin."

Reluctantly, I take the seat beside Alayna and pull her hand into my lap. She squeezes mine back, and it nearly undoes me. I've missed her.

"Before second period, Alayna and another student were caught trying to leave campus. Since they were stopped before they actually left—and because neither has a history of disciplinary issues—I wanted to offer a chance to explain."

If I weren't so worried about Alayna, I'd be melting. Roman in this role—measured, compassionate, in control—is dangerously attractive. But my niece is pale, visibly shaken, and I'm just as eager to hear her side.

"Thank you for the grace," I say. I don't want to believe he's giving her special treatment for my sake, but I trust him. He wouldn't compromise his integrity.

"And the other student?" I ask.

"I can't say," Roman replies. "But I assure you, they're being treated fairly."

I nod and turn to Alayna. "Okay, let's hear it."

She avoids our eyes, chewing on her lower lip. Her knee bounces anxiously.

"It was stupid. I'm really sorry. I'll never do it again," she says, eyes filling with tears. "It wasn't Derek's fault. Please don't punish him. He was only trying to help."

Roman leans forward. "Why were you trying to leave campus in the first place? I'd like to understand what led to that decision, Alayna."

She glances at me before looking back at her lap. "We finished our math test early, so Mrs. Michaels let us sit in the hall to practice lines. We were working on the street brawl scene, and we started talking about how silly the feud is after all the tragedy. It reminded me of divorce..."

Roman offers her a tissue. I release her hand so she can take it, my heart aching as she wipes her eyes.

"What happened next?" I ask gently.

"I started crying. I told Derek it felt like my parents got divorced and I didn't know how to handle it."

Roman's brow furrows. "Did your parents recently divorce?"

Alayna lifts her chin. "Not my mom. I'm talking about Frankie and my dad."

The words hit like a gut punch. Of course she saw it that way. I hadn't even thought about it from her perspective.

"Oh, baby girl." I pull her close as she cries into my shoulder.

The door opens, and Clay steps in, eyes wide with concern. He's polished as always—perfect tie, crisp suit—but his expression is anything but calm. His blue eyes pin me with questions.

"I came as soon as I got the message. What's going on?"

Roman stands, extending a hand. "Mr. Phillips. Thank you for coming. Alayna was caught attempting to leave campus. We're giving her the chance to explain."

Clay steps behind us, resting a hand on Alayna's shoulder. Roman sits again.

"Alayna? Would you like to continue?" he prompts.

She sniffs, "I got really upset. I told Derek that Frankie moved out and it felt like losing my mom." Her words are shaky but honest, her voice breaking on *mom*. "I couldn't stop crying and I was embarrassed. I told Derek I was going to walk home. He wanted to cheer me up, so he said he'd take me to Jake's for a milkshake and bring me back after lunch so we wouldn't miss the whole day. He was just trying to be a good friend. We shouldn't have tried to leave, but I was so upset..."

When she's done, silence stretches.

"Who is this Derek kid again?" Frustration bleeds through Clay's voice.

"Romeo, from the play," I answer quietly.

Roman clears his throat. "What I'm hearing, Alayna, is that you were in need of someone to talk to, and your friend was kind enough to listen and offer comfort. I can't, in good conscience, punish either of you for that. I do believe you see the error in judgment and won't repeat today's decision. However, I'd like you to make an appointment with the school counselor if you feel you have more to get off your chest."

Alayna nods, relief flooding her features. "Yes, Dr. Clarke. Thank you. I promise it won't happen again."

Roman stands. "I'll leave you three to talk. Alayna, you can head back to class when you're ready." He slips out, quietly closing the door behind him.

Alayna and I both stand, turning to face a red-faced Clay.

"Let me get this straight." Clay's anger is barely restrained. "You were upset because of Frankie, and now it's affecting school? You could've called me."

Alayna's cheeks are already pink from crying, but I watch the flush deepen. "I'm sorry, Dad. I thought Frankie would live with us forever, and when she left—and you were so upset—it made me feel helpless."

Guilt crashes over me like a cold wave. "I'm sorry, too, Alayna. I wish you'd called me, or answered any of my messages. I'm not leaving you. I'm two streets or a phone call away. You're not getting rid of me, kiddo." I pull her into a hug, letting her bury her head in my neck.

"If you'd given us more time..." Clay's voice hardens as he turns to me. "You had already picked out a place before you even told us you were leaving."

I exhale, forcing myself to stay calm. "You're probably right. I should've told you I'd been thinking about it for a while. But, Clay, it's been eleven years since I moved in. Don't you think I deserve a life of my own? I love you both and I always will—but it's time for you to be a parent to your daughter, and for me to be the best aunt I can be. Just... not under the same roof."

Clay's jaw tightens. "But I love you—"

The words hit like a slap, and I recoil. Alayna pulls away, shock flashing across her face. How many times do we have to go over this?

"No, Clay. You love Tasha. And you always will." My voice softens. "There are some loves you don't recover from. And that's okay."

I'm still in love with Roman—a fact that becomes clearer every time I'm with him. If Clay's feelings for Tasha run deeper than mine for Roman, complicated by the fact that they share a child... I can only imagine the kind of mark that leaves. I don't blame him. But I know he can never love me in the way I need to be loved. And I can't pretend anymore that I could love him back in that way, either.

Alayna's gaze bounces between us, realization dawning. "Wait—you were trying to be together-together?"

Clay crosses his arms, jaw ticking. "It was clearly a mistake."

Alayna lets out a breathy, almost hysterical laugh. "Dad, you're an idiot."

"Excuse me?" Clay's tone is sharp, but his arms drop slowly to his sides. Some of the fight drains from him. The slightest hint of a smile tugs at his lips.

"I get it—Keke is gorgeous and smart, and a staple in our lives—but you don't love her like that."

Clay lets out a long sigh. "You're a teenager. What do you know about love?"

"I know enough." Alayna's chin lifts with her declaration and Clay stares at her, weariness etched into the deepening lines of his face.

"We have to fix this. This"—he gestures around the office—"can't become our normal."

"Absolutely not." I add, as I wipe a stray tear from Alayna's cheek. When did she grow up so much?

Clay's shoulders sag, his expression softening. "I miss you."

Swallowing back the lump in my throat, I nod. "Can I come back to Sunday dinners?"

Alayna grabs my shoulder, pressing me toward her dad, pulling us all into a tight group hug. "Let's make them mandatory, okay?"

"Done," Clay says, holding us close. "And I'll try to stop being such an idiot."

"Sorry, Dad."

"No, kid, you're right. I needed to hear it."

For the first time in a long time, things feel right. We'll have to heal from this—but at least now, we're trying. And that's a start. Our foundation is solid; we have good bones. We can survive this renovation.

"My girls need me to be better—I get it." Clay rubs a hand over my back before stepping away. This time, when he calls us *his girls*, it doesn't feel wrong. "Alright, kid, get yourself to class before they change their minds and kick you out of that play you're so excited about."

Alayna stretches up on her tiptoes and kisses her dad's cheek. Some of the color has returned to her face, and she looks lighter, like a weight's been lifted. I can only hope that seeing her dad and me communicating eases some of the anxiety she's been carrying.

"And maybe after school today, you can come see my new place?" I offer cautiously. "I'll drive you home after. But only if you're up for it." I hold my breath, waiting.

Alayna hesitates for only a moment before nodding. "Yes. I'd like that." She kisses my cheek, then slips out of the office.

As soon as the door clicks shut behind her, Clay claps his hands down on my shoulders. His touch is familiar, grounding. A sense of relief washes over me, like puzzle pieces finally clicking into place. We still have healing to do, and I'm not sure Clay's fully admitted to himself that he isn't in love with me—but for the first time, it feels like he could get there.

"I owe you an apology," he says, exhaling. "Apparently, I've been an idiot, and it took a fourteen-year-old calling me out to make me see it." He gives my shoulders a small squeeze.

He's one of my oldest and closest friends. For a minute, I think we both forgot that. Things got complicated—but that doesn't mean we can't *un*complicate them.

"We both made mistakes," I say. "Let's just agree to communicate better moving forward—especially for that girl."

Clay nods, rubbing a hand over his jaw. "She's important. But so is your happiness, Frankie. I was selfish with you, and that wasn't fair."

His words catch me off guard, a fresh wave of emotion rising in my chest. "Thank you for saying that."

"I should've said it a long time ago."

He leans in, presses a soft kiss to my forehead, then steps back. Taking his hands from my shoulders, he gives me one last lingering look, then turns and walks out, leaving me alone in the office.

I stagger back into one of the chairs, letting my heart rate settle. Less than an hour ago, I walked in here with anxiety clawing at my ribs, unsure of how this would play out. But now, a quiet peace begins to settle over me.

Things are going to be okay. I'm not sure how I know. But I do.

CHAPTER 29

WHEN I FINALLY STEP out of Roman's office, only Kate is left at her desk. She swivels in her chair, tapping her manicured nails against her lips.

"That seemed dramatic. Everything okay?"

I bite back the smartass remark bubbling on my tongue and nod. "Yep, everything's fine." And it is. But even if it weren't, Kate Payton would be the last person I'd confide in. She's the president of the rumor mill, and I'm not offering up headlines.

"I haven't seen Clay Phillips in the flesh for a while. Man sure takes good care of himself."

I think about telling her that if she likes him so much, she should say it to his face. But I wouldn't do that to Clay. If he ever manages to move on from my sister and find someone to love, I have to believe it won't be someone like Kate.

"That's nice of you to say." I give her my best fake smile. "Where's Mrs. Brosnan?" It hits me—I haven't seen her since the first week of school.

"Oh, you didn't hear?" Kate makes a face like she's sucking on a lemon. "Her hip was bothering her, and when the doctor suggested she take a break, Dr. Clarke told her he'd give her a sixty-day paid vacation."

Roman's racking up kindness points left and right today. "Wow. And she agreed to that?" I can't hide my surprise. Mrs. Brosnan is the most stubborn woman I've ever met.

"Yes," Kate snaps. "Unfortunately, she did."

"Unfortunately?"

Kate hits me with her iciest glare, like daring me to challenge her royal decree. "Do you know how much work she did around here? It's like they expect me to do five jobs now—and smile while I do it."

Maybe that's her karma. But I keep that thought to myself. "Well, I hope she comes back feeling well-rested," I say instead, glancing around the office. I half expect to see Roman pop back out, but there's no sign of him. Kate notices my search, and that familiar smirk creeps back across her face.

"If you're looking for Dr. Clarke, he's not here. He took the other family to an empty classroom—figured y'all might need a minute. All this small-town drama, I bet he takes that job offer in London. I mean, who wouldn't want to go see Big Ben and the Queen, you know?" She grins. "'Course, it'd be a shame to lose him."

"He's headed to London?" My stomach tightens. Old fears flicker up before I can stop them. We've just started to figure things out again. We're not even steady on our feet yet, and already the thought of him leaving twists something inside me.

But I shake it off. I can't say I've forgiven him and still hold onto the hurt he caused when he left the first time. If we're meant to have a future, it'll happen. I have to believe that.

Besides, I'm not about to feed Kate's gossip machine.

"If Roman has plans, he'll tell me when he's ready." I smile, firm and final. "Anyway, I should get back to the theater. See you later, Kate."

She smirks again—meaning crystal clear—but I just roll my eyes and walk out. I'm not letting her sour my mood. Not today. Not when my girl is finally talking to me again, and I know she's waiting.

Now that I've seen Clay and Alayna with my own eyes, my steps are lighter. My mind drifts to Friday night with Roman. For so long, I've held back—caught between uncertainty and the weight of everything else. But now? I have my own place. A fresh start. A shaky but hopeful fresh beginning with my family. Space to dream about the shop, my future, and maybe, finally, what Roman and I could be.

I'm not obsessing anymore. I'm here, in this moment, and things with Roman are real. Honest. I want to say the words out loud—I love him. Not again, but *still*. It's freeing. And maybe, just maybe, he'll say it back.

By the time I reach the theater, it's buzzing. I catch Alayna's eye through the glass, and she rushes over, throwing her arms around me. Her eyes are still a little puffy, but she looks more herself.

"I really get my own room at your new place?" she asks, hopeful.

"Yep. You can decorate it however you want."

"I'm sorry I ghosted you."

I narrow my eyes, trying to look stern. "I think I can forgive you... on one condition."

She chews her lip. "As long as it's not doing your laundry for life or something."

"Just don't do it again." I ruffle her messy bun. "And actually, you're probably stuck doing your own laundry now. Have you ever seen your dad attempt it?"

Alayna groans. "What if we compromise and you help me on Sundays when you come over for dinner?"

"Points for creative thinking." I laugh. "But nope. You can't save it all for one day. I'll help on Sundays, but you've gotta do at least one load every other day. Deal?"

"Okay, Mom."

She freezes, eyes wide as she realizes what she's said. The way she'd compared me leaving to a divorce earlier... the way she talks about me. It hits me then—how deep this bond runs. How much we've always meant to each other.

A lump forms in my throat.

"You know, Layna-bug," I say, softer now, "no matter what we call each other, I'll always be your Keke. And you'll always be like a daughter to me."

She nods and hugs me tighter, then quickly pulls away to change the subject. "Um... you didn't happen to see Derek when you left the office, did you?"

"Smooth redirection," I tease. "No, Ms. Payton said he was meeting with Dr. Clarke and his parents."

I don't miss the way she flinches at that.

"I really hope he's not in trouble. His parents seem cool, but... they're still parents," she says, then quickly adds, "No offense."

"People only say that when they're about to offend someone."

She twists the front of her sneaker into the carpet, chewing her lip like she's trying not to fall apart. "I really like him, Keke. I don't want him to hate me if he gets in trouble because of me."

My girl. She's growing up right before my eyes. The way she talks about him, the light in her eyes—it's all there. These moments will stay with her forever. And I get to be part of them. That's a gift I'll never take for granted.

"He's a sweet boy, huh?"

"The sweetest," she murmurs, blushing. "And Keke?"

"Yeah?" I meet those brown eyes that mirror mine.

"He's an amazing kisser, too. You were right—it's like magic."

With that, she spins and bolts back to her friends, leaving me stunned and grinning. The little twerp knows that conversation isn't over.

A knock at the door pulls my attention. Derek waves through the glass, his eyes bright—doesn't look like a kid who just got in trouble. I open the door.

"You survived?" I ask.

He blushes. "I'm sorry if I got Alayna in trouble. She was crying and—"

I wave it off. "There's nothing to forgive, kid."

His lopsided grin is contagious. Floppy blonde hair, light blue eyes, easy charm—he's adorable. My niece never stood a chance. He doesn't have Roman's dimples, but he's got that same confident glimmer. Sweet, respectful, and clearly smitten. I almost want to hug him myself.

"Dr. Clarke is pretty cool," he says.

"Yeah. I think so, too."

I wish Roman had walked in behind him. I want to thank him properly—for the way he spoke to Alayna, for how he always leads with empathy. That's what makes him great at this job. The kids respect him because he respects them. He listens. He shows up.

Out of the corner of my eye, I catch Alayna watching us, nervous. I keep my face neutral—let her sweat a bit.

"Your parents weren't too hard on you, I hope?"

"Nah." He shrugs. "Dr. Clarke said I'm a good kid and he wasn't worried about me. After that, my parents mostly talked about the play. As long as I keep my grades up, they're chill."

He flips his hair from his eyes. "Mind if I go check on Alayna?"

I grin. "She's convinced you hate her for getting you in trouble."

His face goes serious. "I could never hate her. That's my Juliet."

The cheese. My god. But it's sweet, too.

"Then go get her, Romeo."

He gives me one last charming smile before sprinting for the stage. I watch Alayna's face light up as he reaches her, and it sends me tumbling back to the memory of my first love.

And just like that, I know it again, deep in my bones—my heart is absolutely, irrevocably, still Roman Clarke's.

By the time the school day ends, I'm itching to find Roman. But first, I help Betty clear the stage—gathering tools and folding up tarps, moving everything into the back room where the set pieces will be finished. The crew made solid progress on the flats and larger props, but the stage needs to be cleared before we can start spiking it—marking key positions with colored tape so the actors know their blocking.

With rehearsals shifting from table reads to staging, the actors need to get a feel for the space—where to stand, when to cross, how to move with purpose. The tape marks help them hit those spots on cue, and the tech crew is starting to plan transitions for set changes, too.

The assistant director is already calling students to the stage for a read-through, while the stage manager double-checks everything for a smooth rehearsal. I hear bits of lines drifting through the theater and spot students flipping through scripts, some mouthing cues under their breath.

And Alayna? She's in her element. Watching her work is breathtaking.

Everything's starting to take shape. The set's still rough, costumes are in their early stages, but the energy in the room has shifted. Rehearsals aren't simply lines on a page anymore. The show is beginning to breathe.

Once my duties are wrapped, I head back toward the front office. Relief washes over me when I spot Kate's desk—her purse and collection of half-drunk beverages are gone. She probably bolted the second the bell rang, and I silently thank the universe for the small mercy.

Roman's office door is ajar, and I catch a glimpse of him at his desk, typing away. It's quiet up here, the only sound coming from his keyboard, steady and focused. His brow is furrowed in concentration. I wish I could smooth it with my fingers—ease the weight he's always carrying. I want to pull him back to Friday night at his place, where the world felt far away and uncomplicated.

"Hey, you," I say, knocking gently before nudging the door open.

His head snaps up, a grin breaking across his face. "You're still here?"

"Rehearsals," I remind him, stepping into the office and sinking into the chair across from him. "I'm Alayna's ride tonight."

"Am I interrupting something important?" I ask, nodding toward his screen.

"Nothing that can't wait." He leans back. "I've been trying to catch up on emails. I had more meetings than expected today—the day got away from me."

His smile falters, and I know exactly which meetings he means.

"I hope that wasn't weird for you earlier," he adds, voice softer now. "Me having to step in as principal... being part of your business like that."

Funny thing is, it wasn't weird at all.

I lean in closer, wanting him to hear me clearly. "You were wonderful with her. I was kind of in awe, honestly. The way you handled everything... I can see it now. You're exactly where you're meant to be."

His cheeks flush a little at the compliment. "They're good kids. I just wanted to understand what was going on. Most of the time, if we stop to listen, they'll tell us everything we need to know."

I nod. "I heard Derek's parents took it well?"

"They did," he says. "And when you're working with good kids, you usually get good parents. You'll like them."

"You think I'll be meeting them soon, huh?" I lift a brow. Not really a question. I already know the answer.

Roman's dimple appears, that familiar twinkle lighting up his eyes. "I think that kid's going to be around as long as Alayna wants him. Those Hale girls? Not easy to forget."

God, I hope he never forgets me.

"They're lucky to have you," I say, watching his face. "All of the kids are."

Roman circles back, clearly not ready to drop the earlier thread. "I knew things between you and Clay were... undefined," he says carefully. "But you never mentioned moving out. Why is that?"

"I was too busy kissing you Friday night to tell you," I say, smirking. The half-truth slips out easily. The whole truth? I'd been scared. Saying it out loud—telling him I'd finally moved out, that Clay and I were officially a non-start—made it real. Only Sarah and Clay knew, and that felt safe.

Roman chuckles. "Friday was pretty great, but you still could've told me."

"I would have. Eventually. I told you about the hardware store—that was a big deal. You're still the only one who knows."

"I'm honored," he says, his smile softening. "I can't wait to see it all come together. I'll even take a class—especially if you teach one on wallpaper removal. As charming as that old house is, those creepy horses in the upstairs bathroom have to go."

I laugh. "They really do."

He leans forward, a little more serious now. "But beyond the house and the store—how are you doing with everything?"

"It was time," I say quietly. "Moving out... it was a long time coming. Alayna and Clay took it harder than I expected. I didn't realize how much Alayna was struggling. I thought she was just mad. I didn't know it was more than that."

Even saying it makes my chest ache. The idea of her trying to process everything alone kills me.

"Kids are unpredictable," Roman says. "But the good news? They're resilient. Alayna's smart. She's kind. She's grounded. She's a lot like her aunt." He winks. "She'll be okay."

The tenderness in his voice makes something warm bloom in my chest. I don't want to leave. Not yet.

"When are we going on another date?" I blurt out, the words escaping before I can reel them back.

He doesn't miss a beat. "Do you have dinner plans?"

"Tonight?" Butterflies flutter in my stomach. I love how ready he is—how we're on the same page, wanting more. "As much as I wish I could say no, I promised Alayna I'd take her to see the new place after rehearsal."

Roman crosses the space between us, pulling me gently to my feet. "The kid comes first," he says, brushing a kiss against my lips. "But if you're free tomorrow... I'd like to show you the best pizza in town. Besides, I still owe you a dessert for winning that bet."

I smile against his mouth. "It's a date."

CHAPTER 30

WHEN WE PULL INTO the driveway of my new place, Alayna stares up at the little brick house with wide, adoring eyes.

"It's cuter than I expected," she sighs. "It really feels like home. I guess that means... you're not coming back, huh?"

"Wait 'til you see the inside." I wink as I turn off the car. "I think you're really going to love it."

She tosses her backpack into the backseat before hopping out. She's been unusually quiet during the drive, and I've given her the space to settle after such a long, emotionally loaded day. As I unlock the front door, I watch her closely, heart thudding. I hold it open and let her walk through first.

I hesitate on the threshold—my stomach twisting with something warm and nervous. I want her to see this place as more than just mine.

I want her to feel like it's hers, too.

To know I'm still her home.

Her eyes roam the small living room, lingering on the framed photos and the cluster of plants on nearly every surface. She steps deeper inside, fingertips skimming the back of the couch as she drifts toward the kitchen. I close the door behind us and drop my purse and canvas tote on the entry table.

"It's like someone climbed into your head and barfed it all over this place," she teases, but her voice is thin—and when she turns back to face me, her little face crumples.

"Oh, baby girl." I cross the room in a second and pull her close, holding her tight and rubbing gentle circles on her back. The familiar smell of her shampoo surrounds me, and I blink fast, trying to keep my own tears in check.

"What's wrong?" I whisper.

"It's nothing," she mumbles into my neck. "It's... it's perfect."

"Then why are you crying, Layna-bug?"

She pulls back and wipes her nose on the sleeve of her hoodie. "I wanted to hate this place so I could convince you to come home—but I don't hate it, Keke. I think you're really going to be happy here."

I press my hands to her shoulders and meet her eyes. "You mean we? We are going to be really happy here. You can stay with me anytime you want, okay?"

Alayna nods, her smile watery but real. "Yes, *we.*"

"Alright. Now that that's settled, let's go lie on your bed so you can tell me all about this kissing Derek business." I gently steer her down the hall.

"I *knew* you were dying to bring that up." She laughs.

"What? Me? Never. I'm the picture of restraint," I say, nudging her playfully.

Inside her room, I flick on the light. Alayna gasps at the sight of the queen-sized bed, the bronze frame catching the light just so. I've draped a textured sage green blanket at the foot of the fluffy white comforter, and added floating shelves filled with photos of her and her friends, with a few trailing plants softening the corners. The room smells like clean linen and greenery.

"It's perfect," she breathes, then spins around and crashes into me, wrapping her arms around my middle. "I love it. And I love you."

"Okay, now lie down next to me and spill your guts, kid—I want *all* the details about that kiss."

We snuggle under the throw blanket, her head resting against mine, our hands laced together. She giggles like she can barely contain it.

"It happened last weekend," she begins. "Derek asked me to meet him at the park to run lines, and when I got there, he suggested we sit on that big rock along the walking path so we wouldn't disturb anyone."

"Ah, so he wanted you all to himself?" I bump her shoulder lightly, and she giggles again.

"I guess so. We were sitting on that rock, and he started reciting his lines—then said, 'Let's try Act 1, Scene 5,' and I must've looked like I was about to pass out, because he added, 'or not?'"

"That's the kissing scene you've been so nervous about, right?"

She nods. "But Keke, I wanted to—I really did. So I started saying my lines, and instead of making me feel awkward, he joined right in. And when he said, 'Then move not, while my prayer's effect I take,' I closed my eyes and leaned in..."

My breath catches. I squeeze her hand. "You brave little thing."

"He was so gentle," she whispers. "His fingers felt like flower petals on my cheeks, and his lips were like a whisper against mine. And when he pulled back, I just... I wanted him to do it again. I said, 'Kiss me again, Derek,' and he goes, 'I think that's *my* line.' Then he did it—kissed me again. We just kept kissing, like, forever."

"So it was everything you dreamed a first kiss would be?" I murmur, eyes slipping shut as my own first kiss flickers through my memory—sweet, shaky, and unforgettable.

"It was better. You were right—it was like magic."

"I'm happy for you." I kiss the top of her head. "And now you know—Summer was wrong. First kisses *can* be magical."

"I was so worried it'd be gross. When I told Summer how great it was, she was pretty jealous. I guess she picked the wrong guy for hers."

She keeps talking, her voice light and dreamy—about Derek, the school dance, the play. She hasn't told Clay much yet, but she promises to bring it up over dinner tonight. I'm glad she still wants her dad in the loop. Even though things between Clay and me are still awkward, we'll figure it out. Being a good dad has always come naturally to him.

Eventually, Alayna quiets, her eyes fluttering shut as she snuggles in closer. Even with her growing up, I'm thankful moments like this are still comforting for both of us.

We lay there for a while, hands clasped, soaking in the stillness. I treasure these moments—this fragile, beautiful in-between. My little girl is growing up, and she is somehow, impossibly, cooler than I ever was. Watching her bloom is going to be the greatest privilege of my life.

I let out a soft sigh—then her phone buzzes loudly in her pocket. She startles and pulls it free, glancing at me nervously.

"It's Dad."

"Answer it," I say gently. "It's okay, Layna-bug—we're still a family. Things just look a little different now."

She sits up and gives me a quick, questioning look before answering. "Hey, Dad."

I hear Clay's voice ask if she's ready for dinner, and I nod at her again.

"Yeah, Keke will bring me home now. Her place is really nice—you'd hate it," she teases.

Clay laughs in the background, and I ruffle her hair. "Come on, kid. I'll take you home."

She talks with Clay about tacos and rehearsals while we get in the car, settling back into our rhythm. "Okay, Dad, I'm hanging up. I'll see you in a sec." She tosses her phone into her lap and turns to me. "This was nice—I'm glad I came. Next time I'll bring some of my stuff."

"I'd like that," I say, smiling. "Now pay attention so you know how to get here."

Less than two minutes and three turns later, we pull into her driveway.

"Okay, you're right—we're practically neighbors. It's not far at all." She opens the door and grabs her backpack from the backseat, then circles around to my window.

"I told you, you're welcome anytime. I'll get you your own key this weekend."

She hesitates, pulling that face—the same sheepish grimace she made the day she accidentally lost my favorite scarf. The hair on the back of my neck prickles as she shuffles her feet, kicking at some leaves.

"Uh, by the way, Grandma and Grandpa know you moved out, and they're pretty peeved you didn't tell them yourself. So you should probably call them. Just thought you should know. I love you—bye!"

She sprints toward the front door, blasting past Clay—who waves from the porch—and disappears inside without a backward glance.

All that bonding, all that crying—and she waited until the *very end* to drop that little bomb like a mic.

That little twerp.

She really *is* a Hale.

They say chamomile and lavender tea help with anxiety. So to be safe, I drink a cup of each before dialing my mother's number.

It barely rings once before she answers.

"Oh my word, you're alive." She huffs into the phone like I've been lost at sea. "Frank! Our daughter is on the phone!"

She yells so loud I have to hold the phone away from my ear.

"It's a miracle," Dad chimes in from somewhere in the background, as dry as ever.

"Where have you been? I don't like having to hear about your life from my granddaughter. Especially not when she shows up at our house Friday afternoon in tears, talking about how you moved out and didn't tell anyone. Clay brought her straight from school, the poor thing was just a mess. And he didn't look much better."

So that's where she went after school the day Betty said Clay picked her up early. She hadn't just skipped out—she'd gone to them. Told them everything.

"She kept saying she didn't understand, that you were just gone. That you packed up your room and left them behind. We kept her here all weekend, trying to reassure her, but honestly, we were hoping you'd call. Every time the phone rang, I thought maybe it would be you."

Guilt tightens around my chest, sharp and familiar.

"I've been around. I was going to talk to you about everything eventually, Mom."

And then Mom launches into her tirade, right on schedule. "Eventually? You moved out. You moved out and didn't tell anyone. What kind of person does something like that? How could you just leave Clay and Alayna without discussing it with Clay first? And not even a call to your own parents? Did I raise you this way? Was it something I did wrong?"

Classic Mom—somehow making it about her.

"Mom, put me on speaker so I can talk to you both," I say, massaging the bridge of my nose. I set the phone on the counter and tap it to speakerphone.

"Hello, my sweet daughter," Dad says warmly. "Glad to finally hear from you."

"Hi, Dad." I press my forehead against the cool countertop, taking a breath. "How's the shop? I talked to Mike on Friday when I stopped in for building supplies. He said things were running smoothly. Was he lying to save face?"

Dad chuckles, low and easy, and some of the knots in my chest begin to loosen. "I could run that store in my sleep, kid. We're fine. How's set design coming? Anyone lose a finger yet?"

Mom shrieks in horror, and I can practically see her smacking his arm. She's seen enough real accidents over the years—she doesn't do injury jokes.

"We're actually ahead of schedule. And, knock on wood, no injuries to report."

"That's my girl. I knew you'd run a tight ship."

"Alright, you two have talked shop enough. Now answer my questions," Mom scolds. I hear Dad mutter something about being nice, but we both know it won't help.

"You're asking why I didn't say anything about moving?" I start pacing, dragging a hand through my hair. "Because I knew you'd try to talk me out of it."

"Well, of course we would have!" Mom snaps. "What were you thinking?"

"I was thinking it was time I got my own place. And you know what? It's pretty great. And to be fair, I didn't just leave. I tried to talk to them about my choice over dinner, and they didn't take it well. But I didn't just pack up and slink off into the night, okay?"

"Proud of you," Dad says, and another shriek escapes from Mom.

"You're renting Mel's place?" she asks after a beat, the edge in her voice softening. "That little brick house on Elm?"

"Yes." I exhale slowly. "It's charming, it's clean, and it's only two blocks from Alayna."

Mom sighs—long and dramatic, the kind she's perfected over a lifetime of mothering. "Fine. But stop leaving me out of the loop, Frankie. I'm your mother. I don't want to hear about your life secondhand. I want to hear it from you."

"I love you, kid," Dad says. "I'm heading to bed."

"Love you too, Dad."

The line clicks off speakerphone, and Mom's voice shifts into something softer. "I don't want you to be alone your whole life," she admits quietly. I hear the crinkle of a tissue box, know she's pulling out two tissues just in case. "I want you to have someone to boss around the way I do your father. You'd be great at that."

I laugh, despite myself. "I mean, yeah, I probably would."

She chuckles through her sniffles. "Listen, honey. If you're hurting, or confused, or if something's wrong—just tell me. I don't need the whole soap opera, but I do want to be part of your life."

"I have some plans in the works," I say, choosing each word with care. "Things I want to share with you and Dad. About the hardware store and..."

I hesitate. Does saying it out loud tempt fate? Roman and I are still... undefined. But I've kept Mom in the dark for so long, and maybe this moment is a thread I should tug.

"And what, sweetie?" she prods gently.

"And there's someone who means something to me," I say, quiet but sure. "If things go the way I hope, I'll tell you all about him."

It's not the juicy gossip she's dying for, but it's what I can give her right now.

"I'd like that," she says, her voice watery.

Guilt pinches at my chest. I've ghosted her the same way Alayna ghosted me earlier. And I know how that feels. It sucks.

"I'm sorry I've been distant. I'll do better. I promise."

We talk a little longer—about her garden, Dad's stubborn knees, and the new brunch place she's obsessed with. By the time I agree to plan a family dinner—including Clay and Alayna—and stop by this weekend to talk about the shop, she's scribbled dates into her calendar like they're binding legal contracts.

One more family drama, sorted.

Even if Alayna totally meddled and forced my hand, I guess... all's well that ends well. Or however that saying goes.

CHAPTER 31

AFTER I HANG UP with my parents, I jot down a few bullet points for my hardware store pitch this weekend—just enough to quiet that corner of my brain still craving control. But sleep doesn't come. I lie in the dark, flipping the pillow, kicking off the blankets, pulling them back on. Nothing works.

When my phone buzzes on the nightstand, I roll over, flooded with relief. At least someone else is awake tonight.

I pull the covers up to my chin and unlock my phone.

My pulse stutters.

Roman.

ROMAN

What are you doing?

The ceiling fan stares down at me like it's judging all my life choices. *Get a life,* it seems to say. I snort softly and type back.

> ME
>
> Watching the ceiling fan go around and around.

His response comes immediately.

> ROMAN
>
> Why?

> ME
>
> Can't sleep. Pretty sure my parents think I'm the worst daughter ever.

> ROMAN
>
> Are you?

> ME
>
> Debatable.

> ROMAN
>
> What are they upset with you about that would warrant that title?

> ME
>
> I maybe didn't tell them I was moving out of Clay's house.

> ROMAN
>
> Maybe, or you didn't?

I roll my eyes. Semantics. But still—admitting I'd done it intentionally makes my stomach twist. It's the truth though. Time to stop adding lies to the pile.

ME

I didn't. I didn't want my mom to try and talk me out of it. She's a meddler. Like, Olympic-level meddling.

ROMAN

I always liked your mom.

ME

Well if you see her, maybe you can put in a good word for me then.

ROMAN

Can't Patchouli Sarah charm them for you?

ME

She could. But I think "Dr." in front of your name carries more weight.

ROMAN

What are you doing up?

ME

You mean besides spiraling? Why are you up? Did you forget it's a school night, Dr. Principal?

ROMAN

I can't sleep either. I miss you.

My heart does a slow, deliberate flip.

ME

You saw me a few hours ago.

ROMAN

I did. But we've been doing this weird dance and I want to clear the air... no more hiding.

ME

Dancing can be fun.

ROMAN

Have you been drinking?

ME

Only my weight in anxiety tea. Why?

ROMAN

Want to come over?

Do I want to come over?

Yes. God, yes.

Better than lying here counting how many times my heating unit kicks on. Better than staring at the fan and waiting for dawn.

But... what does he mean? What kind of *come over* is this?

> **ME**
> Is this a booty-call? Because I don't answer those.

> **ROMAN**
> No, Frankie. It's not a booty-call.

> **ME**
> Okay good, just checking.

I laugh quietly at myself, shaking my head. Why am I like this? His next message dings through, and I sit up in bed, my breath catching.

> **ROMAN**
> Just come over. We don't have to have all the answers. We don't have to fix everything tonight. I just want to see you. I don't know what tomorrow will bring, but right now I know I want to be with you. When I'm with you, nothing else matters.

> **ROMAN**
> Please, Frankie. Come over.

His voice seems to rise out of the words, as if I can hear him saying it—pleading, quiet but certain. I can picture the way he rubs a hand over his jaw, eyes intense, focused entirely on me. Roman rarely begs. But he's asking now. Not just for company. For me.

What does this mean?

Does it even matter?

I'm going. He asked. And I'm going to show up.

No more running. No more hiding. We've both done more than enough of that.

I glance down at my pajamas—a cozy matching tie-dye shirt and shorts set—and briefly consider changing into something hotter. But in the end, I fluff my hair, swipe on a bit of mascara, and brush the lingering chamomile off my teeth.

My nerves are buzzing. It's not like I haven't spent the night at his place before—wearing *his* clothes, no less. But this time is different. This time, I'm walking in not because I'm lost, but because I'm choosing to.

I'm in charge of my own future now. And maybe—just maybe—this is a piece of it.

And suddenly, everything is sharp-edged and real. Our connection never died. It just hibernated. And now that it's awake, it's ravenous.

But does Roman want the same future I do? Is he staying in Pinewood, or is London—or something else—still on the table?

I grab my coat and keys, fingers trembling enough that they jingle in my hands. I glance down at my phone.

Does it matter what the future holds?

Maybe it does. But right now, I know one thing with complete clarity: I want to spend every second I can with him. Even if it ends in a spectacular, flaming dumpster fire.

At least I'll know I didn't walk away from what I wanted.

I send one final text.

ME

On my way.

Roman is watching from the window when I pull into his driveway. I tuck my coat around me and run from the car to the porch steps. He looks comfortable, in a black shirt and plaid pajama pants, and I'm glad I stayed in my own pajamas.

As the front door opens, I launch myself into his arms. He laughs and spins me around, pulling us both into the warmth of his home.

Once the door closes behind us, Roman wraps his strong, tanned arms around me, holding me with a delicate kind of reverence, like I'm something precious and breakable.

"I'm glad you came."

I press my lips to his neck, breathing in the familiar scent of his soap and cologne, his hair still slightly damp from a recent shower. Roman brings a hand to my face, tilting my head up until our lips are a breath apart. He holds me there, still and close, until all I can hear is my own heart pounding.

And then he kisses me.

It's not urgent like the others we've shared. This one is slow, deliberate, like every part of him is trying to tell me something in a language only our bodies understand. Something cracks open in my chest, and the warm, gooey center of it all spills into every inch of me.

This kiss feels like love.

Not the fiery kind that blazes and burns. But the kind that stays. That sees. That chooses. The kind of kiss that leaves your soul naked and says, *Finally. I don't care who sees. I choose you.*

We sway together, kissing like we're both remembering something we never want to forget. When we finally pull back, Roman rests his forehead against mine.

"Wow," I whisper.

The fireplace is going again, soft light flickering across the room. The warmth of it seeps into my bones, mingling with the rush of everything I'm feeling.

Roman presses a kiss to my forehead, then leans back with a crooked smile.

"I made us some tea. Do you still like chai?" He gestures to the coffee table.

I nod, slipping off my sandals by the door. "I told you I already drank my weight in tea today, right?"

"You did," he grins. "But I figured if you could drink that much, it must mean you love it a whole lot."

"Well, lucky for you, that's true. And chai is way better than the chamomile I was drinking earlier."

Roman takes my hand, leading me to the couch where two steaming mugs wait beside a plate of chocolate chip cookies.

"Tea and cookies? Is this because you're about to tell me you're moving to London?" I hadn't planned to bring it up unless he did—but the words slip out anyway.

His eyebrows lift, and he shakes his head.

I curl my legs beneath me as I sit beside him. "Sorry. I wasn't going to bring it up. The tea-and-cookies thing kind of triggered it."

"It's okay. I'm happy to talk about it—I'm just surprised you heard."

"You don't have to," I say quickly. "It's just... it's like we're walking a tightrope right now. Balancing between the past and the future, and I don't know which way we'll fall. I've been loving this—getting to know you again—but you don't owe me anything, Roman."

He studies me, his hand flexing gently on my shoulder. "What exactly did you hear about London?"

"Kate mentioned something about you taking a job there. Teaching. Meeting the queen, seeing Big Ben." I try to sound casual, but my pulse is erratic, my skin buzzing with nerves.

"I should've known it was Kate," Roman mutters. "I swear that woman was a mosquito in a past life—one of those nasty little ones that are more like teeth with wings."

"Do mosquitoes even have teeth?" I try not to smile.

"Not the point," he says, flustered. A faint flush creeps up his neck. "I had this whole speech planned. I was waiting for the right moment. But I guess now's as good a time as any."

Silence settles between us, broken only by the soft crackle of the fire and the ticking wall clock. I reach for him, grazing his arm with my fingers. He presses his hand over mine.

"It's true," he says. "I was offered a teaching job in London. One of my old college friends—he went through the whole process, got certified, moved there, all of it. Apparently I made an impact on his career, because he recommended me. But when the offer came... it didn't feel right. Starting over like that—it's not so different from what I did when I left home. But this time, it felt off."

He takes both of my hands in his.

"I was sitting there, trying to write the nicest rejection letter I could, when I got a DM from Principal Garrett. Said he'd read an article I was featured in, wanted me to know how proud he was. It felt like divine intervention. The next thing I knew, I was trying to convince him to let me take his job."

"You gave up London to be principal at Pinewood High?" I blink. "Is the offer... gone?"

He nods. "I left this town and did everything I said I would. I finished school, traveled, built a career. I didn't even know I wanted the 'Doctor' title until I earned it. But something was still missing. When Garrett said he wanted to retire and spend his golden years on a boat with his grandkids... it just clicked."

"You want to be an old man with a boat someday?" I tease.

"Frankie, can you hush before I mess this up?"

"Sorry," I say, laughing. "Continue."

He exhales slowly. "I realized I never stopped hoping you'd come find me. And this was my chance. Not only to keep doing the work I love—but to stop waiting and come back to find *you* instead."

My throat tightens. I blink fast.

"What if I wasn't here anymore?" I whisper.

He smiles. "I figured someone in your family would know where you went."

"And if I was married?"

"Then I guess that would've been my answer," he says simply. "It was a leap of faith. But then, before I even had the chance to go looking, you walked into that school. Like fate was yelling at me."

"Except you thought I had a secret love child."

He smirks. "Seeing you at Jake's with your family, all picture-perfect, it knocked the wind out of me. I was afraid I was too late."

"And now?" I ask softly. "Now that you know it's not too late?"

Roman's hands tighten around mine. His eyes don't waver.

"Yes," he says. "This town, your beautifully chaotic family, *you*—that's what I want."

He clears his throat. "I could've gone to London. But hearing from Garrett, and the chance of you again—it made me realize I've been looking for home in all the wrong places. I didn't just want to come back. I wanted *you* to be here when I did."

I'm still wrapping my head around all of it when he speaks again.

"Can I ask you something?"

"Always."

"If it had been true—if I was leaving for London—what would you have done?"

I've thought about that, so the words come easily.

"I would've told you I wished you wanted to stay, but that I understood. The last time you left, I was ready to abandon everything to follow you. But I'm not that girl anymore. I know who I am. My family needs me, and I have dreams for the store. I love you, Roman. I'd love you across an ocean. But I wouldn't lose myself again to prove it. And deep down, I think I always knew... if we were meant to be, someday we'd get it right."

He nods slowly, eyes full.

"Sometimes I wonder," he says, "if I could go back to that day in the parking lot. Say the right thing. Tell you I loved you. Maybe we could've built a life together then."

I start to respond, but he lifts a hand.

"But I don't think it was our time," he says. "I needed to prove something to myself. And you—you needed those years with Alayna and Clay. You wouldn't trade those memories for anything. And I wouldn't want you to."

His voice softens. "The way you love them—the way you show up, without hesitation—it's one of the things I love most about you."

Tears spill freely now. His words are stitching closed places I didn't know were still torn.

"I'll spend the rest of my life proving I'm ready," Roman says. "That I'm not going to run. I'm yours—if you're willing to take a chance on us again. If you're willing to trust me with your heart."

I lean in, catching his bottom lip gently between my teeth, and he groans softly.

"Are you finished?" I murmur.

"That depends," he whispers, eyes locked on mine. "Are you convinced?"

"Roman, I didn't need any convincing." My voice trembles. "I loved you then, and I love you even more now. Since the moment you ran into me on that soccer field, my heart has always been yours to break."

Relief floods his face. He cups my cheeks, dimples deepening. "I love you, Frankie."

I trace my fingers along his jaw, anchoring us in the present. "Do me a favor?"

"Name it."

"Please don't break it this time."

Roman rests his forehead against mine, voice barely a breath.

"I won't." He says it like a vow.

And this time, I believe him.

CHAPTER 32

ROMAN AND I SPEND the rest of the week alternating houses, neither of us willing to spend a night alone after all the time we've spent apart. We've fallen right back into the early days of our relationship, only this time we're older, wiser, and things are even hotter than I remember. We can't keep our hands off each other, and in the sweet moments before falling asleep, I get to know the man I love even more. I could get used to this feeling—every night like having a slumber party with a best friend.

And as for best friends, Sarah hasn't stopped harassing me for spicy details since I filled her in on everything that's happened between Roman and me. Details she's never going to get, but I love her for her enthusiasm and for being almost as happy for me as I am myself. Our next ladies night is going to be one for celebrating.

Over the course of weeks, our relationship has come full circle. The past has healed in a way that only love can accomplish. We've cleared the air, and the more comfortable we get around each other, the more I'm confident the connection between us is as solid as the ground beneath my feet. And I'm hopelessly, endlessly, completely in love with Roman Clarke. Maybe I always have been, but this time around, things are different. Better. Complete.

I love Roman Clarke. And Roman Clarke loves me. The world is finally back on its axis, and everything is how it was always meant to be. Sure, I'll have to smooth things over with Clay, because I don't imagine he'll take this news easily, despite us speaking again. And Alayna might need a little time to get used to the idea, though I suspect her feelings for Derek will help bridge the gap there. She knows Roman is my first love, and that's something she can relate to now.

There will be growing pains ahead, I'm certain of that. But I'm not afraid of any of that anymore. I'm excited, and giddy, and ready to face everything head-on. Because love has finally come back to me, and it's more than I ever imagined.

On Saturday morning, Roman makes pancakes in my kitchen while I write notes down on a notepad. It's hard not to be distracted by the sight of him, barefoot and rumpled from sleep, cooking in my tiny kitchen. He looks like he belongs there, wearing sleep shorts and a T-shirt, humming along with the radio. In the glowing sunlight, he looks peaceful and at ease, confident in his own body. A body I could get drunk on.

As if he can read where my thoughts have gone, Roman gives me one of his sexiest grins, dimples flashing and eyes crinkling deeply. I avert my gaze back to the notepad.

It's almost time to get dressed and meet with Dad about my ideas for the shop, and while it's technically my business to run, I won't be happy until I have his full support and approval. After all, this is a family business, and it was Dad's place long before it was my own.

"Nervous?" Roman plops a plate of steaming pancakes covered in whipped cream and strawberries down in front of me.

I nod as I look up at him. "I just really want him to be excited about the idea."

"I was thinking..." Roman drums his long fingers on the counter, leaning toward me.

"That sounds dangerous," I laugh, taking a bite of my pancakes. The flavors burst on my tongue and I hum appreciatively before waving a hand for him to continue.

"My house still needs a lot of work. I had planned to hire someone to make the repairs and help me restore it to its former glory, maybe make a few style changes while I'm at it... that horse wallpaper—" Roman shudders.

"I can help you with all of that, you don't have to hire someone."

Roman comes around the counter, taking my face in his hands and landing a quick kiss on my lips. "I was hoping you'd say that."

"Free labor, a discount on supplies, and all the tools we need at your disposal? I'm not surprised you were hoping I'd agree." I laugh, leaning into his touch.

"But you haven't even heard my idea yet." Roman gives me his best Cheshire cat grin, fingers drawing lazy circles on my cheekbones.

"Oh, there's more?"

"I've been thinking about how you want to teach classes at the store, but what if you went a step further than Pinewood? What if you also made yourself a website, or a YouTube channel, put some of your tips and tricks on social media..."

"You really think people would watch my videos?" I chew my lip, thinking the idea over.

"Are you kidding? Renovations and repairs are expensive—most people will at least research ways they can do it themselves before taking out a loan or paying crazy fees to hire a professional. I've seen you with the theater and woodshop kids; you're a natural teacher. People are going to love learning from you."

"You're a genius," I squeal, jumping up from my chair to wrap him in a hug. His excitement is catching, and it feels good to know he believes in me.

"Mike has been running the main shop well, so you'd have time to plan and prepare for your in-person classes. And when you aren't working on those, you could be at my place, renovating on camera and pulling in another stream of income from outside of Pinewood. Imagine the reach Hale Hardware could have."

"Dr. Clarke, all that schooling paid off for you," I tease. "And I'm damn glad you're home."

Home.

That place I've been searching for but couldn't quite pin down. It's more than the place where you keep your things and sleep at night. It hits me with the strength of a bulldozer, and I suck in a breath.

"You're my home." I sigh, locking eyes with the man my heart has chosen.

Roman hoists me up, my legs wrapping naturally around his waist as his arms anchor me to him. "And you're my home."

I blink back tears. "You really don't mind me tearing up your house and making it a construction zone for my own personal gain?"

"Figured we've been going back and forth between your place and mine anyway. I can just stay here while we get the house sorted. And as long as you promise to remove that nightmare-inducing horse wallpaper, I'll give you full control over the design choices."

My mind races with ideas, excitement bubbling up inside me like carbonation. "You're sure I'm the girl you want for the job?"

"Hale, yeah, it's you." Roman winks. "You're the girl I want, for all the jobs."

"Wow, that's cheesy." I laugh. "But also clever."

"Yeah, you like it?"

"Hale Yeah, You Can DIY!" I cry out as the ideas hit me, one after another. "Help for all your home improvement needs!"

"Yes! Now we're talking." Roman grins, kissing me deeply before setting me back on my feet. "Now go take a shower and get dressed. We have a man to see about your future."

Mom and Dad sit across from me at the picnic table in their backyard an hour later, a pitcher of sweet tea and Mom's famous potato salad sandwiches between us. I'm still full from pancakes, but I take a small sandwich to avoid offending her.

They listen quietly while I explain my vision—an online presence, renovation classes, reaching beyond Pinewood—and the longer they stay silent, the faster I talk. Nerves creep in, and my hands have grown clammy by the time I finally finish.

"Well, what do you think?" I ask, picking up my tea to give my hands something to do.

Dad lifts his glass. "Well, baby girl, you don't need it, but you've got my Hale seal of approval."

I glance between them. Dad's cheeks are red from working outside, his overalls smudged with dirt or oil, a thin shirt beneath despite the crisp fall air. His expression's unreadable as always. But Mom, bundled in three sweaters and still shivering, is beaming like the sun just rose for me.

"You really like the idea?"

Mom nods, patting Dad's back. "Your dad's been nervous, Frankie."

"Gracie," he mutters, clearly annoyed she's told me.

"Be quiet and drink your tea, Frank," she snaps playfully. "When you moved out of Clay's and said you wanted to talk about the shop... well, he thought maybe you were ready to move on."

"Move on from the shop?" I place a hand over my heart in mock horror.

"Don't be a smartass, daughter of mine." She points a finger at me, but she's smiling. "But yes. We thought maybe you'd realized you were meant for bigger and better things."

"We'd understand," Dad adds, folding his hands, "if you wanted something else."

I shake my head. "The hardware store is part of me. This idea—it's like everything I've learned is finally coming together. I want to help people love their homes again, give them the tools to do it themselves. That's exciting to me. That feels right."

Dad narrows his eyes slightly. "You're sure this is the life you want?"

"Yes," I say without hesitation. "I'm the next generation of Frank Hale. Of course it is."

"Well," Mom grins, "now your father can stop stressing before he gives himself an ulcer."

Dad laughs, then slings an arm around her shoulder. "Now. You going to tell Roman he can stop hiding in the car and come join us?"

"What now?" Mom twists around, trying to see the front yard.

"He's been in her car the whole time," Dad says, like it's no big deal. "Same boy who used to buzz around her in high school."

"This is why you left Clay's?" Mom's eyes widen.

"Part of it," I admit. "But I was already planning to leave. It was time. I know you wanted us to be more..."

"No, Frankie," Mom interrupts gently. "I wanted you to be happy."

Her words melt something inside me. She's not disappointed. She's... happy for me.

I text Roman to come around back, my heart beating fast. He'd wanted me to give the speech alone, so my parents could focus on my dream, not our relationship. But knowing he was right outside, silently rooting for me? That meant everything.

"That's who you were talking about the other night?" Mom's voice lifts with excitement. "You've rekindled things with Roman?"

"Yes," I say, already smiling. "It's almost like we picked up right where we left off. Like we were always meant to find our way back."

"I may get more grandchildren after all," Mom teases, elbowing Dad.

"Let's not count chickens," Dad grumbles, but there's a glimmer of amusement in his eyes.

The gate creaks open and Roman steps into the yard, looking a little stiff, formal. "Good afternoon, Mr. and Mrs. Hale."

"None of that, boy," Dad says, shaking his hand. "It's Frank and Grace."

"I heard you were back in town," Mom says warmly. "Nice to see you again. Are you enjoying the new job?"

"I am. I love working with the kids." Roman still looks uncomfortable, until I take his hand under the table. His grip softens.

"You met our Alayna?" Dad asks, pouring him a glass of tea and nudging the plate of sandwiches toward him.

"She's a great kid," Roman says, more relaxed now.

"And also a meddling little brat," I add.

"Frankie Mae," Mom scolds. "Don't talk about your sweet niece like that."

"Oh, come on. She gets it from you."

"Ladies," Dad chuckles, "let's not run the boy off."

"Dr. Clarke," I correct, for Mom's benefit.

Mom's eyes sparkle. "A doctor? Your parents must be proud."

"I think they are," Roman shrugs. "But we've never been close. Not like you Hales."

"Well, dear, *we're* proud of you," Mom says, patting his hand. "And happy you and Frankie found your way back to each other."

Dad leans in. "What are your intentions there?"

Roman freezes mid-bite, clearly caught off guard.

"Alright, Dad," I warn. "No scaring him off."

"It's okay," Roman says, swallowing his bite. He straightens, his voice steady. "Frank. Grace. I love your daughter. I've loved her since we were kids in your shop, and I fully intend to spend the rest of my life proving it—if she'll have me."

Mom tears up instantly, leaning against Dad. My own vision blurs, but my heart is soaring.

"Was that a proposal?" I tease, trying to keep it light despite the lump in my throat.

"Not yet," Roman says, smiling at me like I hung the stars. "But expect one very soon."

"You better mean it, Dr. Principal," I say with a grin, "because you're never getting rid of me now."

Dad lets out a rumbling laugh and claps Roman on the back. "Don't worry, son. We're glad to have you back. Our girl thinks the world of you—that's enough for us."

My heart swells. This is it. The dream I never dared to name out loud, finally within reach.

Love, family, purpose—it's all here, right where it's always been.

And the best part?

This is only the beginning.

EPILOGUE

ROMEO AND JULIET – PINEWOOD HIGH SCHOOL FRESHMAN PRODUCTION – OPENING NIGHT

THE AUDITORIUM IS PACKED, a low hum of anticipation crackling beneath the quiet. Stage lights cast a dreamy glow, catching in the dust floating through the air like tiny gold flecks. I nudge Mom's elbow as the final scene begins, cutting off her whisper about Alayna's hair mid-sentence.

"Shh, Mom, it's the finale."

Spotlights snap into place, locking onto Alayna and Derek as they take center stage. The set is transformed into a candlelit tomb—arched stones, ivy-painted walls, and enough eerie gloom to transport us into Shakespeare's world. I hadn't seen the final set with the art department's finishing touches. The students insisted on handling it themselves, earning the right to bring their vision to life without me hovering. Watching it now, I couldn't be prouder.

You can hear a pin drop. Even the creak of an old seat or a quiet cough seems like a violation of the moment. I steal a glance at Alayna, then at Roman across the aisle with the rest of the faculty. His expression is still, but I can tell he's tracking every movement his students make. Or maybe he's remembering the way we used to look at each other, because I swear, the way Derek gazes at Alayna right now—it's the same look Roman gave me once, long before life got in the way.

"O, happy dagger—this is thy sheath. There rust, and let me die." With a slow collapse, Alayna falls over Derek's body, the trick dagger still clutched in her hand. A collective gasp swells and breaks, and then, silence. My vision blurs with tears.

Sarah leans in, resting her head against mine. "Your niece is amazing. I think I hear Hollywood calling."

"She really is," I whisper, my throat tight.

So is my best friend. Her next art show is weeks away, and I already know the world's about to notice her the way I've always seen her. Bright. Brilliant. Brave.

As the lights fade up and the cast take their bows, thunderous applause shakes the room. Around me, friends, family, neighbors— they're all gathered to celebrate these kids. I reach down for the bouquet I stashed under my seat, and Mom and Sarah do the same, our flowers crinkling in their plastic sleeves.

Before we can stand, Mrs. Betty strides onto the stage, microphone in hand.

"Good evening, ladies and gentlemen," she begins, her voice warm and bright. "Thank you for joining us tonight for the Pinewood High freshman production of *Romeo and Juliet.* Our cast and crew worked tirelessly to bring you this show, and I think you'll agree—it paid off."

The crowd erupts again, and I glance toward the stage, ready to dash up and find Alayna. But Betty keeps talking.

"If I could borrow one more moment of your time," she says, smiling knowingly, "there's someone else we'd like to thank tonight."

I freeze. The stagehands emerge with a long, rolled banner. The cast lines up, giggling, hiding the message from the audience.

My stomach flips.

"As you all know, the arts don't always get the funding they deserve—especially in small towns like ours. But we've been lucky. Lucky to have a neighbor who gave not only her money, but her time, her tools, and her heart."

Sarah squeezes my hand, and I feel her lean in before she shoves me upward. "Stand up," she whispers, smirking.

Betty beams at me. "Ms. Frankie Hale, would you please stand?"

The spotlight swings into the audience, catching me like a deer in headlights. I squint through the glare, face flaming, heart thundering.

"This show wouldn't exist without her," Betty says. "Thank you, from all of us."

The cast turns the banner around.

WE LOVE YOU, FRANKIE!

The kids shout in unison, "We love you, Frankie!"

I drop the bouquet into Sarah's lap, pressing both palms over my heart. "I love you!" I shout back, my voice cracking with emotion. Around me, people rise to their feet. The clapping goes on and on. Tears stream down my face. Gratitude cracks open inside me like sunlight through a window.

Sarah's arm slides around my waist, and Mom pulls me into a hug. "I'm so proud of you, Frankie," she whispers.

I look down the row—Clay gives me a nod from beside Dad. A small but sincere smile. We're doing better. We're rebuilding. When he asked for advice about Alayna and Derek last week, it had felt like a new beginning. Two blocks away or not, he still lets me be a part of her story.

And Roman—he's just stepped onto the stage beside Mrs. Betty. Calm, steady, already in principal mode. But when his eyes meet mine, there's a softness that no job title can hide.

He thanks the crowd again, then releases us to go hug our kids and take a thousand blurry pictures in the lobby.

I tug Sarah up by the hand. "Alright," I say, grinning through the tears. "Let's go congratulate our girl."

And just like that, I step into the wings of my own second act—surrounded by love, laughter, sawdust, and fresh beginnings.

SIX MONTHS LATER

"That last video you did, the one where you showed everyone how to remove wallpaper? It got over two million views in six hours, Frankie. You're becoming a household name." Sarah beams at me from across the table, her eyes alight with pride.

My favorite food truck has finally graduated into a full-blown restaurant, and Roman and I have been coming here so often, Sarah insisted I bring her here instead of our usual bar for this month's girls' night. We're tucked in a booth near the back—her choice, so she could people-watch for artistic inspiration. The smell of grilled beef and garlic aioli lingers in the air, same as it did that first night Roman and I sat across from each other at the crowded picnic table in the post office parking lot. This place grew up, just like we did.

Tonight, I'm wearing a soft white sundress Sarah "suggested" I put on earlier today. It hugs all the right curves and flares out enough to make me feel like I'm floating. The fabric kisses my skin with every movement, and for once, I don't tug at the hem or second-guess the way I look. I feel beautiful. Not just because of the dress or the effort—but because I'm loved. And when love is real, it roots you. Makes you glow from the inside out.

"Roman was starting to think I'd never remove that horse wallpaper," I laugh. "I had to put the poor guy out of his misery."

"Misery?" Sarah rolls her eyes, I swear her outfit gives her a new level of sass. The red dress she's wearing is probably a little too hot for this casual spot, but she's a walking flame, and she knows it. "He's the happiest man on the planet. He snagged my bestie—boy better remember how lucky he is, or I'll remind him."

"I think he knows." Most days, I feel like I'm the one who hit the jackpot. My chest swells with the thought. We're happy, and not in a fairytale way, but in the real, quiet kind of way that's earned—and we can finally trust that this love is here to stay.

After weeks of bouncing between our places, Roman moved into my rental full-time while his house undergoes what we now jokingly call "the world's slowest renovation." We didn't like spending nights apart anyway. The theater class still lets me drop in, and I take every opportunity to watch him in his element. The kids adore him. It makes me proud in ways I didn't know I could be.

Even Alayna has adjusted better than I could've imagined. She and Roman now share a deep bond built on movie trivia and mutual respect, complete with strict no-nonsense rules during school hours. Clay took a bit longer to come around, but I understood. Two weeks ago, he finally invited Roman to join us for Sunday dinner. We met at Jake's instead of his house, and

I had to fight off tears the whole night as we laughed and ate like the family we are still learning how to be.

It's not perfect. But it's ours.

"How many followers do you have now?" Sarah asks, sipping her mojito.

The *Hale Yeah, You Can DIY* channel—and all the related socials—have exploded. "Over six million across all platforms," I say with a grin. "Which is wild, considering most of those people have now seen me turn bright red while explaining how to snake a toilet."

"And your dad's antics? Iconic," she adds, laughing. "That video where he trips over the bucket and says he's demonstrating why safety matters? I nearly cried."

Things took off fast. Brands reached out. Videos went viral. We launched DIY kits with the same materials I use in my tutorials, and when orders got overwhelming, I hired six more people—both for fulfillment and for the growing in-person class demand. Hale Hardware is officially on the map. And Dad? He's never looked prouder.

The restaurant is buzzing around us, but we still haven't ordered. "Where's our waiter?" I murmur. "I swear I've never waited this long."

Sarah shrugs. "I'm not in a rush. I'm gonna run to the bathroom."

"Okay, don't fall in," I tease, nodding toward her empty glass.

"If I do, you can always snake the toilet and fish me out," she says with a wink, tapping my shoulder as she passes.

I chuckle and take a sip of my drink, the condensation cool against my fingers. A second later, a hand lands on my shoulder again.

"Wow, did you even wash your hand—"

"Should I have?" Roman's voice cuts in, low and familiar.

I turn—and everything inside me stills.

He's in *that* suit. My favorite. The dark gray one that makes the green in his hazel eyes practically glow. And he's on one knee.

Behind him stands Sarah, smiling like a cat who got into the cream. And when I scan the restaurant, I see it—every table filled with people I love. Alayna. Summer. Clay. Mom and Dad. Mike and Mel. The game night girls. Mrs. Betty and Mrs. Brosnan. Familiar faces from Pinewood High. Even Roman's old soccer teammates.

It hits me all at once—this is *it*.

The nails. The sundress. The restaurant choice. It was all part of the plan; Sarah orchestrated it beautifully. My heart is a rushing, roaring thing.

I glance down at my hands—these hands that once fumbled with a hammer and swung it anyway. The ones that pried up broken tile, built something new from the ruins. Hands that held onto Roman as he carved our initials under the table at the hardware store: R + F 4ever. Forever. We hadn't dared to say the word out loud then...

But I hear it now, loud and sure.

Roman looks up at me, and suddenly, it's just us. Him and me. The world and all its noise fades.

He takes my hand, steady despite the emotion in his eyes. His voice is low, but I feel every word settle deep in my chest.

"Frankie Hale," he says, "I love you because you're fierce and kind, because you always know how to fix what's broken—even when it's not tiles or shelves, but people. I love the way you fight for your family, for your friends, for yourself. I love the way you chew your lip when you want to kiss me but are trying to play it cool. I love that you never stop trying—even when it's hard, even when it hurts."

He swallows, blinking fast.

"I knew you were the one a long time ago—I just didn't know how to hold on. But now I do. I want to build a life with you, Frankie. A messy, joyful, full-of-cat-hair-and-half-finished-renovations kind of life. I want the chaos and the quiet. I want babies with your eyes and your fire. I want Sunday dinners and rainy kisses on the back porch. I want it all, even if it means arguing over which restaurant has the best pizza in town for the fifth time. I want it all, as long as it's with you."

He pulls out a small black box and opens it, revealing a ring I can't even see through the haze of emotion blurring my vision.

I stare down at him, heart pounding, my breath shaky as I try to find the words that have always felt too big for me to say. But now, here, with him on one knee, it's easy.

"I love how you put your whole heart into your job, how you treat each kid like they matter. I love watching you on the soccer field, blasting those balls like you're still in your prime. I love how you get how important Alayna and Clay are to me, and you never make me feel bad for including them in our lives. I love how you look at me like I'm the only woman you see, how you believe in me even when I can barely believe in myself. And you think I can wield a jackhammer, but you know better than to trust me with the grill. But most of all, I love the way you love me. It's a way I never knew was possible."

He waits for me to finish, his dimples deep in his cheeks as he asks, "So, what do you say? Will you marry me, Frankie?"

There's only one answer.

I drop to my knees right there with him, cheeks wet, heart full, and shout:

"Hale, yeah!"

Acknowledgements

My loyal readers, thank you for coming along on this journey with me! After two young adult novels, I wasn't sure who would follow me into the world of "Adult Romance" but here you are! I hope you loved this one just as much as the others! And if this is your first journey with me, welcome!! Thank you for taking a chance on a new-to-you author. I hope you have enjoyed the ride.

As always, I need to thank my husband, Josh, for putting up with my scattered brain. I know when I'm working on a project the house suffers, the family gets neglected, and I don't always get dressed for the day, but I'm so thankful that you support this dream of mine despite all of that. I've loved you all these years, it only makes sense I write love stories for the masses. You've shown me what it means to go the distance. I love you.

My sweet children, I hope someday you find your own epic love stories. You, after all, are the legacy of my own love story. All four of you.

Grandma, thank you for allowing me to steal all the romance novels I could read off of your hallway shelf. It was those books that sparked a love of happily-ever-after. I love you to the moon and back.

Bestie, Thanks for believing in me even when I'm struggling. For being my biggest fan. For asking questions while you read that make me think up better endings, even when you don't know you're doing it.

Mom, Lori, Tiffanie, Kayla, Sommer, Amanda, Andrea, Breanna... thank you for constantly pushing me to write the next chapter and to believe in my talents! I love you more than words.

My amazing BETA readers: Eliana, Melissa & Kaylyn, Stephanie, Brittany, Katie, Gabby, Page, Heather, Loren, Leslie, Whitney, Brittani, Kelly, Crystal, Abbie, Jessica, Marissa, Andrea, Susan, Ashley, and if I forgot anyone, please know, I appreciate each and every one of you more than I can say. Your feedback makes me a better writer, and I always enjoy your commentary!

Kayla, thank you for listening to me cry about writing at any time of day. For never letting me give in to the imposter syndrome burnout, and for being an amazing friend. You inspire me every day.

To my amazing editor, the lovely Tori Freeman, I cannot even begin to explain how glad I am that our paths crossed. The advice and changes you suggested have absolutely made me a better writer and helped give this book the polish it deserved. Working with you was a dream and I cannot wait to do it all over again! Here's to more 5 a.m. meetings at the coffee shop!

To my talented cover designer, Brenna Jones. Girl, this is the most gorgeous book ever, and I cannot thank you enough for your hard work! And for putting up with all my requests. I'll be back for the next book!

And for everyone still reading.... writing books is something that I hope I can always do, and you are the ones who make that dream continue. Thank you for your support.

All my love,
XOXO – Nic

Also by Nicole Reeves

Crimson Hearts
Young Adult / Contemporary Fiction.
A coming of age story of first loves, sibling bonds, and unconventional families. Shedding light on the journey of grief, loss, and the resiliency of the human spirit.

What Remains
Young Adult / Apocalyptic Science Fiction.
A gripping tale of survival, self-discovery, love, and the indomitable human spirit in the face of an apocalyptic world.

Learn More about Nicole:
Instagram: @nic_reeves_writes
Tiktok: @authornicolereeves

Website: www.nicolereeves.com

About The Author

Nicole Reeves lives in Texas, but grew up in Southeast Alaska, where she thought swimming in glacier-water and running from bears was a perfectly normal childhood.

When she's not writing or chasing her kids around with her husband,  you'll find her balancing book stacks on her high-heels and sharing the shenanigans on #bookstagram.

www.ingramcontent.com/pod-product-compliance
Lightning Source LLC
Chambersburg PA
CBHW021006260626
47169CB00006B/1966